"Josh is your son. When I left Chicago, when I thought you were dead, I was pregnant with your son."

He was a father. He had no solid reason to be proud, but he was…a father. The realization knitted through his consciousness, drawing his fragmented self back together. He accepted her statement without doubt or question. On a cellular level, he must have known. Being a father changed everything. "Eden, why did you pick this moment to tell me?"

"Because I'm afraid." But her voice sounded strong and defiant. "I thought we might be killed, and you deserve to know before you die."

"No more negative thoughts." He rubbed his hands up and down her arm. "We're going to make it."

"How can you be so sure?"

"Because I've got to meet my son."

Dear Harlequin Intrigue Reader,

Yeah, it's cold outside, but we have just the remedy to heat you up—another fantastic lineup of breathtaking romantic suspense!

Getting things started with even more excitement than usual is Debra Webb with a super spin-off of her popular COLBY AGENCY series. THE SPECIALISTS is a trilogy of ultradaring operatives the likes of which are rarely—if ever—seen. And man, are they sexy! Look for *Undercover Wife* this month and two more thrillers to follow in February and March. Hang on to your seats.

A triple pack of TOP SECRET BABIES also kicks off the New Year. First out: *The Secret She Keeps* by Cassie Miles. Can you imagine how you'd feel if you learned the father of your child was back…as were all the old emotions? This one, by a veteran Harlequin Intrigue author, is surely a keeper. Promotional titles by Mallory Kane and Ann Voss Peterson respectively follow in the months to come.

And since Cupid is once again a blip on the radar screen, we thought we'd highlight some special Valentine picks for the holiday. Harper Allen singes the sheets so to speak with *McQueen's Heat* and Adrianne Lee is *Sentenced To Wed* this month. Next month, Amanda Stevens fans the flames with *Confessions of the Heart*. **WARNING:** You may need sunblock to read these scorchers.

Enjoy!

Sincerely,

Denise O'Sullivan
Associate Senior Editor
Harlequin Intrigue

THE SECRET
SHE KEEPS

CASSIE MILES

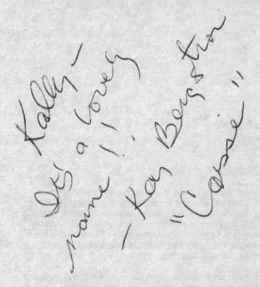

Kally —
It's a lovely
name !! — Kay Bergstrom
"Cassie"

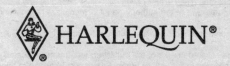

HARLEQUIN®

TORONTO • NEW YORK • LONDON
AMSTERDAM • PARIS • SYDNEY • HAMBURG
STOCKHOLM • ATHENS • TOKYO • MILAN • MADRID
PRAGUE • WARSAW • BUDAPEST • AUCKLAND

ISBN 0-373-22694-2

THE SECRET SHE KEEPS

Copyright © 2003 by Kay Bergstrom

Visit us at www.eHarlequin.com

Printed in U.S.A.

ABOUT THE AUTHOR

For most of her life, Cassie Miles has lived in land-locked, beautiful Colorado, which is about a thousand miles from family in Chicago and an equal distance from fun in Las Vegas. She likes to travel, but has never been fond of airplanes. Her favorite way of getting from here to there is the road trip, especially the kind of leisurely ride where you can go off the highway and explore all the historical markers, roadside attractions and local eats.

It's the very best kind of trip to take with someone you love. Writing *The Secret She Keeps* was an absolute joy because she had a chance to revisit the great Midwest via car, train and horseback, with a short hop to Vegas in a puddle jumper.

Books by Cassie Miles

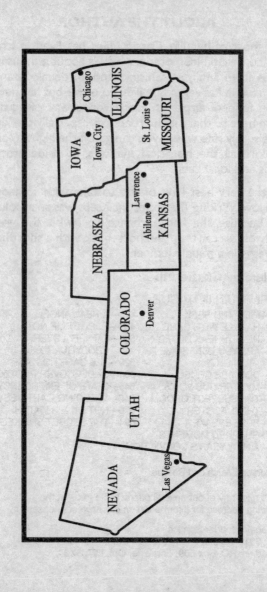

CAST OF CHARACTERS

Payne Magnuson—Alias Peter Maggio. The undercover federal agent, supposed to be dead, was on the run, framed for murder and targeted for vengeance.

Eden Miller—Alias Candace Verone and Susan Anthony. The Denver soccer mom escaped her violent crime-family background to protect her son.

Josh Miller—The eleven-year-old son of Eden had no idea about his heritage.

Danny Oliphant—Also known as Danny-O. A traitorous federal agent whose cleverness led to disaster.

Gus Verone—The patriarch of the notorious Verone crime family.

Sophia Verone—Eden's grandmother and Gus's wife, she struggled with family loyalty.

Luke Borman, Chuck Sonderberg and Samuels—Federal agents, who were both good guys and bad guys.

Sister Max—A kindly old nun who occasionally worked for the FBI.

For my wise and patient editor, Patience Smith,
and Denise O'Sullivan at Harlequin Intrigue.
And, as always, for Rick.

Prologue

Bitter cold inhabited the last days of April like an unwanted guest who didn't know when to leave. The vestiges of sleet had melted off the streets of Brooklyn, but a veil of ice remained, sparkling in the headlights of slow-moving traffic on the narrow streets. Payne Magnuson turned up the collar on his black overcoat and adjusted the lapels across his shoulder holster.

He seldom wore his gun anymore. A senior agent at Quantico, his regular assignment was in the classroom. Today, he was in New York for a consultation and seminar, teaching other special operation personnel how to go undercover and get out in one piece. Payne had the practical knowledge. Twelve years ago when he was twenty-four, he'd infiltrated the upper echelons of a Chicago crime family and lived among them for eighteen months. His tapes, wire taps and sequestered testimony had taken down seven minor crime bosses and toppled the Verone family. He should have been proud. In certain FBI circles, Payne was considered a legend.

Yet, he never thought of that time without regret. His efforts hadn't ended corruption in greater Chicago. He'd barely made a dent. When the Verones stepped down, another family arose to take their place. Crime was a many-headed hydra, voracious and unstoppable. Now, a dozen years later, Gus Verone, the old patriarch, had regained supremacy. Except for two men still serving time in federal prison, it was as if Payne's undercover operation had never happened.

"You're going to love this restaurant," his companion said.

"Why's that, Danny-O?"

"It's Italian."

Danny Oliphant, like many of the younger agents, assumed that Payne was of Mediterranean descent. Because of his black hair and dark eyes? A superficial resemblance to Al Pacino? It wasn't true; Payne wasn't Italian. His surname, Magnuson, was Scotch, and he'd grown up in Wisconsin where the culinary fare was mainly meat and potatoes. His only association with Italian cooking was during his undercover assignment when he immersed himself in the culture and passed as Pete Maggio.

As a general rule, Payne avoided the Italian scene. He'd met a lot of people in Chicago he couldn't face again. Not that they'd be expecting to see him. Payne, in his incarnation as Pete Maggio, was supposed to be dead.

Danny Oliphant—a husky redhead with an innocent, snub-nosed face—held open the door to the corner restaurant, Mama Paisan's. They shook off the cold in the foyer and stepped inside where a pleasant warmth surrounded them. In keeping with the neighborhood location, the decor was casual with red checkered tablecloths and woven Chianti bottles used as flower vases. A long bar traversed one wall. Above the noise of conversation, Payne heard the background music of a tarantella.

Instinctively, he scanned the faces of restaurant patrons, looking for enemies. He recognized one man. Not an enemy. Another agent from today's seminar.

"Luke Borman." Payne turned to Danny-O. "I didn't know we were meeting anyone."

"Me neither." Danny-O waved and approached the

other man. "Hey, Luke. Good to see you. What are the odds we'd end up at the same place?"

Too high, Payne thought. As he reached across the table to shake hands, Luke's jacket gaped open and Payne noticed the handle of the gun in his shoulder holster. Not standard FBI issue. This casual dinner was beginning to feel like a setup.

"Join us," Danny-O offered.

"Thanks, but no," Luke said. He checked his wristwatch. "I'm waiting for my girlfriend. She's late, as usual."

His reason for being at Mama Paisan's sounded innocent enough. Luke's presence was nothing more than coincidence, except Payne didn't believe in random chance. Everything happened for a reason.

He led the way to a table in the middle of the restaurant and sat with his back to the wall. Though he remained alert to potential danger, the comfortable atmosphere soothed him. The mouthwatering fragrance of rich sauces and fresh bread tickled his senses and took him back in time. He remembered a candlelit dinner in his Chicago apartment. Twelve years ago. And he remembered a woman, *the* woman, Candace Verone. Slender with long coltish legs, she swept through his small one-bedroom apartment with sinuous grace. Wisps of long chestnut hair escaped her ponytail and curled at the edge of her high cheekbones. She wore no makeup, didn't need any. Her hazel eyes were ringed with thick, black lashes. Her full lips glistened with a soft, natural pink. She was only nineteen but seemed more mature. The constant drama of the Verone crime family would be enough to age anyone, especially a sensitive coed with a strong sense of justice and truth.

Candace Verone. Payne thought of her often. The atmosphere at Mama Paisan's brought her back to him with unbearable vividness. He remembered her leaning across the table in his apartment, holding out a serving spoon for him to sample the tomato sauce that had been bubbling on the stove for hours. In memory, his tongue tasted the perfect blend of fresh tomatoes, onions, peppers and garlic. In her eyes, the candlelight reflected a winsome glow.

He'd wanted to be honest with her, to explain his undercover work. To do so would have been dangerous. For both of them. He figured that when his assignment ended, he would come back for her. But such solace was not to be. She vanished after the final takedown. Though it seemed impossible, she was gone without a trace, never to be heard from again. Her disappearance was a tribute to the national and international connections of the patriarch, Gus Verone. He'd hidden his granddaughter so effectively that even the FBI couldn't locate her. Payne had followed every lead, every hint. He would've done anything to see her again, to taste her lips, to feel her delicate body cradled tight against his—

"Payne!" Danny-O called him back to reality, nodding toward the waitress. "Should we get wine with dinner?"

"Burgundy," Payne said. Candace had preferred red wine, full-bodied and rich. "A liter."

There was no reason to avoid alcohol. He wasn't on duty. This afternoon's consultation and seminar on undercover procedure had gone smoothly, and he planned to head back to D.C. tomorrow morning.

Danny-O planted his elbows on the checkered tablecloth and leaned forward. With his red hair and freckles, he looked like Opie grown up. "What was it really like? Being inside?"

Payne shrugged. This wasn't the place to be discussing undercover ops. "Just a job."

"Did you ever, you know, get too involved? Did you ever think of dumping the assignment and joining the family?"

What kind of question was that? A test of loyalty? He

wondered if Danny-O had an ulterior motive when he volunteered to show Payne the town. "Why do you ask?"

"You got to admit, the families have a certain appeal. Lots of money. Good wine. Great food." He gestured to the table in front of them where the waitress placed a basket of warm crusty bread. Danny-O winked up at her. "Beautiful women."

She smiled back at him and moved away. Her graceful hips undulated as she wove through the half-filled tables. It was a decent-sized crowd for a Thursday night when the weather was dismal. Payne watched as the waitress swished through the swinging door into the kitchen. What lay behind that door?

He glanced again at Luke Borman whose girlfriend had not yet arrived. Something about this dinner was wrong. Payne's instincts, honed from years of ferreting out deceit, warned him to move on. He held up his wristwatch and made an excuse. "Sorry, Danny, I don't really have time for dinner. I'm meeting someone at ten."

"Who?" Danny-O challenged.

"Someone." His tone was clipped, final. He'd say no more. Explanation was unnecessary; a senior agent deserved respect.

"At least have a glass of wine." Danny-O raised both hands in a conciliatory gesture. "Come on, Payne. You can spare time for one glass, can't you?"

Was he stalling, trying to buy time to keep Payne at the table? "You sound anxious, Danny-O. Been under stress lately?"

"To tell the truth, I can't believe I'm here with you. You're one of my heroes. I want to get into—" He stopped himself before blurting a specific reference to undercover work. "—your field. I've read every word of your reports, all the transcripts."

Those documents were supposed to be sealed, top secret. How had a young agent, like Danny Oliphant, gotten clearance? Payne wanted to know more. He purposely relaxed his features, pretending to be seduced into indiscretion by the flattery. "Which part interested you the most?"

"Had to be the final takedown when you set up Locksmith and the guy they called The Nose."

Payne capped his suspicions with a false smile, irritated that Danny-O knew the code words which meant he had accessed top secret, sequestered transcripts of testimony. This did not bode well.

The wine bottle was placed on their table, and Payne went through the ritual tasting before pouring a glass of dark crimson liquid, the color of blood. "Who have you been working with on this?"

"Nobody really."

"You're being modest," Payne said. "Somebody had to give you clearance to read those documents."

"I shouldn't say this." Danny-O tried to look sheepish but failed. This baby agent was more like a wolf. "I'm kind of a computer whiz. I hacked into the files."

Unlikely. Very few amateur computer jockeys possessed the level of skill required to breach FBI security. Something was up, something treacherous.

Payne lifted his wineglass as he gazed toward the door. Three men entered. Two were unfamiliar, but Payne knew the tall man in the black leather jacket. His waist had thickened and his features had hardened. His opaque black eyes absorbed the light, sucked the energy from the cheery restaurant and turned everything dark. He was Eddy Verone. Candace's brother. The up-and-coming boss in Chicago. Why was he here? What did this mean? No time to think.

Payne reacted instantly. His gun was in his hand. Damn it! He didn't want a shoot-out in the middle of a crowded restaurant.

Danny-O had already pulled his weapon, identical to Payne's. The young agent fired at Eddy Verone.

With a shove, Payne overturned the table. He focused on Luke Borman. From halfway across the restaurant, the barrel of Luke's .45 caliber revolver aimed directly at the center of Payne's chest.

The first shot was Payne's. Borman went down.

Payne dodged through the tables, through the screaming, terrified patrons. He hit the kitchen door and kept running. Undercover, again. He'd been set up.

Chapter One

Dressed in a black skirt, white blouse, black sweater and the black and white headdress of a novice nun, the woman who had once been known as Candace Verone hurried along the sidewalk outside St. Catherine's parochial school. Head down, the folds of the wimple obscured her features. She rushed as though late for an important appointment. In the carefully tended soil near the school's entrance, she noticed the green blades of new dahlias, a harbinger of springtime, a promise of new life. Yet, her mind was consumed by thoughts of death.

She still couldn't accept her brother's murder. Eddy was too young to die.

Quickly, she mounted the steps at the arched stone entryway of St. Catherine's, a school she had once attended a long time ago in another life. Her name was Eden Miller now. She was thirty-one years old, a single mother, currently living in Denver, making an honest living from smart investments and part-time work for a caterer. The key word there was "honest," a description not often associated with her past in this quiet Chicago suburb.

Inside the school, Eden flattened her back into an alcove beside a plaster statue. Her plan was to sneak through the bowels of the school into the church next door where her brother's funeral would take place in a few hours.

She had risked everything by coming here. If recognized, twelve years of carefully constructed anonymity would be erased.

Cautiously, she peeked out from behind the Blessed Virgin statue. Had the hallways always been so narrow? Years ago, the school had seemed much more impressive, filled with whispers and laughter. In a rush, she remembered spelling bees and notes passed in class and best friends and boyfriends. But now was not the appropriate moment for nostalgia. She needed to slip through the school undetected. It shouldn't be too hard. Classes were in session, and no one should be in the halls. The tricky part would be to avoid the nuns and secretaries who worked in the main office.

Before she could make her move, Eden was caught. A large hand clasped her shoulder and spun her around. She faced Sister Maxine who was uncharacteristically dressed in her full regalia—a flowing black habit with a carved rosewood crucifix the size of a baseball bat hanging from wooden beads around her ample waist.

Silently, Eden cursed. She should have remembered that Sister Max had always been able to creep silently and appear out of nowhere. The joke was that, like the Lord, Sister Max "moved in mysterious ways."

The old nun peered through her rimless eyeglasses. "I don't believe we've met. May I help you?"

Eden hoped Sister couldn't see her too clearly. From a distance, Eden could pass for a novice nun. Up close, her white blouse was definitely silk, and the sweater showed a stylish cut. "I'm new here," she said. "A math teacher. I transferred from, um, another parish."

At the sound of her voice, a smile softened Sister's stern visage. Gently, she chided, "You were never a good liar, Candace."

Her arms spread wide like the wings of a wise black bird, and she pulled Eden into a hug. The soft warmth of

Sister Max felt like a wonderfully safe haven, and Eden hugged back with all her might.

Sister Max had been a comforting presence in the background of her life. When her mother died from natural causes while Eden was in fourth grade, Sister Max had pulled her from class and had given her the news. The same with her murdered father in seventh grade, but Eden hadn't wept on that occasion. The Verone family tragedies had become too regular, almost expected. Still, she appreciated the solace offered instinctively by Sister Max, and Eden wished she could have stayed in touch. "I'm sorry, Sister. I left without saying goodbye."

"I understand. Your family… Let's just say, I understand why you had to depart so abruptly, Candace."

"Call me Eden. Eden Miller. That's my name now."

Sister Max stepped back. With a clean white hanky that had appeared from nowhere, she daubed at the corners of her eyes behind her glasses. "Eden it is. I've been expecting you."

"You have?" Tension shot through her. Was it so obvious that she'd return for her brother's funeral? "Why?"

"Come with me."

Eden balked, fearful of a trap. If Gus Verone sank his talons into her, she'd never escape. "Sister, I can't see my grandfather."

"Of course not. I might be a nun, but I'm not an idiot." Bitterness tinged her voice. Though Sister Max believed judgment was the province of the Lord, she thoroughly disapproved of Verone family activities. "There's someone else who wants to see you. And I promise you'll come to no harm."

"Who is this mysterious person?"

"You'll see."

Her grandmother? Eden's heart leapt. She missed her grandmother, Sophia Verone, so very much. As soon as Eden heard of Eddy's death, she'd called her grandmother.

On the phone, Sophia sounded desolate and weak. She'd outlived both of her own sons, and now she'd lost her only grandson, Eddy. Granddaughter Eden felt guilty to be living so far away; she was as good as gone. She'd left her grandmother alone in a nest of vipers.

Sister Max led her down the stairs, past the cafeteria and into a tunnel that connected with the church. It was the route used by students attending Mass during snowy weather. "I'm sorry for your loss, Candace. I mean, Eden. Your brother chose a dangerous path."

His life in crime, supposedly serving the family, had killed him. Just as it killed her father and her uncle. And her one true love. His name whispered through her conscience like a forbidden breeze. Peter Maggio. Over the years, Eden had tried not to think of him, to force his presence from her mind. But her senses would never forget his gentle caresses. Her ears always listened for the rich deep timbre of his voice, speaking to her of love, promising he would never leave her. Her eyes were reminded of Peter every single day. Their son, Josh, who was nearly twelve years old, looked more and more like his father as he matured. Sometimes, Josh would cock his head at a certain angle when asking a question, and she would see the reincarnation of Peter in the dark eyes of a son who had never met his family. And never would, Eden swore. Her primary goal in life was to keep Josh safe from the Verones.

In the basement of St. Catherine's church, Sister Max pushed through one closed door and then another. She paused outside a third door. "This may be difficult for you, Eden. But I believe this meeting is necessary. For what it's worth, I've always known in my heart that he was a good man."

He? What good man was she talking about? "I don't understand, Sister."

"My prayers are with you. Be strong." Sister Max guided Eden inside and closed the door behind her.

In the smallish room where racks of choir robes and vestments were stored in plastic dry cleaners' bags, the light came from a single forty-watt bulb. It wasn't dark, but Eden squinted, unable to comprehend what she was seeing.

She focused on a rugged man in a worn brown leather bomber jacket. Every detail came into stark clarity. She noticed the shine on his oxblood loafers, the stitching on his jeans, the buttons on his white shirt, the slight bulge of his jacket concealing a shoulder holster. His jaw set hard as granite. His dark eyes shone with unspoken gravity. Lightly etched crow's feet touched those eyes.

"Peter," she whispered.

He looked older. His high cheekbones and jawline were more sharply chiseled. A touch of gray streaked his thick black hair.

She must be dreaming. He couldn't be here. Peter Maggio was dead. He'd been dead for twelve years, the entire life span of their son.

"Candace," he said.

"Eden," she corrected automatically. Her heart beat fast, speeded by the pressure of a thousand emotions. It felt like her rib cage would explode. "Candace is dead. Like you. You're dead."

"I didn't want to meet like this. I would have given you time to—"

"Stop!" The music of his voice was overwhelmed by a roaring in her ears. She'd lost her mind. Gone insane. "You're dead."

"Touch me."

When his hand reached toward her, she shied away in horror. This handsome spectre might pull her into the grave beside him where they would rest together for all eternity. Too often she'd dreamed of such peace, being in Peter's arms one more time. Forever. But she couldn't leave her son to fend for himself. She had to protect Josh. For his sake, she had to stay alive.

The ghost stepped toward her, leaving the shadows.

"Keep away from me," she gasped.

"Eden, it's all right. I won't hurt you."

The glow of the forty-watt bulb glistened in his hair. She stared, incapable of absorbing the miracle that stood before her. He was here. Alive! Peter Maggio had returned from the grave. A miracle or a curse, she didn't know which.

Eden closed her eyes. Her head whirled. Her knees went limp and she felt herself falling, falling into a bottomless abyss.

Kneeling beside her, Payne cradled her head against his arm. Though he hadn't intended to shock her into a dead faint, he should have expected her reaction at coming face-to-face with a living, breathing ghost.

He should have asked Sister Max to prepare Candace, but there wasn't time to gently ease her into acceptance. Too soon, his enemies would arrive for the funeral. Payne was investigating on his own, looking for proof to charge the corrupt agents who had killed Eddy and sabotaged Payne's career. At the same time, he was on the run. His identity had been revealed to the Verones—the criminals he had secretly prosecuted so long ago. They wanted his blood.

Every minute Payne stayed in this church increased the odds against his survival, but he had desperately needed this time alone with the woman who had haunted his heart for twelve years. Candace Verone was the ghost, the vanished lover, the only woman he had ever truly cared for.

He stared into her face—a perfect oval, framed by the white headpiece of a novice nun. Her black eyebrows arched delicately over thick, sooty lashes. A stubborn jaw and a straight Roman nose lent character to her features. In her teens, she'd been adorable. Now, in the prime of her life, she was a breathtaking beauty.

Her lashes fluttered, her eyelids opened and she gazed

dreamily, not yet fully conscious. Her full lips parted as if she were about to smile. He wanted to kiss those lips, to embrace her and pretend the last twelve years had never happened.

Her expression transformed. All gentleness left her face as she snapped, "You're supposed to be dead."

"Sorry," he said.

"Twelve years ago, you died."

"I was shot and in the hospital for a week, but—"

"Basta!" Her hazel eyes flashed. Her beautiful lips compressed in a tight, angry line. "I should kill you myself. With these hands."

"Candace, I tried—"

"Don't call me that." She shoved away from him with a wild flailing of arms and legs. "I'm Eden Miller now."

"Fair enough." He had a confession of his own. "And I'm not Peter Maggio. I never was. My real name is Payne Magnuson."

"Pain?" she said, her voice rising on the single syllable. "Pain! How appropriate!"

She bolted to her feet. For a moment, she wobbled. Her hand rubbed against her forehead and she yanked off the wimple. Her fingers raked through her shoulder-length chestnut hair, streaked with blond highlights. Very sophisticated, Payne thought.

She glared at him. "Why are you smiling?"

"A nun?" That sure as hell wasn't the way he remembered her.

"A schoolgirl disguise didn't cut it. The plaid uniform skirt I wore when I was fourteen didn't fit."

"You're the first nun I've seen wearing a silk blouse and cashmere sweater."

She stiffened. "The outfit worked well enough to get me inside the school without being noticed."

"You look good, Eden."

"So do you," she said grudgingly. She hated the way

he looked. His body was hard and strong. His face had grown even more attractive with age. Damn him! In a righteous world, he would've been physically punished for deserting her while she was pregnant, even though he hadn't known about her condition. He should've guessed. He should've gotten word to her. Instead, he abandoned her! Even worse, he lied about his name…and what else? What other lies? Peter, or Payne, should be forced to wear his deceptions and cruelty on his face. He should be hideous.

After all she'd been through, she would never forgive him. She'd given birth alone, a frightened nineteen-year-old in a strange city. And she'd raised their son. Alone.

Rage sluiced hotly through her veins as she paced back and forth in the small vestment room, slapping at the plastic garment bags, seething. "You let me think you were dead! You deserted me!"

"I couldn't find you." He stood and casually brushed the dust from his Levi's. He looked classy, even in jeans and a beat-up bomber jacket. "I searched every damn computer file, every record. I followed slim leads all around the country. I even went to Sicily."

"I don't believe you."

"Give me a break, Eden. Nobody could find you. Not even your grandfather. You pulled off the disappearing act of the century."

She'd done too good a job. When Candace fled, she withdrew all the money from her accounts. With insurance payouts for both her mother and father and college funds, it had been a considerable amount. Not knowing where to go, she turned to her grandmother who referred her to friends in Denver. However, after the initial contact, Candace buried herself more deeply. She changed her name, her vital records, her identity. No one could find her. She was completely alone. "I had to do it. I had to break away from them."

"I understand," he said.

She stalked away from him and stood, staring at the corner of the room where the walls met the ceiling in mathematical ninety degree angles. She yearned for logic. Seeing Payne had turned her world upside-down. Nothing made sense.

She didn't dare to turn and confront him directly, not while she could still feel his intense magnetism. If she gazed full into his eyes, she'd be helplessly drawn to him, unable to resist.

Eden tossed her head. "If you really wanted to find me, you could have. All you had to do was talk to Grandmother Sophia. I had a post office box where she could contact me."

"You're right. I should have paid more attention to Sophia." Twelve years ago, he'd concentrated his search on associates of Gus Verone, but he hadn't ignored Grandmother Sophia. Undercover, in disguise, he kept her under surveillance as she puttered in the marketplace or sat in the front pew at Mass. He wire-tapped her private telephone. He'd intercepted much of her correspondence to no avail. "Unfortunately, I couldn't approach Sophia with a direct inquiry from Peter Maggio who was, as you pointed out, supposed to be dead."

"You're a coward," Eden muttered, "too afraid to return from the dead and face the Verone family."

He shrugged. Undercover work was no place for heroes. The job required stealth, not macho bravery. It was time for another confession. "I was undercover, Eden. I'm a senior agent for the FBI."

As she whirled to face him, her hazel eyes narrowed. "Another lie. You were never honest with me."

He might have defended himself, might have told her that every syllable he'd uttered in praise of her beauty, intelligence and wit had been truth. The language of his emotions had been pure.

But she had a right to her anger.

And she unleashed her rage, full-force. Eden rattled through a barrage of Italian invective before facing him directly, fists on hips. "So you're a fed. It was your work to bring down my family."

He wouldn't blame her if she hated him. She'd been raised to put family above all else, and Payne had betrayed the Verones.

Instead, she gave a curt nod. "Good. At least you had the right idea, saving the family from crime."

"But it didn't work," he said.

"Not for Eddy." Her jaw tightened as she struggled to maintain her tough attitude. "Eddy used bad judgment. And he paid for it."

The sorrow in her eyes belied her harsh judgment. No matter what she said, he knew that Eden considered her brother's death to be a tragedy. Palpable grief surrounded her. Payne had known that she couldn't stay away from her family at this terrible time. He'd counted on her need to be with them. Hoping to console her, he reached out and touched her arm.

She yanked away from him. "Don't."

Somehow, in the back of his mind, he'd always imagined that when he saw her again, she would melt into his arms and allow herself to be carried away on clouds of bliss. Apparently, he'd been wrong. In the vernacular, he could *forgeddabouddit*.

"Okay, Eden, here's the story." Payne opted for facts. This time, there would be no lies between them. "I'm undercover, again. This time, it's more complicated than before. I was framed by another agent. Inside the Bureau, I'm considered a renegade. They're looking for me, want to take me into custody. Plus, your family knows I'm alive."

"So, you're wanted by the Verones *and* the feds?"

"Essentially."

"Nice work," she said sarcastically.

"I didn't see the double-cross until it was too late."

"What double-cross? I want more explanation," she demanded. "And don't even think about lying to me."

"The setup happened at a restaurant in Brooklyn. I saw your brother shot."

She gasped. Her hands flew to cover her mouth. She whispered, "Who killed him?"

"An agent. His name is Danny Oliphant. That snubnosed, redheaded bastard shot Eddy in cold blood." He wanted her to hear this information from his lips. "No matter what anyone tells you, I didn't kill your brother."

"Why would people say such a thing, if it wasn't true?"

"Part of the setup. Danny-O delivered me to the meet in Brooklyn. I suspected something was wrong, but I didn't understand until I saw Eddy walk through the door. Danny-O drew and fired." Payne had since learned that Danny-O had used an exact duplicate of his own weapon, right down to the serial numbers. "His gun was identical to mine."

"So it would be assumed you were the shooter," Eden said. "And what were you doing while this Danny-O person killed my brother?"

"There was another agent in the restaurant. Luke Borman. He was aiming at me. My guess is that his gun was a match for Eddy's. When the ballistics people analyzed the crime scene, they'd assume that I shot Eddy and he shot me."

"But there were witnesses," she said.

"Parents and kids having dinner. When the bullets started flying, they dove for cover. They were scared, hysterical. I doubt any of them could say exactly what happened." Especially not when Danny-O was directing the investigation. "Here's how it's going down. I'm accused of killing your brother and shooting Agent Borman."

"Did you?" she asked. "Did you shoot the other agent?"

"Yes."

"Is he dead?" she asked.

"Alive and recovering," Payne said. "He's a hero."

"And you're the goat."

She leaned her back against the wall and regarded him steadily as if she were weighing his words against her standard of truth. He trusted her instincts. Though raised in an atmosphere of base treachery, Eden had a finely tuned moral compass.

"If you had met my brother on the street," she said, "and he recognized you, would you have killed him?"

"If it came down to him or me," Payne said, "I'd shoot."

She frowned, considering. Then she glanced at her wristwatch. They were both aware of the ticking clock. Soon, the Verone family would gather for the funeral in the upstairs sanctuary. "Why did you come here, Payne?"

"I wanted to see you."

She brushed away his comment. "I've never heard of a fed who was so sentimental. There must be another reason."

"Surveillance." By observing those who attended the funeral, he might be able to connect the dots and figure out the connections that led to Danny-O. "Your brother was killed for a reason. I want to know why."

"Why does this make a difference to you?"

"Until I have proof to implicate Danny-O and Luke Borman, I'm out in the cold."

"Because the feds think you're the corrupt agent who's working with the Verones."

"Eden, we don't have time to talk about this. Not right now. I want you to meet me after the funeral. I'll be at this motel." He handed her a card. "I'll wait until four o'clock."

"Before four o'clock," she repeated. "At this motel."

Eden glanced at the card, aware that he was literally trusting her with his life. If she betrayed him by giving his location to her grandfather, Payne would be trapped in a motel room with no escape. The Verone family would take their revenge without mercy.

It was what he deserved for deserting her. A slow and horrible death. But she knew, in her heart, that she would never cause him to suffer. Besides which, he might have another motive in revealing his location. What if Payne expected her to pass on the name of his motel? He might be arranging a sting to catch the Verone assassins. Or, if she came alone, he might be plotting to kidnap her, using her for leverage against her family.

With sudden alarm, she realized that Payne's apparent trust might have something to do with Josh. Did he even know about their son? His son? Though he hadn't mentioned Josh, this might be part of a plot to steal her child. So many devious possibilities lay beneath the surface. As a daughter of the Verone family, she had learned to navigate the Byzantine twists and turns of the criminal mind. She must always beware of murky deceptions.

And yet, as she had stated, Candace Verone was dead. She was Eden Miller, a law-abiding citizen who expected honesty.

She looked up at Payne again. Frankly, she demanded, "Why should I come to this motel? Why should I believe a single word you've told me?"

An infinitesimal twitch at the corner of his left eye was the only warning before Payne closed the space between them with a few quick strides. His arms surrounded her. His mouth slanted across hers.

Furiously, she fought his kiss. She twisted her body, but his strength was too great. He held her even more tightly. Her breasts crushed against his chest.

Eden wrenched back her head and prepared to scream.

"Trust me," he whispered.

His dark eyes shone with mesmerizing light. He was the man she had dreamed about, night after lonely night, the only man who had ever touched her soul. God help her, she wanted his kiss. With every fiber of her being, she yearned for him.

He held her nape gently. His lips pressed against hers.

Her resistance ebbed, swift as the retreating surf across smooth, shimmering sands. Her eyelids closed in a swoon. Lifted beyond reality into a netherworld, she welcomed the flow of passion through her veins, awakening dormant sensation. Her arms clung to him. She kissed back, releasing years of longing.

He was alive and in her arms. She treasured this precious moment.

He ended their kiss and stepped away from her. Silent as a shadow, he went through the door and closed it behind him.

Eden was left wondering if this meeting had really happened. Her fingertips touched her moist lips where the taste of Payne still lingered. She had to see him again. Slipping the card with the name of the motel into her bra, she went to the door and prepared herself to face her brother's funeral.

Outside, at the end of the first hallway, Sister Max stood waiting, fidgeting with her rosary. "Are you all right?" she asked.

Eden nodded. "How did you come to be friendly with Payne Magnuson?"

"Like you, I first knew him as Peter Maggio. When you two started seeing each other, he came to me for advice."

"Why?" What sort of man sought dating advice from a nun?

"Well, he couldn't very well talk to your grandfather. Gus Verone had let it be known that you were off-limits."

Eden was well aware of her grandfather's decree. Most men ran in terror when they learned her name was Verone. But not Payne. He hadn't pursued her, but he certainly hadn't pushed her away. "He told you about our relationship?"

"Remember, my dear child, that you were very young. Only nineteen. Only a year out of high school. And he was a grown man of twenty-four. He didn't want to take advantage."

"What did you tell him?"

"The truth," said Sister Max. "You had to grow up more quickly than most girls. In your nineteen years, you'd experienced more than your share of sorrow and responsibility. I assured him that you were capable of making your own decisions and taking care of yourself."

"You were correct."

Sometimes, Eden thought she'd been born an adult. She'd met Peter, now known as Payne, with her eyes wide open and would never regret their earth-shaking nights of passion. She wasn't sorry for moments that felt so right, lovemaking that brought her a son, Josh, the light of her life.

"Now, you have another decision," Sister Max said. Her tone was brisk, almost businesslike. For a woman of the Church, she seemed far too comfortable with all this undercover subterfuge. "Your grandmother is here. She's alone in an anteroom off the sanctuary with the coffin. Do you want to go there?"

"Yes." She answered without hesitation. Eden owed her escape to Grandmother Sophia.

Once again, Sister Max showed her to a closed door and stationed herself outside. "I'll make sure no one bothers you."

Eden stepped inside. The air was redolent with the mysterious scents of the church and a blanket of white flowers that covered the lower half of an ebony coffin fitted with gold trim. Beside the casket sat a tiny gray-haired woman wearing a neat black pillbox hat. Her head drooped. Her eyes closed. With a small withered hand, she caressed the gleaming coffin.

"Grandmother," Eden said.

Sophia rose slowly to her feet. Though she looked not a day older than when Eden had last seen her twelve years ago, sorrow kept the smile from her grandmother's face. Despite her diminutive size, she held herself erect. A proud woman, much stronger than anyone expected, Sophia had learned to cope with tragedy. "Come."

Eden stepped forward. There would be no embrace. No show of emotion. The women of the Verone family accepted their fate without weeping.

Sophia took both of Eden's hands and squeezed hard before nodding toward the coffin. "Say goodbye to your brother."

Drawing from her grandmother's dignified example, Eden straightened her shoulders. Woodenly, she moved to the open top of the coffin. Eddy's eyes were closed. His cheeks, sunken. His skin was colored by an unnatural pallor. Eden barely recognized the grown man. Instead, she saw a dark-haired boy, her older brother, who had defended her on the asphalt playground outside St. Catherine's after their mother passed away. The other kids had taunted that her mother deserved to die, that all Verones were poison, especially her. Poison Candace. Poison Candy. With his fists and hot temper, Eddy made it clear that anybody who messed with his sister would face his wrath.

Not that Eddy had always acted as her protector. She remembered his sly, teasing grin when he yanked her ponytail or chased her with a bleeding hunk of liver when she proclaimed herself to be a vegetarian for two months. A typical big brother, Eddy loved to torment her. But when she needed him, he was there for her…except at the very end of their time together when she left the family to have her baby. Eddy would never have understood why she needed to escape the clutches of the Verones. Family was everything to him. Above all, he was loyal, and that loyalty had killed him.

Eden fought the hot tears that threatened to spill from her eyes and moisten Eddy's crisp white shirt. Her skin felt hot, flushed with the effort of self-control. *Oh, Eddy, you could have been so much more.*

She placed a final kiss on his cold cheek and stepped away from the coffin to face her grandmother.

"He had no children," Sophia said. "His wife was barren."

Eden nodded. In infrequent letters from Sophia delivered to the anonymous post office box, her grandmother had made clear her disappointment with Eddy's wife, a beautiful but annoying twit who was not worthy of the family name. Secretly, Eden suspected that Eddy's wife was infertile by choice and not ready to give up the flashy nightlife for the role of motherhood.

She reached into the pocket of her skirt and pulled out two snapshots, her latest pictures of Josh. "These are for you."

As she gazed at the photographs, Sophia's lips almost smiled. "Such a handsome boy."

"And he's doing well in school. All A's and B's on his report card."

"What about sports?"

"He plays soccer and baseball. He's a shortstop." She glanced back at the coffin. "Like Eddy."

"You've done a good job," her grandmother said. "You were right to leave Chicago, to protect your child. But now, things have changed."

"What do you mean?"

"Eddy is dead," she said simply. "Your son, Josh, is the only male heir."

"Heir to what?" A shiver chased down Eden's spine. Apprehensively, she watched the hint of a smile fall from her grandmother's face. "What are you telling me?"

Sophia said, "I'm sorry."

A small rear door swung open. Gus Verone strode into the anteroom. Though in his early seventies, his fierce strength remained undiminished. With broad shoulders thrown back, he looked like he could wrestle a lion. His thick white mane bristled with energy. He stood before her, blocking any chance of escape.

He didn't bother to say hello or welcome back. His mouth barely moved as he issued his implacable proclamation.

"I want the boy."

Chapter Two

Betrayed! Eden's last thread of trust—the bond she'd shared with Grandmother Sophia—was severed. Eden had no allies, no support, nowhere to turn. All alone, she stood at the foot of her brother's coffin and faced her grandfather, the patriarch of the Verone family.

Her gaze locked with his. She would never allow him to take her son. Never!

"Where is he?" Gus Verone asked.

"With friends back in Denver." Eden glanced toward her grandmother. Not even Sophia knew the identities of these friends. For the moment, at least, Josh would be safe.

"Contact them," her grandfather said.

"I can't," Eden said. "They've gone camping in the mountains. There's no way to reach them."

"On a schoolday?" her grandfather questioned. "You allow your son to miss school for a camping trip?"

"Not usually." She didn't have to defend her mothering skills to him. "But this was a special occasion. A birthday."

"After the funeral, you will help me find these friends. I wish to speak to my grandson."

Never! "I'll try," she lied.

Though willing to fight to the death, Eden knew that obvious resistance was useless. To defeat her grandfather, she must outsmart him, to be even more sly and crafty than Gus Verone. She was forced to lie. And she would, gladly and successfully. If it meant saving her son, she'd wage a war of duplicity. She could do this! Verone blood flowed through her veins. Deception was her birthright. She'd use every necessary untruth to hide her anger and her fear. There was no other choice.

Eden took the photographs of Josh from her Grandmother Sophia. With a false smile, she presented them to her grandfather. "This is my son, Josh."

As he looked at the snapshots, the blaze in his eyes diminished. Gus Verone studied both pictures with obvious pleasure. For a moment, she thought her ferocious grandfather was on the verge of sentiment. "He looks like your father. And your brother."

Both dead. Eden steeled herself against her natural affection toward this man who had held her as a child and taken her to the zoo and told her bedtime stories. She could not allow herself to love him.

When Gus raised his head, his lower lip quivered. He held his arms wide. "My prodigal granddaughter, come to me."

She stepped into his arms, aware that she was dancing with the devil. Yet, she felt comforted by his acceptance. A strange warmth spread through her. This was where she belonged. This was her heritage, preordained by centuries of tragic Verones.

He whispered, "When I heard Eddy was killed, I thought I would die myself."

"I know." She'd felt the same way. Despite her loathing for her grandfather and all he represented, her natural grief rose up and joined with his. Tears swelled at the corners of her eyes, and she longed to give vent to her intense sorrow, to weep hysterically, to tear her clothes and beat her breasts in a primitive ritual of mourning.

She fought for control, needing to keep her wits about

her. More important than her sadness was her son's future. In order to insure he had a future, she had to escape the clutches of Gus Verone.

He held her at arm's length, searching her face for signs of acquiescence. "Things are different now with the Verones."

She didn't believe him. If "things" were different, there would have been no reason for Eddy's murder.

"You'll see," Gus said. "We have legitimate businesses. An accountant. I've opened a wine shop."

"A liquor store," Sophia corrected sharply.

He shot her a hard glance. "I provide all the wine for the church. Free of charge."

"As if a few bottles of wine will buy God's forgiveness," Sophia said.

He turned back to Eden. "Your grandmother is a hard woman. But you'll understand. You'll see. Your son will be safe with us."

Like Eddy? Through gritted teeth, she lied, "It's good to be home."

"That's my girl!" He clapped her shoulders and beamed. His attitude reminded her of a beast toying with his prey before he tore limb from limb and devoured his hapless victim. "Come with me."

"Of course." There was no other option. All doors would be guarded by her grandfather's foot soldiers. She must time her escape carefully.

Wrapping an arm around her waist, he guided her toward the exit from the anteroom. With every appearance of innocence, Gus said, "I have more unfortunate news."

She braced herself. "Yes?"

"You once were fond of Pete Maggio. You remember?"

Had Payne been caught in the basement? Was he dead? Though she felt a burst of alarm, Eden showed no sign of apprehension. "I remember him."

"We thought he'd been killed, but it wasn't true. It was Pete Maggio who murdered your brother."

Payne had warned her that this would be the accepted story, and she was more inclined to believe him than her grandfather. "I can't believe it," she said. "Why would Peter Maggio shoot Eddy?"

"I don't yet know."

Liar! Surely, her grandfather knew that Peter Maggio was really Payne Magnuson, a federal agent.

He continued, "But I'll find out why. And I will have my revenge. Pete Maggio will pay with his life."

Eden could hold back no longer. "Two minutes ago, you said things were different. Now you're talking about another murder. Which is it, Gus? Are you a legitimate wine merchant or a crime boss?"

"I take care of my family."

That was always the reason, the excuse for inexcusable crime. Locked in her grandfather's iron grasp, she went through the door into a corridor, leaving Grandmother Sophia alone with the coffin to mourn. Nothing had changed. Nothing ever would.

As she and Gus walked slowly along the side aisle through St. Catherine's magnificent sanctuary, Eden searched for a way out. Beneath the vaulted ceilings and stained glass windows, men in dark suits stood guard beside the marble statues of saints with hollow, sightless eyes. Awaiting her grandfather's orders, his men sat stoically in polished oak pews. Their presence—obscene in this cathedral—emphasized the futility of any attempted flight. As Eden passed a shrine of votives, she offered a silent prayer. *Help me. Keep my son safe.*

Her grandfather escorted her down a flight of stairs to a room near the front of the church where a bride might make final preparations for her ultimate walk down the aisle. It was also where the immediate family waited before a funeral. Several people had gathered. Their nervous chatter ceased when Gus Verone entered. Furtive silence ensued. Every gaze slid toward Eden and her grandfather.

Gus spoke without raising his voice. "Into every dark sorrow comes a ray of light. My granddaughter, Candace Verone, returns to the family."

He nodded for her to speak to this gathering of strangers who were all too familiar. Distant cousins, aunts and uncles—all ages and sizes—ranged before her like a family portrait come to life. She couldn't hate them, but she would never willingly take her place among the Verones.

What should she say? Only the truth. "I loved my brother, Eddy, and I regret the years we've been apart. He should not have died so young. On this day, I share my grief with all of you."

A stoop-shouldered woman with silver hair piled high beneath a black lace mantilla took Eden's hands and kissed both cheeks. "Welcome," she said.

Then came another and another in a bizarre ritual, bringing her back to the fold. The prodigal granddaughter had returned; it was time to slaughter the fatted calf and celebrate. Each greeting piled on another heavy layer of remorse, suffocating her lungs, killing her gently with their forgiveness.

Fifteen minutes before the funeral was scheduled to begin, she found herself talking to her cousin, Robert Ciari, who had been only a year ahead of her at St. Catherine's. A former football player, Robert's muscle had gone to fat. His hair thinned, he looked much older than thirty-two.

Eden would've expected Robert to be next in line after her grandfather, but he wasn't being treated with the deference reserved for a boss.

"What have you been up to?" Eden asked.

"This and that," he said. "Went to college. Busted up my knee real bad so I couldn't play football anymore. Got married."

"Kids?"

"Three daughters." He shrugged. "I guess I got lucky because they take after their mother. They're real smart. My oldest wants to be a lawyer."

They were joined by a statuesque, raven-haired woman in a snug black jersey dress. She had a figure to die for. Angela Benedict, another cousin, was probably ten years older than Eden. "Little Candace," she said in a husky voice. "I used to baby-sit for you and Eddy. Remember?"

"How could I forget?" Angela had been the coolest teenager in the neighborhood. A cheerleader. The star of the high school play. "I idolized you, Angela. I wanted to be you when I grew up."

"Things change." An edge of bitterness marred her precise beauty. Eden remembered that Angela's husband had spent six years in prison after the shoot-out when she thought Peter, now Payne, had died.

"Where have you been?" Angela asked.

"Out west." Eden didn't want to give particulars that made her easier to find. "I work for a caterer."

"You always loved cooking," Angela said. "Is there a husband?"

"Not yet," Eden said. "Tell me about your kids."

"My boys are nearly grown. Both in college." She linked arms with Eden, sweeping her away from Robert Ciari. "Come with me to the ladies' room. We need some girl talk."

There was nothing girlish about this strong, well-dressed, attractive woman. Power radiated from Angela Benedict. If she'd been born male, Angela would certainly have been ruling the family roost.

The plain, three-stall bathroom was empty, and Angela wasted no words. "Peter Maggio has come back from the dead. He was your lover, wasn't he?"

"Angela, that's ancient history."

"He gave you a child." Her dark eyes bored hard into Eden's face. "A son."

"I have a son," Eden said, careful not to acknowledge that Payne was the father.

"An heir to the Verone family name. Your grandfather wants the boy here."

"I don't understand why," Eden said. "It's not like we're royalty or anything. If my grandfather wants to groom an heir, why not look to Robert Ciari. He has—"

"Female children," Angela said harshly. "We call Robert the girl-maker. He's not a leader."

She turned away and studied her reflection in the bathroom mirror. She placed her black leather purse on the counter beside the sink and removed a tube of lipstick. As she prepared to reapply her makeup, she avoided Eden's gaze. Cousin Angela was hiding something. A clenching in her jaw betrayed her tension. What did she want? Power and wealth, Eden deduced, because Angela was not the sort of woman who cared much about loving or being loved. She wanted her boys to rise to power in the family.

The thought disgusted Eden. She couldn't imagine thrusting Josh into this arena. Any woman who would sacrifice her children was a frightening creature.

Quietly, Eden asked, "What about you? You could run the family."

"I didn't marry the right man," Angela said. "Gus doesn't like Nicky. No one can doubt his loyalty, but my husband is difficult. Angry. Brooding. After prison, he was never quite the same."

As Angela applied blood-red lipstick with an unshaking hand, Eden had the impression that this woman was strong enough for both herself and her husband—ferocious enough to lead an army into battle, taking no prisoners.

The question was: Why had Angela made a point of seeking her out? Her intention in bringing Eden into the bathroom was certainly not for girl talk. "Was there something you wanted to say to me?"

"I want to stay in touch." She removed a small gold

case from her purse and took out a business card. "This is my personal cell phone. Call me any time."

Though Eden slipped the card inside her skirt pocket, she couldn't imagine they'd ever be friends. "I appreciate the gesture, Angela."

"But you really don't plan to stick around, do you? You don't care for the family business. Twelve years ago, when it came time for us to stand together, you ran." Her alto voice resonated with disdain. "I suspect you don't want your son to be involved with the Verones."

"Very perceptive," Eden said coolly.

"I suspect," Angela said, "that you would run away again if given a chance."

As she replaced her lipstick in her purse, she removed a set of keys which she left on the countertop. "It's the black Corvette in the first row of the church parking lot."

Turning on her heel, she left the ladies' room.

Eden snatched the keys. She turned toward the garden level casement window. It'd be easy to climb out and escape. Almost too easy.

No doubt, Angela was setting her up. If Eden ran, she'd be out of favor with her grandfather. She would also be beyond his protection. Whoever had killed Eddy might come after her.

But if she stayed, Eden was trapped. Josh would be brought here. He'd be indoctrinated into the family business.

She had to take this chance.

INSIDE THE MOTEL ROOM, Payne stood at the edge of the window, peering through the slit between the nubby brown curtain and the stucco wall. The Riverside Inn was a two-story structure with rooms on both sides. He'd chosen a spot on the first floor near the end of the building. From this vantage point, he could see the motel office and the asphalt parking lot. His own rental car was parked on the opposite side of the building, ready for a quick escape if Candace, who now called herself Eden, chose to reveal his location to her family.

Arranging a meeting with her had violated every principle of undercover work. Payne had allowed his emotions to overwhelm common sense. He'd revealed too much. Like a rookie, he'd risked his entire operation for a few moments of gratification. For one kiss.

But what a kiss! He didn't honestly regret one second of the time he'd spent with her in St. Catherine's basement. She was everything he remembered and more. Strong, principled and vivacious, she was even more lovely than when she was a nineteen-year-old virgin who gave her love so sweetly to him. He treasured that indelible memory. Their first night together had become a fantasy. If he closed his eyes, Payne could remember the feel of her satin skin. He could see her surprised look of arousal. Her hazel eyes widened. She gasped. And then came her soft cries of delight.

His dream woman. She stirred his blood. The mere thought of her excited him.

He stared at the motel parking lot. Once again, he was violating the dictates of undercover work. He had trusted a potential enemy and left himself vulnerable, but he didn't care. Candace Verone was worth the risk.

Not Candace, he reminded himself. She was Eden. A strange name. Did she identify with Eve who was too smart to stay in a supposed Paradise? Maybe she'd picked Eden because the name reminded her of Eddy. Poor guy! In that Brooklyn restaurant, he never stood a chance. Danny-O had been lying in wait. But why?

That discovery was Payne's mission—a job not sanctioned by the FBI or anybody else. Other law enforcement people were involved. Other agents. And members of the Verone family. Who were they? And why, damn it, why had the Verones arranged a hit on Eddy?

He checked his wristwatch. Two forty-five. He'd promised to stay here until four. In the next hour and fifteen minutes, the course of his future might be determined. Either she would come to him or not. He hardly dared to hope. If she came to him…

A black Corvette with temporary tags roared into the parking lot and squealed to a stop outside his window. Eden bolted from the car. Her confused gaze darted. She didn't know which room was his.

A well-trained undercover agent would've stayed inside, not revealing himself with anything more than a subtle gesture. He would've exerted caution and patience. But Payne wasn't thinking like a federal agent. He was only a man.

He flung open the door to his room and strode toward her. His arms enveloped her. He inhaled the clean fragrance of her hair. My God, she was everything he'd ever wanted.

"Back off!" she ordered.

"You came to me." Ignoring her protest, he embraced her more tightly, hanging onto a dream that just might come true. "You're here."

"Well, duh!" Forcibly, she shoved free. "Listen, Payne. Or whoever you are. We've got to move. Now."

"Damn, you're beautiful." Her chestnut hair was mussed. Her white silk blouse had come partially untucked from the black skirt. Her breath came in gasps. Her cheeks flushed pink with excitement.

She wanted him. He knew she wanted him.

"Payne!" she shouted. "Did you hear me?"

He nodded, not trusting himself to speak without bursting into a sonnet to describe her melodious voice and fantastic—

"We gotta go," she said. "My grandfather's men could be here any minute."

"Why?"

Eden rolled her eyes. "Because I escaped from the funeral. I snuck through the bathroom window and stole a car.''

"Nice wheels," he noted.

"But a little obvious," she said. "Somebody could have followed me."

He doubted her logic. If she'd picked up a tail, they'd be here by now.

And there they were. Two full-sized sedans rounded the motel office and tore across the motel parking lot, aiming directly for them. Payne snapped a mental Polaroid, memorizing make, model and license plate number for future reference. Then, he grabbed Eden's hand and dove into his motel room.

"I told you so," she said.

"Yes, you did." And it was a little grating for her to mention that fact. He didn't need to be reminded of his tactical errors.

Crossing the motel room, Payne went through the door into a hallway that ran the length of the building. Pulling Eden along with him, he used his key on a room at the opposite side of the hall which he had also reserved. They entered a room that was a mirror image of the one they'd just left, except it opened onto a rear parking lot where his rental car awaited. "We go out this way."

"Got it," she said.

He went first. He could already hear gunfire from the opposite side of the Riverside Inn. Payne yanked his pistol from the holster attached to his belt.

At his car, he signalled to Eden. "Get in the passenger side and duck down."

She quickly obeyed.

He slid behind the wheel of a midsize rental car with just enough juice for decent acceleration. If the fates were with them, their assailants would be busy on the other side and wouldn't realize they'd fled until they were on their way.

No such luck! A bullet pinged against the side of the car.
He lowered the window and fired back, then glanced at
Eden who was crouched on the floor under the dashboard.

"Give me your gun," she said. "I'll return fire."

He'd prefer if she stayed in a more protected position.
"No."

"Give me the damn gun!"

Another bullet. He handed over the pistol. While he
drove, she poked the gun through the open window and
fired blindly in the direction of their attackers.

Payne raced to the end of the parking lot and merged
into a steady flow of traffic. Less than a mile from here
was the entry ramp to a major interstate highway. Dodging
from lane to lane, barely squeaking through every amber
light before it turned red, he drove past the interstate. "Are
they tailing us?"

Eden craned her neck to see through the rear window.
"I don't think so. Where are we going?"

He'd studied the maps but hadn't made firm plans. They
approached the intersection of two routes, offering three
possible directions for their escape. He made his decision
and turned left. "We're headed south."

The four lane road stretched past strip malls and gas
stations before narrowing to a two-lane. Payne pulled into
a cafe parking lot to watch the flow of traffic.

"What are you doing?" she demanded.

"I'm making sure they're not coming this way." None
of the passing cars matched the description he'd memorized. Though their flight had been sloppy, it had worked.
His advance planning had paid off. "I think we're okay on
this route. Give me my gun back."

"I don't think so," she said.

He took his eyes off the road and stared into her beautiful
but determined hazel eyes. What the hell was going on?
"Give the gun back. Now."

"It doesn't make sense for you to have the gun. You

need to concentrate on driving. I'm riding shotgun. That's what the passenger seat is called, you know. Riding shotgun.''

"Cute." But she wasn't an agent. Eden was the woman of his dreams. "Are you a marksman?"

"That's not the point," she said. "And shouldn't we be moving on?"

He couldn't believe that she was questioning his authority and trying to call the shots. However, she was correct. He ought to be on the road, putting distance between them and the Verones.

Silently, he put the car in gear, exited the cafe parking lot and headed south, unsure of their final destination. For now, he needed to stay in the Chicago area to pursue his investigation. Tomorrow, he planned to pick up the surveillance cameras he had placed at St. Catherine's to find out who had attended Eddy's funeral. He wondered if Danny-O had the guts to show up, to stand beside the coffin of the man he'd murdered. If Danny-O was there, who was with him? Who were the other agents who allied themselves with the Verones?

As he drove, he became aware of Eden staring at him. "What is it?" he asked.

"I'm trying to decide if I can trust you."

"Are you kidding? I've been in law enforcement all my adult life. I'm a senior agent. I teach classes at Quantico."

"That doesn't mean you're trustworthy," she said. "Twelve years ago, you were good enough at deception to fool my whole family. And me."

"That was my job."

"And now? What's your current assignment?"

"This time, it's personal," he said. "I need to find out why your brother was murdered."

"I see." Eden hadn't expected that response. She'd thought he was, once again, working on an elaborate takedown of the Verones.

She leaned back in her seat and stared through the windshield. Though she didn't believe in her grandfather's brand of vengeance, she was strangely touched that Payne was concerned about finding justice for her brother. "I didn't think you even liked Eddy."

"He was your brother." Payne shrugged. "That made him important to me."

And how would he feel when he learned he had a son? Eden wasn't sure she should tell him. Josh was her child, her baby. She'd raised him all by herself and had done a fine job for a single mother who showed up pregnant in Denver, not knowing a soul. Introducing a brand-new father would be traumatic to say the least.

She looked down at her lap. Her hands curled around the handle of the black automatic pistol. Her fingers were visibly trembling. She willed herself to stop but couldn't. Detached, she observed this strange quaking in her hands. Was she in shock? Her breath caught in her lungs and came in shallow little gasps. She forced herself to sigh. Exhale. Inhale. Get a grip!

This was a belated reaction to having her life threatened. When they were escaping from the motel, she hadn't acknowledged her fear, didn't allow herself to imagine that she could've been shot or killed. The reality sank in. My God, she could be dead right now. Like Eddy. Cold in his coffin. Dead like all the other Verones. The tremors marched up her arm, and she shivered.

"Are you cold?" Payne asked.

"A little scared." Defensively, she added, "Just a little."

"I never would've guessed. You handled yourself like a pro."

"A professional agent or a criminal? Do I remind you of someone who regularly engages in gun battles? Who goes for high-speed chases in stolen Corvettes?" She hadn't intended to snap at him, but she welcomed the outburst of anger that stifled her fear. "I am a Verone, you know."

"As if I could forget."

The tone of his voice cooled by several degrees, and she could feel him pulling away from her. Good! She didn't need Payne Magnuson, no matter what his mission. "I'll always be a Verone."

"I meant to compliment you," he said. "When those guys were coming after us, you were smart and quick."

That wasn't how she felt right now. She wanted to scream hysterically at the top of her lungs and give vent to the unbearable tension building inside her. Her nerves stretched tight as the head of a snare drum. Her pulse beat a sharp rat-a-tat-tat. She was nervous for her own safety and terrified for Josh. "I need to go to the airport."

"Not possible."

"Do I need to remind you that I'm the one with a gun in my hand?"

"There's no way you can catch a flight from O'Hare without someone noticing," he said. "We're being pursued by two different factions. Your grandfather's men. And a group of FBI agents who have convinced the Bureau that I'm the renegade. They'll want to bring you in for questioning."

"But I haven't done anything," she protested.

"Life ain't fair."

Implacably, he continued to drive along the southern route leading to nowhere. His hand on the wheel was steady. No tremors there. Payne was accustomed to danger. With his dark eyes trained on the road, he drove at a sane, responsible speed. His calm manner reassured her. Payne seemed like a man who could handle any crisis. He radiated a masculine aura of capability.

Eden ordered her lungs to exhale again, slowly. Her panic had begun to wane. Studying Payne soothed her. His features were sharply chiseled and his deep-set eyes held a lifetime of unspoken expression. She could see a strong resemblance to her son. Not a bad thing. She wouldn't mind if Josh grew up to look like his father with broad shoulders and strong wrists.

Eden wished she could simply ride along and admire the scenery, but she had important things to do. "I have to get back to Denver."

"How?"

"Airport," she repeated, exasperated by his unwillingness to comprehend. "O'Hare."

"I told you before. The FBI is looking for you. That means you can't take any form of public transportation. With the current level of airport security and surveillance, you wouldn't make it to the ticket counter before somebody picked you up." He glanced toward her. "The best way to get across country is to drive."

"It'll take forever," she said. There wasn't that much time. Her grandfather would track down the friends Josh was staying with. The Verones would grab her son before she could rescue him. "Isn't there a faster way? Maybe I could charter a plane."

He shook his head. "Surveillance, again."

How could she keep Josh safe? She had to find a way. "I need to be in Denver."

"What's the big rush, anyway? Your job? A boyfriend?"

There was no way to convince him of the urgency of her situation without inventing a stinky bouquet of lies. She had to tell him the truth.

At least, mostly the truth. She wouldn't reveal to Payne that he was the father of her son. Instead of saying that Josh was almost twelve, she'd subtract a year from his age. Payne would never guess the truth.

She stared at Payne's handsome profile and said, "The reason I need to hurry back to Denver is that...I have a son."

Chapter Three

"You have a son." Payne repeated her words, allowing them to sink into his consciousness like a depth charge blasting the hull of a torpedo.

She had a son? How had that happened? Well, of course, he knew how. He just didn't like to think of it. The idea of Eden and another man didn't fit his view of the world. She was *his woman.*

His fingers tightened on the steering wheel as he imagined this other man. This faceless interloper. Payne's foot tromped the accelerator pedal as he raced through an amber light. *She had a son.* "I didn't know you were married."

"I'm not. And I wasn't."

"The father?"

"He's out of the picture," she said. "Long gone. I've told my son that his father is dead."

From the snarly tone of her voice, Payne deduced that she'd be glad if this guy actually was deceased. That was some reassurance. At least she wasn't in love with the jerk who'd seduced and abandoned her.

He hit the accelerator again to pass a slow-moving vehicle before the route narrowed into a two lane ribbon wending through open fields. He buzzed open the window, thinking he might clear his head with the scent of new growth, but the only smell was the hot metal, gas-dribbling stench of traffic. Not pretty. Not perfume.

Her revelation would take some mental adjusting on his part. "How old is your boy?"

"He has a name," she said. "It's Josh. Josh Miller. And he's almost eleven years old."

Another bombshell struck. It didn't take a calculator to figure the timing. Twelve years ago, Eden fled from Chicago and settled in Denver. Approximately a year later, she gave birth. She must have met Josh's father within a few months after arriving in her new hometown.

While Payne had been recovering from his wounds after the final shootout with the Verones and then initiating a frantic search for her, she'd been with another guy. The woman of his dreams hadn't wasted much time before moving on with her life. A few lousy months was a damned fast turnaround, even if she'd thought he was dead at the time. A guppy would have been more faithful to his memory.

Harshly, he asked, "How did you get pregnant? You told me you were on birth control."

"I thought I was protected. If you remember, I wasn't very sophisticated when it came to sex. Apparently, I was doing something wrong."

"Apparently," he echoed. Sleeping with another man when she should have been mourning Payne's supposed death in Chicago was wrong. Dead wrong. They'd shared the love of the century. True love. Couldn't she have waited? At least a year. Maybe two years.

His perfect fantasy woman was turning into someone he didn't know. Eden Miller. A single mother from Denver with a complicated life.

"My son," she said, "is why I need to get back home. Do you understand?"

"Not really. I'm sure you left him with somebody responsible."

"Of course, I did," she said huffily. "I happen to be a very good mother."

The two-lane highway ahead was blocked by an ancient rattletrap truck forcing him to slow down. Forty miles per hour. Thirty. He crept along with no chance to pass on the winding road, stuck in second gear, frustration building on every level. "So, what's the big rush to get back to your son?"

"When Eddy was killed, my son became the only direct descendant of Gus Verone," she explained. "My grandfather wants to bring my son to Chicago so he can be groomed to take over the family business."

"And you don't want that to happen."

"Never," she said vehemently. "I've taught my son the difference between right and wrong. I didn't raise him to be a criminal."

Though Payne agreed that Gus Verone was a bad influence, he had another interpretation of the situation. It was possible that Gus only wanted to meet his grandson and have a chance to love the boy—a perfectly natural urge for a grandfather. "Have you told Gus how you feel about the family business?"

"According to my grandfather, things have changed. The Verones are on the up and up. They have an wine shop. Blah, blah, blah. It's all a lie."

"How do you know? You've been gone."

"Nothing has changed. My grandmother sits beside the coffin, silently mourning another tragic loss, tearing another piece from her soul. My cousins circle like sharks waiting to gain influence. My brother is murdered. Have you forgotten so quickly, Payne? We were pursued by armed men. They came after us with guns blazing."

"We don't know your grandfather sent them," he said. "In fact, I consider it unlikely. No matter what you think of Gus, he wouldn't put out a hit on his own granddaughter."

She sank back against the passenger seat. When he glanced over at her, she seemed deflated. Some of the wind had left her sails, and he couldn't help feeling a little bit sorry for her. Though Eden wasn't the tender goddess he remembered, Payne sympathized with her confusion. Somebody was after her. She didn't know who. She didn't know why they wanted to harm her.

Her dilemma wasn't too far removed from his own position as a supposedly renegade agent. However, Payne had years of experience in dealing with subterfuge and undercover operations. Plus, he didn't have a kid to worry about.

Slowly, she shook her head. Her thick, chestnut hair fell forward and obscured her face. She still held the gun in her lap. "If not my grandfather, then who? Who sent those thugs?"

It was the same people who ordered the hit on Eddy. The obvious conclusion solidified in his mind. There was another faction in the Verone family who wanted to take over the family crime business. With Eddy gone, there was only Gus to contend with. And Eden's young son. The boy might be in real danger.

Payne decided against revealing this logic to Eden. She'd only get more hostile. Instead, he probed for information. "Suppose there's someone in your family who wants to take over from Gus. Who do you think it might be?"

"Angela," she said without a second thought.

He clarified, "Your cousin, Angela Benedict. Why her?"

"I didn't steal her car. She kind of gave me the keys."

"Kind of?"

"She left them where I could take them and mentioned that she drove a black Corvette." Eden's fists clenched as if she were trying to hold onto a viable conclusion. "I suspected a setup at the time. Now, I'm sure of it."

"You're probably right," Payne said.

"She pretended to be so friendly. Even gave me her card

with her cell phone number. Can you believe she set me up? My own cousin!''

Payne wasn't too shocked by anything that happened within the Verone family. When it came to intrigues, they made the Borgias look like slackers. ''I've had my eye on her husband, Nicky.''

Eden shook her head. ''Nicky doesn't have the temperament for a boss. Angela said he was never the same after prison. Trust me on this. Angela is the strong one in that family.''

Though Payne didn't have computer access to FBI files, he remembered Angela—an incredibly beautiful woman with the temperament of a she-tiger. But could she stage a successful takeover? ''I don't think the Verone men would ever accept a woman as boss.''

''Maybe not,'' Eden said, ''but Angela could be the power behind the throne, shoving her husband forward to take over.''

''What about Robert Ciari? He's another cousin.''

''Everybody laughs at him. He has three daughters, and they call him the girl-maker.'' She rolled her eyes. ''My family is so politically incorrect.''

''Engaging in organized crime generally has that effect,'' Payne said.

''If they're coming after me,'' she said, ''imagine what they'd do to my son. I can't stand this!''

Driving behind the slow-moving, decrepit truck was making him crazy. The line of cars behind them had grown into a snaking caravan. Some were honking.

Up ahead, he spotted a diner, so designated by a sign that said: Diner. The letters were lit in neon pink, even in broad daylight, and the sign featured a picture of a pig with a knife and fork and the notation in quotes, ''Welcome to Hog Heaven.''

He flicked the turn signal and exited. ''Hungry?''

''How can you think of food at a time like this?''

"It's almost five o'clock. Chow time."

"I don't want to stop," she said. "If we keep driving, twenty-four seven, we can make it back to Denver by late tomorrow night."

"That means highway driving."

"Of course," she said. "Did you have some other route in mind? Planning on a little sight-seeing?"

"Cruising the interstate is risky. There could be patrol cars with an APB, looking for us. Not to mention aircraft surveillance. Besides, I have some business to take care of in the Chicago area before we leave."

"Fine," she said. "Drop me off. I can manage by myself."

He was tempted to do exactly that. Chauffeuring her across the Midwest interfered with his investigation. But he couldn't abandon her. Not when she was a target for the Verones. "Here's the deal, Eden. I'll get you back to Denver in one piece. And I have some ideas on how we can take care of your son in the meantime."

"Okay, let's keep going."

"Not going to happen." He parked the rental car in the rear lot behind the diner. "Your part of this deal is that you do what I say. No whining. No second-guessing. Agreed?"

"I don't have much choice." She glared at him. Her lips were tight, but for once she didn't argue. "Agreed."

Was she actually conceding? Or did she have something else in mind. He said, "I want my gun back. Now."

Again, she obeyed. Her suddenly docile attitude made him suspicious. All day long, she'd been sniping at him. Now, Eden was acting like Miss Congeniality.

He tucked his gun into the holster, got out of the car and slipped into his leather bomber jacket. Circling the rental car, he inspected the damage to the rear fender. Three bullet holes. One was only a few inches away from the gas line.

It could have sparked an explosion, could have been a lethal hit.

Eden stood outside the passenger side door, tucking in her shirt and fussing with her hair. "I don't suppose you have a hairbrush, do you?"

He pulled a black plastic comb from the back pocket of his jeans and handed it over. "Don't ask for my lipstick."

She didn't crack a smile. Something else was on her mind, and he figured that whatever she was plotting meant bad news for him.

In the diner, they sat across from each other in a red plastic booth. The pig theme on the sign was echoed by a dancing swine pattern on the curtains and a hog-shaped menu. The specialty of the house was, predictably, pork.

As she gazed down at the menu, he studied her. The delicate arch of her eyebrow and the line of her chin still brought to mind the youthful beauty he'd fallen in love with twelve years ago. But his attitude toward her was different. He no longer saw a fantasy woman. "What do you do for a living in Denver?"

"Part-time work for a caterer. I made some smart investments when I first moved to town and that pays most of my bills." She glanced up at him. "I spend most of my time with my son. You know, volunteering at his school. Driving car pools."

"You're a soccer mom."

"He plays baseball, too. And he loves computer games."

She was definitely *not* his fantasy woman. Eden had both feet planted on the ground. "How about you?" he asked. "What do you do for fun?"

She regarded him blankly. "I told you already. I spend time with my son."

"You used to dance."

She frowned and looked away. "Not anymore."

After they ordered, he leaned across the Formica-topped table toward her and spoke in a low voice. "I still have a

few federal contacts who I can trust.'' Payne's mentor—
the guy who'd taught him everything—was in Vegas. ''We
can use them to have your son taken into protective custody
until we get to Denver.''

''No, thank you. I'll take care of my son.'' She rear-
ranged her silverware on the table and took a sip of water
without looking at him. Avoiding his gaze?

''You're going to handle this all by yourself?''

''All by myself. That's how it's been from the minute
he was born.'' She slid out of the booth. ''If you'll excuse
me, I'm going to the ladies' room.''

He watched as she strode toward the rest room at the
rear of Hog Heaven. Shoulders straight and head held high,
she looked like a woman with a purpose. Which was? Once
before today, she'd slipped out a bathroom window and
stolen a car. Was she planning to do it again? Payne
couldn't remember if he'd double-checked the locks on the
rental car.

He signalled to the waitress. ''Make that order to go.
And give me a couple of bottled waters.''

Five minutes later, he paid at the register for their burgers. Eden still hadn't returned from the rest room.

He left the diner and walked around back. Though no
one appeared to be inside his rental car, a window at the
rear of the diner hung open. He opened the driver's side
door and saw Eden leaning across the gear shift and messing with the panel under the steering wheel.

She looked up at him with wide, surprised eyes. Scram-
bling, she assumed a more normal position in the passenger
seat. ''I can't quite remember how to hot-wire a car.''

''Technology has improved in the last twelve years,'' he
said. ''Grand theft auto is a lot more difficult these days.''

He slid behind the steering wheel and passed her the bag
containing the burgers. He was seriously ticked off. No way
would he get into this kind of game-playing with her. His
career was at stake. His very life was in danger.

If he was smart, he'd drive back to Chicago and dump her on the doorstep of Gus Verone. That was what she deserved. That was where she belonged.

Beside him, she took a bite of her hamburger. "Good," she said.

He couldn't believe her attitude. He'd found her trying to steal his car, and she wasn't even going to apologize. She expected him to accept her idiotic behavior without rancor or complaint. *Think again!* "You already betrayed our deal. Give me one good reason why I shouldn't dump you right here."

"Can't think of one." She sipped her bottled water. "Why don't you tell me?"

Her flippant remark grated against his last nerve. Payne devoured his hamburger so fast he barely tasted the grease. He stuck the car key in the ignition and started the engine.

"Where are we going?" she asked.

"Back toward the city." His tone was clipped and terse. "I have work to do."

"But I need to be in Denver."

Payne didn't bother to respond or reassure her that he intended to make sure her son was safe. He was calling the shots. If she didn't like his game plan, that was too damned bad.

EDEN DIDN'T MUCH CARE for the motel Payne had selected for the night, and she hated that they were stopping. Her need to get back to Denver and take care of Josh had become an obsession. He was her son, her responsibility. Like a ferocious mother hawk, she wanted to swoop home, gather him under her wing and soar away to the distant ends of the earth where no one would ever find them.

Sitting at the edge of one of the double beds, she watched avidly as Payne used a cell phone he'd taken from one of the suitcases he unpacked from the trunk. He punched in an interminable series of numbers, waited for a moment, punched in more numbers and then hung up.

"What are you doing?" she demanded.

"Taking care of business." His dark eyes regarded her coldly, and his mouth pursed slightly in a sneer. He looked like he wanted to spit. Ever since she'd tried to hot-wire the car, he'd been angry. "I'm arranging for your son to be safe. I need the name, phone number and address of the friends your son is staying with."

Eden hesitated. Giving this important information worried her, but she had no choice. If Payne could provide protection for Josh, she couldn't hold back. She grabbed a motel notepad and wrote down the data. "I should call my friends and let them know it's okay to let Josh leave."

"Fine."

She glanced at the cell phone. "Is it safe to talk on that thing? I thought cell phone signals could be picked up."

"This is a secure instrument."

Though she wasn't quite sure what that meant, his glower didn't encourage further conversation. "Would you mind telling me what's going to happen next?"

"This phone—the secured cell phone—will ring," Payne said. His impatient tone suggested that she was a complete moron. "I'll ID the safe contact on the other end. He'll arrange for someone in Denver—probably an agent—to pick up Josh and take him to a safe house."

"How can I trust this person?"

"Because I said so." He glowered at her.

"What's this supposed safe house like?" she asked. "It sounds kind of scary. Will my son be frightened?"

"If he's like most ten-year-olds, he'll be excited to play along with a federal agent." Payne rifled through one of his suitcases, sorting through equipment. "Kids love this stuff. It's like a game of cops and robbers."

He removed a handgun from his case and checked the ammunition clip. There was another gun—bigger with a long barrel—and other mechanical objects of varying size and shape, including a laptop computer.

"Boys and their toys," she said. Payne's studious interest in these gadgets reminded her of Josh. From the time her son was a baby, she'd encouraged him to read books and play with a variety of educational toys designed to enhance his intelligence. It had been a futile effort. Within minutes, Josh and his little boy buddies transformed the Microscope for Pre-schoolers into a machine gun and attacked each other with Tiny Toddler Slide Rulers. The only time Josh sat still was when he played computer games.

The phone rang. Payne exchanged information quickly and efficiently. He disconnected and tossed the cell phone over to her. "Call your friends. An agent will be on their doorstep within the hour."

Eden contacted her friends, made a purposely vague explanation about something weird happening on her vacation and assured them that it was okay to let Josh leave with the federal agent who would come to their home to pick him up. Then she asked to talk to her son.

"Hey, Mom. What's up?"

"I'm fine," she said. "Listen, honey, I've run into a little problem here. You need to stay with somebody else until I get back to town, okay?"

"Got it. So, who am I supposed to stay with?"

This was the hard part. She didn't want to scare him, but she had to tell him the truth. "The man who will come to pick you up is an FBI agent. He's going to take you to a safe house."

"Way cool."

He sounded far too calm...even a little bit happy. Probably, he was covering up his fear so she wouldn't worry. Gently, Eden said, "Everything is going to be okay. You don't need to be freaked out by—"

"A real fed? A g-man?"

"Yes, dear. But don't worry, I'll—"

"With, like, a real gun and handcuffs and stuff?"

"I suppose so," she said.

"Can I tell people? Or maybe not, huh?" His voice cracked. Nearly twelve years old, he was almost a man with a grown-up baritone. "Is this, like, top secret stuff?"

"Let's go with that. Let's call it top secret."

"You got it, Mom." She could almost see him puffing out his skinny chest as he whispered into the phone. "You think they'll show me their guns?"

"I'll be back in Denver as soon as possible," she answered quickly, purposely ignoring his question. "I love you, honey."

"Back at ya, Mom. Bye."

She disconnected the call, annoyed by her son's blatant enthusiasm for hanging out with a fed in a safe house. She would rather he'd been somewhat scared. Slightly cautious.

"How's your son?" Payne asked. "Is he okay with this?"

"He's thrilled," she said glumly. "He seems to think that real guns and handcuffs are way cool."

Payne grinned. "I might like this kid."

"Of course, you would." *You're his father.* She silently stumbled over the thought, glad she hadn't spoken aloud. "Why wouldn't you like Josh? I've brought him up well."

"You seem overprotective. Like the kind of mom who buys unisex dolls for a boy."

"I tried that," she admitted. "He tore off the doll's arms to look inside. Then he threw her on the roof to see if she could fly."

"That's good," Payne said. "Doesn't sound like he's suffering from not having a man around the house."

"In my opinion," she said archly, "the presence of a male role model is highly overrated."

"That's because you had one. No matter what else might

be said about Gus Verone, he's an archetypal male. Like those old silverback gorillas who rule the pack."

"Charming analogy," she said.

Searching her memory, she tried to remember if Payne had a male role model while he was growing up. He'd claimed to be an orphan, but that was when he called himself Peter Maggio. "I don't know anything about you."

"Sure you do. We used to talk."

"I talked to Peter Maggio." She had desperately loved Peter Maggio. He had been the center of her life. "I don't know Payne Magnuson."

"I'm not all that different from Pete Maggio."

"Tell me about your family."

He eyed her curiously. "Why do you want to know?"

Because you were once everything to me. It was impossible to look at him and not see the younger man she'd fallen in love with. Long ago, she'd memorized the masculine but elegant planes of his face, watching him at night while he slept beside her, always on his back. She knew his hands—a jagged scar across the knuckles on the right. She knew his body. Intimately. In a dusty, cobwebbed corner of her heart, she wondered if it could happen again. Could lightning strike twice in the same place?

On a more practical level, she rationalized that she ought to take these moments together to find out about his real family, the Magnuson family. She owed it to Josh to find out if there were any medical histories to watch out for.

She asked, "When you were growing up, did you have a male role model?"

"My father died when I was ten. Car accident. My mother remarried when I was thirteen. My stepfather was a decent man, but I never got real close to him."

"Why not?"

"He was a teacher at the local high school, and I always felt like he was spying on me." He grinned at the memory.

"I got real good at sneaking around. Maybe that's why I went into undercover work."

"And your birth father," Eden asked, "what did he do for a living?"

"He was an English professor at the university in Madison, Wisconsin. But he wasn't a poetry-spouting wuss. He was a real Hemingway kind of guy. Every weekend, we'd go camping or rock climbing."

Eden was pleased with this heritage. Josh had a professor in his background. Excellent! "Your father sounds like a macho guy."

"He wasn't obnoxious about it, but he was definitely a guy." Payne shrugged. "Male role model. It's good for kids to be around men who aren't afraid to act like men."

Unfortunately, that wasn't always possible. Eden had no choice in the matter. Peter Maggio had been dead. In her own defense, she said, "A woman can provide that kind of competitive, assertive model."

"Yeah? But would a woman get into a burping contest? Stick straws up her nose and shoot milk? Leave her socks on the floor?"

"Probably not, but—"

"Women don't understand the Three Stooges. Nyuk, nyuk, nyuk."

Definitely irritated, she was about to react when she noticed the twinkle in his eye. He was baiting her. Eden smiled to herself. Two could play at this game. She was very capable of being a tease. "You have a point, Payne. And let me tell you something else. It's not just about kids."

"What's not?"

She rose from the bed and came toward him, swinging her hips just enough to be subtly sexy. Her hand reached up and lightly patted his cheek. She purred, "Women like men who aren't afraid to act like men."

His eyebrows hiked high on his forehead. His mouth twisted in a surprised grimace. "I take it you're joking."

Tossing her hair, she said, "Take it any way you want."

She turned away from him and returned to the bed where she collapsed backward, lying flat. Though it wasn't a feather mattress, stretching out felt fantastic. She closed her eyelids. Relief flowed through her, washing away her inner tension. Josh was taken care of. The Verones didn't know her location. For the moment, anyway, everybody was safe.

"Don't get too comfortable," he said. "We need to go out and buy you some clothes and a jacket."

"Now?" She groaned. "Can't it wait until tomorrow?"

He was silent for a moment. "I guess so. Tomorrow starts early. We're leaving here at two in the morning."

"Why?"

"We need to stop at St. Catherine's to pick up a couple of surveillance cameras I placed at your brother's funeral. Between two and three in the morning sounds like a safe time to break into a church."

She kept her eyes shut, not wanting to think about breaking and entering at St. Catherine's. Or Eddy's funeral. Or Payne. She wasn't sure how to deal with the fact that he was still alive. Or that he was the father of her son.

Eden shuddered and sat up on the bed. "I ought to take a shower before I fall asleep."

He tossed an extra large T-shirt toward her. "You can use this for pajamas."

"And what will you wear?"

His dark eyes fastened on hers. "I think you remember how I prefer to sleep."

Nude! He slept in the nude! Oh dear, she most definitely didn't want to think about his long, muscular body stretched out on white cotton sheets. His broad chest, lightly sprinkled with springy hair. His lean torso.

Eden swallowed hard and lurched off the bed toward the small bathroom. She splashed water on her face and dragged Payne's little black comb through her tangled hair. It was important to stay in here long enough for him to get into bed, safely under the covers. If he started parading around the motel room naked, she didn't know what she'd do.

She confronted her sparkling eyes in the bathroom mirror. Could she sleep with him? No way! She'd done that once before, and look what happened. She rubbed his toothpaste across her teeth and rinsed her dry mouth with water. Her heart was beating too fast for someone who had no intention of making love tonight. Nor any other night. Not with him.

Cautiously, she peeked out from behind the bathroom door and saw him sitting at the circular table by the window, concentrating on the laptop he had opened before him. The lamplight reflected off the touch of silver in his black hair. He looked studious, like the son of a professor.

Wearing his T-shirt—which hung almost to her knees— she felt dangerously exposed. The short walk to her bed seemed like an impossible distance.

Eden straightened her shoulders. *Stop acting like a nervous little virgin!* Apart from the kiss when they first met, he'd given no indication that he was even attracted to her anymore. They were older now. Their lives were different. He was a senior agent who taught at Quantico. She was a soccer mom.

"Are you going to get in bed?" he asked. "Or spend the night lurking behind that door?"

"Don't watch me," she said.

"Okay."

But when she emerged from the bathroom, he faced directly toward her. His dark eyes devoured her. His gaze felt palpable as a slow caress, touching every part of her body. "You promised," she said.

"I lied."

"How am I supposed to trust you, if—"

"You're a beautiful woman," he interrupted. His voice was warm and intoxicating as aged cognac. "I wouldn't be a man if I looked away."

Utterly self-conscious, she walked to the bed, yanked back the covers and slipped inside. The sheets cooled her skin. She was trembling from her scalp to her toes. "Good night, Payne."

"Good night, Eden."

He turned off the light at the table, and the room became as dark as a midnight fantasy.

Chapter Four

At ten minutes past two in the morning, Payne was wide awake—dressed and showered with his suitcases repacked. Though he wasn't being careful about keeping quiet, Eden hadn't stirred. Sleeping like a rock, she lay on her back with one arm thrown above her head on the pillow. The glow from the bedside lamp shone on the delicate flesh of her inner arm, so pale her skin seemed luminescent.

Payne looked away from her. He didn't want to be attracted to Eden Miller. She wasn't the perfect fantasy woman he once remembered; she was the mother of another man's child. Barely trusting Payne, she'd tried to run from him, to steal his car and leave him stranded in Nowhereville. She wasn't an angel.

Driving her cross-country to Denver would take at least three days of fairly constant road time on back routes. Three days in hell. He slammed down the lid on his suitcase of high-tech surveillance equipment and weaponry, then glanced over at her sleeping figure. She still hadn't moved. Any normal human being would have been roused by his banging around in the motel room. Conclusion: She wasn't normal.

Eden was a supernatural succubus determined to test his patience and remind him that dreams never came true. Why else would she be here? There had to be a reason; everything happened for a reason.

He went to her bedside and stood over her. Her chestnut hair framed her face with careless curls. Her lips parted slightly. Full, kissable lips.

Though he'd intended to grab her shoulder and shake her awake, he couldn't bear to touch her. One touch would lead to another, and she'd murmur his name, and Payne would be lost to the nascent desires that teased his senses.

"Eden." His voice was husky. He leaned over her.

An adorable frown creased her forehead. "Izzit morning?"

He wanted to tell her that it was time—now was the moment when she would waken and see him for who he really was. Not a twelve-year-old memory, but a real man, matured and worthy of her trust. In spite of everything, he wanted her. "Eden."

"Wanna sleep more." But Eden felt herself swimming toward wakefulness. She took a gulp of air. Her eyelids lifted and she gazed up into a pair of warm, deep brown eyes. He smiled down at her. A halo of light surrounded his head.

"It's you," she said. She reached up, hoping this vision wouldn't vanish when she tried to touch him. The palm of her hand rested on his freshly shaved cheek, and she felt the solid bone beneath his skin. He smelled clean and wonderful. His black hair was damp as if he'd just come from the shower to her bed, come to make love to her.

"Peter," she whispered. Her eyes drifted shut. She lifted her chin, waiting for his sweet, soft kisses.

"Wake up, Eden."

His voice turned harsh. Why was Peter angry with her?

Eyelids still closed, she felt him moving away, disappearing again into the dark void. And she remembered reality. Peter Maggio was gone. Dead. Never to return.

She sat up on the bed and looked around the homely

motel room with scratched furniture and bland beige walls. Payne Magnuson stood at the edge of the window, peering through the space where the drapes met the wall. His back turned toward her as if he couldn't stand the sight of her.

Fine! She felt the same way about him. Eden could never be as close to Payne as she'd been to Peter, the man she'd loved with the wholehearted abandon of youth. They were older now; their lives had taken on all manner of complications.

"The shower is free," he said gruffly. "We need to get moving."

She glanced at the bedside clock. "It's two-twenty."

"I know."

She threw off the covers and stalked to the bathroom with none of the coy reticence she'd felt last night when intimacy tinted the air like a magical pink cloud. A new day set a new focus. There were tasks to be done. The sooner they got on the road, the sooner she'd be back in Denver with Josh. "I'll be ready in fifteen minutes."

Quickly in and out of the shower, she found a gray sweatsuit hanging from a hook on the bathroom door. In the nighttime chill, these sweats would be more practical than her skirt and sweater. She put on the huge clothing and rubbed a hole in the steamed-up mirror to look at herself. What a joke! In the over-large sweats, she looked absolutely absurd.

Stepping out of the bathroom, she allowed the long arms of the sweatshirt to droop over her hands and waved at Payne. "Look at me. I'm one of the Seven Dwarfs."

In spite of his cranky mood, he grinned. "Dopey?"

"Baggy," she said. "That was the dwarf with no fashion sense."

"Ready?" He'd already packed his two suitcases but left them on the bed as he put on his leather jacket over his shoulder holster. He nodded toward the door. "I've already warmed up the car."

"Aren't you going to take your bags?"

He shook his head and tossed her a lightweight parka. "Let's go."

Settled into the passenger seat, cozy and warm in his parka and sweatsuit, she felt an illogical but pleasant rush of excitement. They were starting out on a road trip, an adventure.

The headlights of their rental car cut through the silent, dark night. Few other cars were on the road, and it seemed they had the whole world to themselves. Wide open spaces waited to be explored.

In spite of the ever-present danger and the million and one reasons to be worried, she felt hopeful. "So, Payne. Why did you leave your stuff in the motel room?"

"It's our base of operations," he said. "I have a lot of sensitive equipment in those cases, and I don't want to risk losing it. Something might happen to this vehicle."

"Like what?"

"You never know." He shrugged. "It's best to leave all options open. Always look for a second escape route. Besides, we have to come back in this direction to catch the road we're going to take south to Danville. Then we'll cut across to Amish country."

He must have been busy last night. "Did you map our route on the computer?"

"Yeah," he said. "And I had contact with the agent at the safe house. Your son sounds like he's doing fine. He was kicking butt on the PlayStation games."

"The agent in Denver called last night? I wish you'd awakened me."

"I tried," he said. "I can't believe how heavy you sleep. Like a ton of granite."

"It's a talent," she said.

"If you ask me, it's a little weird."

"PlayStation," she said. Eden wasn't fond of the digitized entertainment her son enjoyed. "I hope the safe house agent isn't letting Josh play those violent animated games with the big-breasted women in tight leather."

"Oh, I'm sure he's not." Payne's voice was loaded with sarcasm. "A federal agent would never ever play with sexy cartoon babes."

He pulled into the parking lot of an all-night convenience store. "Do you still take your coffee black?"

"Absolutely."

He went inside and returned with two extra large coffees and a box of prepackaged powdered donuts that usually would've disgusted her. But Eden was starving. She munched aggressively, disregarding the cardboard taste of the food and the watered-down flavor of the coffee.

"I have more information," Payne said. "I put a trace on the license plates of the two cars that came after us yesterday. The vehicles are registered to Anthony Carelli and Terrance Ameche."

"Titty Ameche." She grinned, remembering a much younger man, kind of clumsy and very shy. His nickname came either from his preference for that particular body part or because he was a heavyset guy with a big chest. "He played football with my cousin, Robert Ciari."

"I thought his name sounded familiar," Payne said as he started the car and returned to the road. "What about the other guy?"

"Don't know him." These two—Anthony Carelli and Titty—were obviously aligned with the bad guys who had been responsible for her brother's death. "Do you think we should let my grandfather know that these men are not to be trusted?"

"That's a negative." He scowled at her. "Why would you think we should contact Gus about anything?"

"These guys tried to kill us. They're dangerous." No

matter how she felt about her grandfather, she didn't want him to be assassinated. "They might go after him."

"Doubtful. If they meant to kill Gus, they would've done it long ago. Besides, if we tell your grandfather, he'll demand revenge." Payne pointed out, "We don't want to be the ones who light the fuse."

"What fuse?"

"For a war inside the Verone family."

"Right." For a moment, she'd forgotten that practically everyone within the Verone circle had reason to mistrust everyone else. Her father once told her that the family that hates each other stays together, always watchful, taking care not to offend. How could she have forgotten the insane family code that dictated harsh vengeance no matter what the consequences?

Eden took another bite of her donut. She'd been thinking of the Verones as if they were normal. Obviously, she'd been away too long.

She was still nursing her extra large coffee when she recognized the streets leading to St. Catherine's. "What's our plan?" she asked.

"You stay right here in the car with the doors locked and drink your coffee."

"I have no problem with that assignment. It looks cold outside." She asked, "And what will you be doing?"

He explained, "I placed two mini-cameras inside the church. Sister Max said she'd try to remove them and would leave them in a prearranged spot. If everything goes right, I'll walk to the pickup point, grab the cameras, return to the car and we'll be on our way."

"Great," she said. "But I do have a request. My own rental car is nearby, parked on Elm Street three blocks from the church. Could we swing past and pick up my suitcase from the trunk?"

"I'll try to grab your luggage," he said. "Do you have the key?"

Eden reached down her collar and fished around inside her bra. Her fingers touched the business card given to her by Angela before she grabbed the single car key. "Here it is. I'll really appreciate if you do this, Payne. I want to get my purse. And my cell phone. And my own clothes."

"But you look so cute in the sweatsuit."

"Baggy the dwarf," she said. "Not a look I'd like to go public with."

He cruised to a silent stop five blocks away from St. Catherine's. Before he opened the car door, he cautioned her again. "Stay in the car."

"Good luck, Payne."

She watched him disappear into the night, moving with great stealth through the shadows between streetlights in this calm, suburban neighborhood. Once she heard a dog barking. Otherwise, there was no indication of Payne's presence.

His skill at undercover work impressed her. He was constantly planning ahead, mapping alternate escape routes and staying in focus as he went after the bad guys.

Somehow, she'd known from the first time they met that he was one of the good guys. Not a fed, of course. She hadn't suspected his secret identity. But he hadn't been a mindless thug or, worse, a sadistic hit man. When he posed as Peter Maggio, he was different from the other men who worked for her grandfather—more mindful, more inclined to talk through a problem than to shoot it.

She wondered if he'd sensed the same thing about her. Perhaps, his initial attraction to her had been the drawing together of two kindred spirits, both of them seeking to do the right thing in an atmosphere where criminal activity was part of daily business. She hoped so. It was nice to believe that there had been something more to their youthful affair than mere lust...not that there was anything wrong with the lust.

She sighed, sipped her coffee and checked her wristwatch. How long had he been gone? Seven minutes. Sitting here alone, the time passed slowly. If she'd still had the key to her rental car, she would've trotted over there herself to fetch her luggage.

A sharp rap at the passenger side window startled her. She turned and saw a man holding an FBI badge in one hand and a gun in the other. In the light of the streetlamp, she noticed that he had red hair. Was this Danny-O? The man who had murdered her brother?

"Open up," he said. "Payne sent me."

She didn't believe him. Intuitively, she knew this fed was not to be trusted. Damn it! She wished that Payne had left her a gun.

GLIDING THROUGH THE NIGHT, silent as a breeze, Payne neared the courtyard that stretched between St. Catherine's church and the school. Thus far, his progress had been unimpeded.

If he'd worn the night-vision glasses that gave a clear scope into every shadow, his approach might have been easier. But he didn't like to rely too much on technology that dulled the instincts necessary for undercover work. At heart, Payne was an old-fashioned spy.

He stepped silently onto the flagstones of the courtyard. At the edge of a recessed grotto on the north end, he recognized a small statue on a pedestal. St. Michael, patron saint of cops. The statue was made of stone. Years of exposure to snow and rain had worn down the detail on the sculpture, but the avenging angel with sword raised still looked fierce. Leading a charge, St. Michael's robes swirled around him. His face contorted in a battle cry. Payne offered a small prayer to this muscular saint before reaching behind his pedestal.

The two cameras were there. Sister Max hadn't let him down. Payne sent a silent thank you to that good woman.

With the cameras stashed in his pocket, he eased to the

edge of the courtyard. Then he spotted the sentry, strolling the distance between church and school.

Payne hid in a shadow, peering through the dark, trying to make out the features on this guy who wore a black jacket and trousers. He was on patrol and had the air of a man doing his duty, keeping watch. His attitude and clothes told Payne this guy wasn't one of the Verones. The sentry was a fed, possibly a former student at Quantico who hadn't paid attention when Payne advised that a stakeout never included marching back and forth.

Easily, Payne slipped past him. A rising sense of apprehension hastened his retreat toward the car where Eden was waiting. The FBI always worked in teams. If there was one fed, there had to be another.

STARING THROUGH the car window down the barrel of a gun, Eden decided to better her chance for escape by getting out of the car. If this guy meant to kill her, she was a sitting duck inside the car. On the street, she might be able to sweet-talk him and then to flee. At least she'd have mobility.

He moved back as she pushed open the car door. Flashing a supposedly friendly smile, she said, "You said that Payne sent you. Is he okay?"

"He's fine." The agent didn't lower his gun. "You're Eden Miller, right?"

"Yes, I am." Though her stomach flip-flopped with the familiar tension that came whenever she was stopped by a cop, Eden put on the straight-forward manner of an upright citizen with nothing to hide. Her internal agenda was very different. She wanted to learn if her first suspicion was correct. Was this burly, red-haired man Danny Oliphant? "And who are you? Do you mind if I take another tiny peek at your credentials?"

"Not necessary," he said. "Ma'am, I'm concerned about your son in Denver."

So was she. Eden wished that Payne had forced her to wake up when the agent called from the safe house. She would've felt much better if she'd spoken directly to Josh and heard, in his own words, that he was kicking butt with the PlayStation games. "What about my son?"

"I'll need the name and address of the people he's staying with. So he can be protected."

"Certainly." But Payne had already taken care of Josh's safety. If this fed was really working with Payne, he ought to be aware of the arrangements.

"Come with me, Miss. We need to insure your son's safety."

"Of course." He was lying. She could feel his deception like an icy fist grabbing her heart. Looking up at him, she wished he'd move into the light from the streetlamp so she could clearly view his face. "Are you Danny Oliphant?"

"My name isn't important."

"You really don't need your gun." She took a few steps back. "Holster your weapon, and I'll talk to you."

"Not a chance. Not while your little friend, Payne, is still at large."

"I thought you were working *with* Payne."

"Might as well be," he said. "I've studied all his operations. I know exactly how he thinks."

"Is that how you got interested in my family?"

"Could be."

Under the streetlight, she stared into the agent's bland face. She saw the glimmer of pure evil in his pale blue eyes. "You're Danny-O."

"That's right."

His lip coiled in a sneer, and she knew the truth. Unadulterated hatred flooded through her. "You killed my brother."

With no thought for her own safety, Eden sprang at him. Fingernails unsheathed, she aimed for his eyes. This bastard shot her brother. He deserved to die.

He dropped the gun to grapple with her. She scratched his face before he caught her hands. He was strong. He could overpower her easily, but she didn't care. She fought him with the fury of pent-up hatred—the vengeful fury of a true Verone. With all her strength, she pummeled his chest. Her legs lashed out with hard kicks. Still, he held her tightly.

She heard a thud. His arms lost all strength. Danny-O crumpled to the hard pavement of the suburban street where dogs had begun to bark.

As Danny-O fell, she saw Payne, gun in hand. He must have knocked Danny-O unconscious with the butt of his pistol. But unconscious wasn't enough. She wanted her brother's killer to be dead.

On hands and knees, Eden scrambled on the pavement, searching for Danny-O's gun. Here! Her hands locked on the handle. Her finger crooked around the trigger. Rising to her knees above him, she aimed into the despised face of a murderer.

"No!" Payne stepped in front of her, blocking her shot. "Eden, don't."

"Step aside," she said. "He's going to die."

"Verone justice?" He caught hold of her wrists and pointed the barrel of the gun downward. "If you shoot Danny-O, you're no better than—"

"I don't care," she said. "He killed Eddy."

"But he's still a federal agent. You'd be charged with his murder. You'd go to prison. Then what would happen to your son?"

"Oh God, you're right." She couldn't commit murder. What was she doing? What had she been thinking? Gasping, Eden released her grip on the gun.

"It's okay." Payne took the weapon, flipped the safety and tucked it into his belt before he handcuffed Danny-O on the sidewalk. If he'd had more time, he would've searched through Danny-O's pockets for his walkie-talkie

and other useful stuff, but the neighborhood was beginning
to wake up. Dogs howled ceaselessly. A couple of porch-
lights had come on. In a few minutes, the good people of
this south Chicago suburb would be dialing 9-1-1.

He grabbed Eden's hand and pulled her to her feet.
"Let's go. We're taking your rental car."

"I can't believe I almost killed him."

There would be plenty of time for recriminations later.
"But you didn't. That's what counts."

She raised tortured eyes to his face. "I should turn myself in before—"

"Later."

He yanked her into motion. She had no choice but to
come along, stumbling behind him in her baggy sweatsuit
and over-large jacket. Not a subtle escape. Not a classic
textbook maneuver.

Two streets to the north was Elm. The ruckus hadn't
quite spread this far. Four cars were parked along the street.
"Which one is yours?"

She pointed. "The little one."

An economy special. Not much power. He hoped they
wouldn't be caught in a high-speed chase.

Payne got behind the steering wheel and unlocked her
door while he adjusted the seat to accommodate his longer
legs. His heart was pounding. He wanted to take off like a
rocket but forced himself to drive carefully. The last thing
he needed was to be pulled over for speeding. When he
turned onto a main road, he checked in the rearview mirror.
No other car was behind him. So far, so good.

"Payne, do you think I'm a flawed person? Geneti-
cally?"

"Because your name is Verone?" He shook his head.
"I don't believe that stuff. Everybody has choices."

"But I was out of control." Her voice trembled. "I really
meant to kill Danny-O."

He checked the rearview mirror again. There were headlights behind them. A tail? He couldn't take the chance of slowing down to see if the car would pass. The odds were against him. Danny-O had been clever enough to post a guard at the church and to patrol the outer perimeter himself. Likely, he had other agents in the area.

Dead ahead was a set of railroad tracks which meant an access road, usually deserted at night. No trains in sight.

In the passenger seat beside him, Eden had buried her face in her hands. She didn't seem to be weeping, but he couldn't really tell. He bounced over the tracks and swerved onto the two lane road running parallel to the tracks.

The headlights in his rearview mirror followed. Definitely a tail.

Payne wished for a train. Some kind of distraction. An opportunity for escape. "Come on, Amtrak," he murmured.

This area was industrial, dotted with several warehouse facilities. At this hour, the only inhabitants were night watchmen. Payne increased his driving speed. The headlights in his rearview mirror kept pace.

They were headed west. A good diversion. His pursuers would assume he was trying to hook into Interstate 80, the most direct route to Colorado. Unfortunately, the fact that he was being followed also meant they had the make of the rental car and his license plate so they could put out an APB with the highway patrol.

Payne heard a train whistle—a lonely cry in the night. Driving parallel to the tracks, he passed an intersection where the black-and-white striped guard post descended and warning lights flashed. It was almost time to make his move.

A few blocks away, he saw the headlight on the train's engine. If Payne darted across the tracks just as the train approached, he could lose the tail. Timing was everything. He had to turn now. Right now!

At the intersection, he made a controlled swerve, avoided the black-and-white barrier and bumped onto the tracks. The locomotive bore down upon them. Tons of steel charged at them. Unstoppable.

As the economy rental car lurched forward, inches from disaster, he heard Eden scream. He dodged the barrier on the opposite side.

They were safe. The car following them was stuck on the other side of the tracks, waiting for the long freight train to pass.

At the first main road, Payne headed east toward their motel. He glanced toward Eden. "Are you okay?"

Her eyes were huge. "The next time you try to kill us, warn me. I deserve at least a minute to let my life flash before my eyes."

"I was losing a tail," he explained. "If I'd warned you, there would have been another minute to be scared."

"Oh, yeah. Total shock is better."

"Here's the new plan," he said. "We'll stop at the motel, pick up my suitcases and then we're on our way. While it's still dark, I ought to steal some new license plates."

He could feel her disapproval. Coldly, she said, "The distinction between the criminals and the feds is real thin. Like soldiers on opposite sides in a war."

"Not exactly. My side is fighting to protect the innocent and defend their rights. And, generally, the feds don't make as much money as the bad guys."

"Except for Danny-O," she said darkly. "He was trying to find Josh. Is there any way he'd know about the safe house in Denver?"

"None at all," Payne said. "The agent taking care of your son is a personal contact. He's not acting for the Bureau."

"Who is he acting for?"

"A friend."

Payne glanced in his rearview mirror. The road behind them was empty. For now.

Chapter Five

Danny Oliphant sat alone at a square table in the Cicero Cafe. Facing the door, he nursed a cup of bitter coffee and a throbbing ache in the back of his skull from stitches and a slight concussion. The doctor had ordered a couple of days' bedrest, but Danny-O didn't listen. The more serious injury was to his pride, and the only way to heal that wound was to apprehend Payne Magnuson and Eden Miller. That little witch! Danny-O touched a scratch on his cheek. It was her fault he'd been distracted. It was her fault Payne got the drop on him.

This incident should *not* have happened. Danny-O had done everything right, had analyzed the situation correctly. He'd known—beyond a doubt's shadow—that Payne would arrange surveillance at St. Catherine's during Eddy's funeral. Since Payne couldn't show up in person, he had to set cameras.

After the service, Danny-O and two other federal agents had swept the sanctuary and found nothing. But he knew, from years of studying Payne's methods of operation, that the cameras had been there and Payne would be back to collect them.

And Danny-O was right; he'd made the smart call. That was important to him. In his gut, he knew he was better than Payne. Smarter.

When Danny-O saw Titty Ameche and Tony Carelli lumber into the diner, he was disappointed. The ache in his head intensified. He'd expected to talk with the higher-ups. Damn it, he deserved their attention. The people who would ultimately run the Verone family business ought to be here, showing respect for the risks he'd taken and acknowledging his clever strategy in setting a trap at the church.

The two thugs pulled out chairs and sat at the small Formica-topped table, surrounding Danny-O.

Titty did the talking. "You let them get away."

"So did you," Danny-O pointed out. "At the motel."

"I got chewed out good for that." His big, angry face nestled on a double chin. His thick shoulders sloped down to a barrel chest. Though Titty wasn't in great shape and probably had a cholesterol count in four digits, Danny-O would be a fool to match muscle with this giant.

"You've got to admit," Danny-O said, "I was right in thinking they'd come back to the church."

"But you let them get away," Titty repeated.

That's right, you big moron! Rub it in! Danny reached for his coffee. Anger sent tremors through his fingers. His hand shook too much to lift the mug to his mouth. Fighting to maintain control, he reported, "I've ordered surveillance on the airport, trains and buses. According to our intelligence, they haven't left the area."

"Unless they're driving." Titty leaned toward him, resting his weight on his elbows and causing the table to tilt. He repeated, "They could be driving."

"I don't think they'll leave Chicago," Danny-O said. Payne was known for being relentless. It would take a lot to pull him off the case. "He'll stay here and investigate."

"Maybe." Titty shrugged his massive shoulders. "And maybe not. We think they're on the run. Candace wants to get back to Denver."

"With all due respect, it's not her decision." Eden Miller

wasn't calling the shots. Payne was in charge. He'd make the decisions. "Payne is the one we have to watch."

"He'll do what she says," Titty predicted.

Like hell he would. Payne Magnuson was the original loner. He didn't rely on anybody else's judgment, least of all the ideas of an untrained female who wasn't even part of the intelligence community. "Why?" he demanded. "Why do you think he'd let her boss him around?"

"The kid in Denver." Titty lowered his voice to a whisper. "Josh Miller is Peter Maggio's son."

"Damn!" Danny-O's head throbbed. In light of this information, he had to adjust his thinking. It was probable that Payne would head for Denver to care for his son personally. He was probably on the road right now.

"The only way they'd stick around here," Titty said, "is if they look to Gus for help."

"Payne won't." Danny-O was sure of that. "His ego is too big."

Protecting his child, Payne would be more determined than ever before, more emotionally involved. And that made him more dangerous.

Danny-O needed to stop Payne, to keep him from messing up this lucrative connection with the Verone crime family. Before now, it had seemed enough to discredit Payne and oust him from FBI protection based on forensic evidence with the murder weapon in Brooklyn and the combined eyewitness reports of Danny-O and Luke Borman.

Now the strategy had to change. Payne had to be apprehended. Then killed. To do otherwise was inviting disaster.

Death was the strategy. Danny-O smiled. He liked when things were settled and final. The tremors in his fingers stilled, and he raised the coffee mug to his lips. Payne's demise would be his ticket to success.

CRUISING ON Route One, parallel to the eastern edge of Illinois, Eden completed a cell phone conversation with

Josh who, indeed, sounded like he was having great fun at the safe house. Though she couldn't stop worrying about her son, she felt somewhat relieved. "Josh is doing well."

"Good." Payne drove steadily on the quiet back route. "I didn't think he'd be scared."

"Not a bit," she said. "Tell me about this safe house. Josh said they were in the mountains."

"I've never been there."

"But you're sure it's safe?"

"Yes," he said.

She gazed through the passenger side window as they crossed a two-lane bridge over the rushing Vermillion River, swelled to its banks in the early spring. A sign at the end of the bridge indicated that the next city of note was Paris.

From a study of the road maps, she knew they were also in the vicinity of Palermo and Scotland, but there was no way she'd confuse this flat Illinois countryside with France, Italy or the British Isles. The rich soil of the nation's breadbasket was dedicated to farming on a vast scale. New fields for soybeans, wheat, carrots, radishes and corn had been plowed in neat furrows. In some places, the fresh green shoots had already begun to leaf, seeking sunlight on this warmish April day while she and the man she'd once loved proceeded on their road trip. It all seemed so pleasantly normal—deceptively so. Peering into the distance, she saw storm clouds darkening the horizon, carrying the threat of tornado or flood. Danger was never far away.

Eden hiked up the sleeve of the over-large sweatsuit and checked her wristwatch. It was nearly eleven o'clock, and her stomach was growling. After they turned west, Payne had promised they could stop for lunch. She folded her arms below her breasts, holding in her hunger.

Her thoughts turned—as they had a hundred times before—to her homicidal rage on the streets near St. Catherine's. She had fully intended to kill Danny-O. If Payne hadn't stopped her, she would have pulled the trigger. For revenge. Her motivation and her behavior were pure Verone. How could she even think of murdering another human being? She was a mother, a decent person. For the last bake sale at Josh's school, she'd made a hundred cupcakes. Did that sound like the work of a psycho killer? Uncomfortable with her thoughts, she fidgeted nervously.

By contrast, Payne was utterly calm. When he talked about what had happened at the church, he was logical. The fact that Danny-O had dragged in a surveillance team and a chase team worried Payne. It seemed that the FBI was taking the job of apprehending him very seriously.

Holding back her hunger, she said, "Tell me about the people who are on our side."

"There are a couple of guys I've worked with who I can trust. Personal friends. But I really can't contact them. It's too obvious that I would. They'll be watched."

His reasoning was a bit convoluted, but she understood. "How did you arrange for the safe house?"

"A long time ago," he said, "I worked with a guy who was smart, tough and honest. I trust him with my life. If I'd been in the military, I'd call him my general. He's my mentor."

"And he runs a secret network of good guys?"

"Nothing so formal," Payne said. "Let's just say that whenever he contacts me and asks for a favor, I do what he says without question. And there are other people like me, willing to help no matter what."

"Is your mentor in Denver?"

"Frankly, Eden, I don't want to give you his location."

"Why not?" Their conversations seemed to constantly see-saw back and forth between truth and deception, suspicion and trust, past and present. "I'm not going to attack him or anything."

"This isn't about you," he said. "It's about intelligence

work. We might get separated. You might be picked up. In that case, the less you know, the better.''

She didn't like the way he tossed out these cryptic comments. *The less you know, the better.* What did that mean? Sarcastically, she said, ''Are we talking about some kind of interrogation? Truth serum? Beatings with rubber hoses? Broken kneecaps?''

''You know your family better than I do,'' he said.

''My family would never hurt me.''

''I seem to recall a couple of guys coming after us at the motel. I doubt they were firing blanks.''

She frowned. It was hard to imagine Titty Ameche purposely harming her. ''We got away, didn't we?''

''If they'd caught us,'' Payne said, ''I wouldn't expect you to hold back information, especially not if they threatened your son.''

Though he didn't come right out and accuse her of being unreliable, he didn't completely trust her, either. And why should he? Yesterday, she tried to hot-wire his car and escape. At St. Catherine's, she'd come within a hairbreadth of shooting a man in cold blood. These were definitely not the actions of a dependable, intelligent person. ''What made you decide to help me?''

''It's the right thing to do,'' he said.

''But you don't think of me the same way you think of your mentor. You don't have that same kind of unquestioning loyalty.''

''It's not the same,'' he said. ''But I have feelings for you.''

''Really?'' She felt inordinately pleased. ''What kind of feelings?''

''Responsibility. I want to protect you.'' He hesitated, considering. ''And there's guilt. Twelve years ago, I should have been smarter. I should have found you.''

''If you had found me, what would have happened?''

''I don't want to live in the past, Eden. There's no point

in nursing a regret or worrying about what might have been.''

But she didn't want to let go of these thoughts. ''Back then, you were in love with me.''

''That was then.''

And what about now? Could he, possibly, be a little bit attracted to her? Eden contemplated this thought, rolled it around in her mind and decided she wouldn't mind if he had a personal affinity for her—a special, sensual yearning born twelve years ago and awakened by seeing her again. Would that be so very impossible? She couldn't deny that when she looked at him, she felt a stirring deep inside— far more powerful than a superficial appreciation for a handsome man. She turned her head and studied him. What would it be like to make love to him now?

She noticed his hands, gripping the steering wheel. Though his fingers were long and sensitive like an artist or a concert pianist, these were definitely the hands of a man accustomed to rough work. There were scars. Calluses. Ridges and sinews. He had strong hands, capable hands. She imagined his touch on her body, skillfully arousing her.

When he was younger, their lovemaking was driven and wildly passionate. And now? She wondered if he would be more deliberate, paying more attention to detail. His caresses would slowly, gradually awaken her desires, delicately peeling back her inhibitions like petals on a rosebud.

As he drove, concentrating on the road, she stared at his face in profile. High cheekbones, straight nose, strong jawline. His bone structure was perfect. She focused on the straight line of his mouth. What would it be like to trace his lips with the tip of her tongue?

When he looked toward her, she peered into his eyes. In their ebony depths, she saw an exquisite, world-weary sadness.

''Hungry?'' he asked.

Eden was starved for his attention but couldn't tell him about those desires. He might reject her. He might abandon her. Again.

She had to be vigilant, to guard against this new emotional danger. She pulled her gaze away from his before her eyes revealed too much. Back to reality, she acknowledged that she was also hungry for food. All this sexual fantasizing was probably the result of low blood sugar. "I could eat."

"Me, too."

"How long until we get to Denver?" she asked.

"You sound like a kid." He grinned. "How many more miles? Are we there yet?"

"I'm not whining, I just want to know the plan. I know you have one. You have a plan and a contingency for everything."

"I figure we'll make it to the St. Louis area today. I'd like to stop somewhere near there and find a new vehicle."

"Another rental car?" she asked.

"Could be a problem," he said. Payne had used his undercover identity driver's license and credit card to rent the vehicle that was now in the custody of Danny Oliphant. "I'm sure the feds will be keeping track of car rentals, and I don't have another ID."

"I do," she said. "I keep another identity current just in case. It's Susan Anthony."

"As in Susan B. Anthony, the mother of women's suffrage?"

"The first real-live female on the dollar coin," she said. "I consider her a role model."

"For her stand on women's rights? Or because she was on the dollar?"

"Both," Eden said.

Though her attitude seemed breezy and offhand, Payne understood the abiding fear that caused her to maintain alternate identities. Candace Verone, alias Eden Miller, alias

Susan Anthony. She'd been undercover for twelve years—
a long assignment.

At the intersection with Route 36, he turned right, heading west. "When this is over, what do you plan to do?"

She leaned forward to peer through the windshield.
"Maybe I'll pick up and start over as Susan Anthony, even
though I hate to do that to Josh. He likes his school and
his friends. It'll be hard for him to understand why we're
moving."

"And why you're using a different name," Payne said.
"How much does your son know about the Verones?"

"Not much," she said. "I've told him, truthfully, that
my mother and father are both deceased. I've mentioned
his great-grandparents and others—aunts, uncles and cousins."

"Have you mentioned the Verone name?"

"Never," she said. "I can't take the chance that Josh
might read something in the newspaper or see something
on the news about the alleged crime family in Chicago.
Like the news reports of Eddy's murder."

"Did you tell your son that Eddy was his uncle?"

"No."

Though she didn't indulge in self-pity, Payne sensed her
loneliness. Breaking free from her family had cast her
adrift. "This has been hard for you."

"I'm okay." She sat up straighter in the seat beside him.
"Anyway, I'll use my Susan Anthony driver's license and
credit card to rent a car. I kind of hate to do it. I might
need the undercover identity later."

"We can find another way," Payne said. Though he
could probably go through his mentor to find a safe contact
in St. Louis, he didn't want to spread knowledge of his
whereabouts unless it was absolutely necessary. They'd be
better off buying another car with cash from a private party.

Actually, Payne knew an agent in St. Louis who might
help. His name was Samuels and he'd been at Quantico for

a while, teaching computer hacking and intelligence. It was a risk to contact him, but—

"I've got an idea." She flung her hands wide then clapped them together. Payne remembered her grandfather, Gus Verone, using the same emphatic gesture. No matter how much Eden avoided her heritage, there were unmistakable family traits. "I know people in St. Louis."

He didn't like the sound of this. "Who?"

"People," she said. "And, if I remember correctly, one of them sells used cars. It's perfect!"

Suspiciously, he asked, "Family?"

"Relatives on my mother's side. But don't worry. They hate the Verones. Since before I was born, there's been bad blood. Like the Hatfields and McCoys."

"Eden, I don't think it's smart to jump into the middle of a family vendetta."

"Not a problem. Aunt Camille and her family don't kill people. Gosh, I haven't seen them in years, not since I was a senior in high school and I stopped in St. Louis on my way to Carbondale to check out Southern Illinois University. I almost went there, you know."

"What changed your mind?"

"I got interested in this guy in Chicago." Her voice softened with nostalgia. "He worked for my grandfather which was a big strike against him. I swore I'd never get involved with a thug like Peter Maggio. But there was something about you."

"Wait a minute," Payne said. "Are you saying that you came after me?"

"Like a homing pigeon to the roost. Like an arrow to a bull's eye."

He couldn't believe it! "You? Came after me?"

"Didn't you think it was strange that I was always hanging around where you were?"

"I thought it was coincidence."

"You know better than that," she chided. "There are no coincidences."

"Everything happens for a reason," he completed the phrase that summed up his philosophy of life. But why? What was the ultimate reason for their youthful love affair? "Amazing. You initiated our relationship."

"You betcha," she said.

He truly hadn't noticed her wiles. And he couldn't blame his blindness on naïveté. He'd been a twenty-four-year-old man, a federal agent. Not a babe in the woods. As he thought back, a series of mental pictures flashed through his mind. A beautiful young woman sunbathing on the patio outside her grandfather's study, washing the car when he pulled into the driveway, waitressing at his table in a family restaurant. He remembered her musky perfume, her flashing eyes, the cascading ripple of her laughter. "You seduced me."

"Well, duh!"

"I can't believe it. Before I asked you out, I was in a moral dilemma, thinking I was too old for you. And you were stalking me."

"You were a definite hottie," she said. "Not that I made a regular practice of stalking."

"Why me?"

"Because." She lightly touched his arm. "I thought you were the one for me. The only one."

"I felt the same way."

An uncomfortable silence settled between them as the past and present intersected. If everything happened for a reason, why were they together right now? Payne knew she was leading him somewhere. Deeper into danger, most likely.

Through the windshield, he watched an Amish man prepare his fields using an old-fashioned horse-drawn plow. The farmer wore plain black trousers, suspenders and a wide-brim hat. Behind the man and team of plow horses were two young girls who carefully scattered seed. They wore plain, solid-colored dresses and little white caps to cover their hair.

"Not even a tractor," he said. The Amish sought to replicate the distant past even now in the new millennium. These plain people understood family. Their traditions were forever. "No cars. No electricity."

"I wonder," Eden said, "if I could come here and join the Amish."

He almost laughed out loud. Even in a baggy sweatsuit, she was too sophisticated. Beauty salon streaks highlighted her chestnut hair. Her attitude was pure city girl. "I thought you were a totally modern soccer mom."

"And a great cook. Don't forget that talent. I could use my cooking skills to fit in with these people," she said. "This would be an excellent environment for raising kids. They'd be safe."

Though he understood her longing for stability, the farming life wasn't for her. Or her son. "Josh is a PlayStation wizard. He'd be bored with horses and fields."

"True. Also, after being raised near the mountains, he'd never settle for prairies. The Amish probably don't go snowboarding."

"Probably not."

Payne exited Route 36 and drove into a small town. Outside a restaurant, he parked beside a hitching post for the horse-drawn Amish buggies. "Lunch," he said.

"I don't think they'll offer a vegetarian nouvelle cuisine menu, so I want some kind of chicken." She was already opening her door. "I need my suitcase from the trunk. It's definitely time to change clothes."

He entered the restaurant where there was a Bavarian atmosphere with a lot of Hummel-type figurines of rosy-cheeked boys and girls. Payne found a seat and ordered chicken dinners for both of them while Eden retired to the bathroom.

Today, he had no fears about her trying to flee from him. Like it or not, they were together until they reached Denver and located her son. He'd arrange for some sort of protective custody. Then, they could say goodbye again. Payne would return to his regular life, free from the fantasy of rediscovering the magic of his undying youthful love for the former Candace Verone.

When she sat down at the table, he hardly recognized her. The light touch of makeup enhanced her features and emphasized her luminous hazel eyes. Just like when she'd dressed as a nun with a white silk blouse, she managed to look stylish in blue jeans with a form-hugging burgundy sweater under a tailored tweed jacket. "Very nice."

"I know." She wasn't bragging, merely stating the facts. She knew how to put herself together. "Did you order?"

"Chicken," he said, still admiring the way she looked. He was seeing the real Eden Miller, single mother and capable human being. And Payne was drawn to her in a different way than in his dreams.

She took her cell phone from her purse. "I have another idea. What if I call Angela on her private cell phone?"

"Bad idea," he said.

"Hear me out, Payne. I could drop a few hints that would make her think we took the other route through Nebraska."

He nodded, considering. A little misdirection might be useful. "What reason would you give for calling her?"

"A thank-you for letting me use her car?"

"The brand-new black 'vette with the temp tags." He reached into his pocket and handed her his secured cell phone. "Keep it short. Don't say too much."

"If we were taking the north route, where would we be right now?"

"Iowa City," he said.

"Okay." Eden grinned as she accepted his cell phone, glad to be doing something useful instead of sitting in the passenger seat watching the scenery. "I'll be careful."

Eden dialed the phone number on Angela's business card. When her cousin answered, she identified herself as Candace.

"My God," Angela said. "Are you all right?"

"I've been better," she said. "Listen, I wanted to thank you for helping me escape. It means a lot that someone in the family understands how I feel."

"You ran off with Pete Maggio," Angela said. "I understand. You love him."

"No," Eden said. She looked across the table at Payne who watched her intently. "I mean, I don't know."

"Love makes women do foolish things." Angela's sigh was audible. "I'm sorry, Candace. You have to let him go. It's not safe for you to be with him. Come back home."

As if it was so much safer to be in the clutches of the Verones? "I don't think so."

"Tell me where you are. I'll come and get you. Personally."

That sounded like a threat. Eden felt a pinprick of anger toward her cousin who had set her up. "The same way Titty Ameche came to get me? With a gun?"

"I would never hurt you. If I did, Eddy would come down from Heaven and haunt me. Oh God, I miss him." There seemed to be a thread of real emotion in her voice. Angela cleared her throat and demanded, "Where the hell are you?"

"We're on the road. I can't really tell. Someplace near Iowa City?"

"You stay there," Angela said. "I'll come and—"

"Gotta go," Eden said. "Peter is coming back."

She disconnected the call and beamed across the table at Payne. "That was fun."

"What did she say?"

No way would Eden tell him about the foolishness of women in love. "She wants me to be safely brought into the family fold. Hah!"

"Do you still think she's the one running the family?"

Eden wasn't as sure as she'd been earlier. There seemed to have been a ring of sincerity in Angela's voice, especially when she spoke of Eddy. "It's hard to say."

"Because she's family," Payne said. "It's natural for you to believe in them. Go ahead and call your uncle in St. Louis. We'll get a different car from him."

Eden felt a rush of pleasure as she looked up Frank Borelli's phone number. She was on her way to visit her family. It felt like a homecoming.

Chapter Six

Eden was related to the Borellis of East St. Louis through her Aunt Camille, her mother's cousin who came to live with her mother's family after Camille's parents divorced—a scandal that still provoked gossip among the matriarchs. Whenever Grandmother Sophia spoke of Camille, she looked down her nose and whispered, "You know, she came from a broken home."

An obnoxious distinction, Eden thought. Especially coming from Sophia Verone whose family tree blossomed with murderers, thieves and nephews in prison. Worst of all, Grandmother Sophia had betrayed Eden at the church, delivering her into the waiting arms of Gus Verone. Eden frowned. It would take a long time to forgive such treachery. To Eden's way of thinking, her Aunt Camille—who had escaped to St. Louis and married an honest man—was a far more successful person than Sophia.

When Payne pulled up to the curb outside the two-story, Tudor-style house with shake shingles and peaked gables, Eden's heart lifted. After her grotesque face-off with the Verones in Chicago, this visit had to be better. What could be worse than escaping her family through a bathroom window, being tracked down and shot at by a thug named Titty? If it wasn't so absurd, Eden would've wept.

Looking out the passenger window, she sighed. "This place hasn't changed a bit. Not in thirteen years."

"Let's go over the plan again," Payne said. "We go in, get the new car and leave. Polite but quick."

"We have to stay for a bite." She opened the passenger side door and stepped onto the clean-swept sidewalk. "My Aunt Camille makes the most unbelievable, melt-in-your-mouth cannolis."

"One bite." Payne circled the car and stood beside her. "Then we're gone."

"We should've brought something. It isn't right to come here empty-handed."

"Eden, this isn't a social call."

"I know." But, just for a moment, she wanted to pretend that she was returning to the glowing family hearth where she would be beloved—embraced without question or demand. Not that her family life had ever been ideal. Of course, there were occasional moments, a few happy memories. A Christmas eve when the Verones sang carols. Dancing with her grandfather at Angela and Nicky Benedict's wedding. Her sixth birthday party when her mother rented a pony. Eden remembered coming home from school and finding her mother waiting with fresh baked ziti and a hug.

"Are you all right?" Payne asked.

"I'm fine." She pulled herself together as they strolled up the sidewalk past the blooming dahlias and a phalanx of garden gnomes. "Don't worry. I told Uncle Frank this was top secret stuff. Nobody else in the family will know we're here. Except for their son, Junior, because he's the one with the car lot."

Before Eden could knock, Aunt Camille flung the door open wide. She was a short, elfish woman with a huge smile. Her ebony, chin-length bouffant hairstyle hadn't varied since the early sixties. "Candace Verone," she squealed. "Omigod, omigod, you're here!"

Her tanned, wiry arms squeezed Eden tightly as she dragged her inside the foyer. Camille loosened her hold and squinted up. "Let me look at you. The streaks in the hair are very chic. You're a regular J-Lo."

"And you. You haven't changed at all." Eden wasn't merely offering a compliment. Her aunt appeared ageless. "You look great."

"A little lifting. A little tucking," Camille confided. "Expensive but worth it."

"Costs me a fortune." Her Uncle Frank strolled into the foyer. He was short with a comfortable potbelly and a shiny bald head. "Your Aunt Camille is no cheap date, *capisce?*"

When he hugged her, Eden smelled the cigar smoke clinging to his sweater vest and khakis. For as long as she could remember, Camille had been nagging him about his stogies.

"Omigod," Camille said. Her dark eyes sloshed with unshed tears. Her manicured fingernails closed around the gold crucifix she always wore. "Candace, you're so much like your dear mother, rest her soul."

"And your brother," her uncle said. "We read about Eddy in the papers. Another tragedy for the Verones. It should be your grandfather who gets shot. He should be the one rotting in his—"

"Knock it off, Frank." Camille turned to Payne. With a lightning change of temperament which was typical of this wildly emotional woman, she flashed her big smile. "Are you going to introduce us to your young man?"

"He's not mine," Eden said. "I mean, we're not dating or anything."

"I thought you were travelling across the country together."

"Well, we are," she said. "But—"

"No need to explain," Frank boomed. "Sheesh, Camille. Kids are different now. They don't get married at the drop of a hat."

"Are you saying you wouldn't marry me if you met me today?" Camille demanded.

He leaned toward her and murmured something in Italian which was, apparently, the right thing to say because Camille giggled.

Watching them, Eden smiled. Her aunt and uncle were boisterous. Their home was always filled with yelling and arm-flapping gestures, but there was never any doubt about their love.

Uncle Frank grabbed Payne's hand and pumped. "I'm Frank Borelli. I sell real estate, and I can't get my wife to move. Twenty years, and we're in the same house. And you?"

"I teach," Payne said. "Advanced classes at a school near Washington, D. C."

"Ah, good." Frank's eyes narrowed, still assessing this stranger. "So, *professore,* you got a name?"

"Peter Maggio."

Eden shot him a surprised glance. They hadn't discussed aliases, but she was pleased that he'd chosen to be Peter—an identity that took her back in time. It almost felt like she was visiting socially, introducing her aunt and uncle to the man she would one day marry. The father of her child.

"Maggio!" Uncle Frank clapped Payne on the shoulder. "A good Italian boy."

"Come to the kitchen," Camille ordered. "You have to eat. *Mangi.*"

The huge, redolent kitchen was the heart of this home with gleaming oak cabinetry, a double oven and double refrigerator, plastered with photographs. The countertops were stacked with every small appliance known to woman. "Sit at the counter," Camille ordered. "I know you're in a hurry."

"We have to wait," Uncle Frank said. "Junior is coming with the car. A little Nissan. Preowned but a real beaut."

Eden reminded him, "And Junior won't file the paperwork for a couple of days, right?"

Uncle Frank took a fat cigar from his shirt pocket and ran it under his nose, obviously wanting to light up but knowing he wasn't allowed to smoke in the house. "This car transaction. It better have nothing to do with Verone family business, *capisce?*"

"It's the opposite." Though Eden knew she should explain as little as possible, she ought to give some reason. "I went to Chicago for Eddy's funeral. My grandfather wanted me to stay. I didn't want to. I'm running away."

"Again?" Camille questioned, "What about your little boy? Do you have pictures?"

Of course, she did. Eden always carried a photo of Josh in her wallet, but she couldn't show the picture while Payne was around. He might see the resemblance. Who was she kidding? Josh was nearly identical to Payne; he couldn't miss the similarity which would cause serious problems when they got to Denver. She'd have to figure something out before then. "Sorry. No photos."

"I still have the baby picture you sent." Camille went to the refrigerator and studied the array. "He must be almost twelve now."

"Almost eleven," Eden corrected. Panic fluttered inside her. If Camille found that baby picture, it had the date of birth. Payne would see it. He would know. And she didn't want him to find out like this.

"I'm sure he's almost twelve," Camille said.

"Sheesh!" Uncle Frank rolled his eyes. "I think the girl knows when her own *bambino* was born. Are we going to eat?"

Camille frowned. "I must've put the picture in an album. I'll find it."

"Smells like lasagne," Frank said.

"You get salad," she said as she opened the oven and pulled out a pan of rich lasagne smothered in mozzarella.

"Beautiful!" Frank said. In fluent Italian, he extolled the virtues of his wife, her cooking and the wonders of pasta.

With an amused expression, Camille listened. Heat from the oven flushed her cheeks, and she looked very pretty as she nodded to her husband. "Maybe a tiny piece of lasagne for you, Frank."

"A big slab," he said.

"We'll see," she said as she heaped lasagne onto plates to serve Eden and Payne.

There was something endearingly intimate about the way her aunt and uncle related to food. Camille teased. Frank demanded. Their interaction was almost like foreplay.

Eden found herself smiling again. She really felt comfortable here, being part of a family, and she wished this experience could be a full-time part of her life, something to share with Josh. A family of her own. More children. A husband. A real home.

She tasted a forkful of the lasagne. The thick pasta layer and rich ricotta cheese balanced the garlic and oregano tang of the sauce. Magnificent! Maybe even better than sex.

She glanced over at Payne who chewed with his eyes closed, savoring the taste. He swallowed and exhaled a satisfied moan. "Camille, you're a goddess."

"My goddess," Frank said possessively.

"And you, Frank, are a lucky man," Payne said.

Slyly, Camille said, "I could give this recipe to my little Candace. I know she can cook."

"She's a fantastic cook," Payne said.

When he looked warmly toward her, she knew he was remembering the dinners she made for him so long ago. She'd fed him from her own fork and kissed away the last traces of sauce from his mouth. At this moment, as she met his gaze and saw her own memories reflected there, Eden felt extraordinarily close to him.

Aunt Camille said, "Cooking is the way to a man's heart."

Impulsively, Eden reached over to pat Payne on the belly. "Through his stomach."

He grasped her hand and lightly squeezed her fingers. "What's the way to a woman's heart?"

"Through her head," Eden said. "Women are much more practical than men."

With his free hand, he caressed her cheek. "I'd like to test that theory."

The front door crashed open and there came a shout, "Where is she? Where is my beautiful cousin?"

Leaving Payne behind, Eden hopped from the counter stool and ran to greet Junior. He was probably six inches taller but, otherwise, looked much like his father, including the bald head. Junior's enthusiastic temperament also showed Uncle Frank's influence as he scooped her off her feet and spun her around.

Junior had not come alone. With him was his wife and four children, all under the age of ten. The kids dashed into the kitchen to greet their grandparents, then scattered like jumping beans. Junior's wife, a buxom redhead, chatted like she'd known Eden forever. "Junior's told me all about you," she said. "He thought you were the prettiest, smartest thing in the world, you know."

"I never would've guessed," she said. "I seem to remember him chasing me with spiders."

"Because I liked you." As his wife followed her brood into the kitchen, Junior's expression turned serious. "I'm sorry about Eddy."

"Me, too."

"I sent flowers," he said. "I hope that was okay."

Eden was touched by his gesture. No matter how much the Borellis hated the Verones, they were relatives. Junior had tried to do the right thing. "I'm sure Grandmother Sophia appreciated them."

While Junior took Payne outside to close the deal on the preowned Nissan, another cousin and her husband arrived.

More lasagne was served, and the noise level in the house rose several decibels.

If this was Uncle Frank's idea of a top secret, low-key greeting, Eden couldn't imagine what a real party would be like. All these people, talking and laughing, surrounded her with a pleasant, poignant happiness. She wanted to gather up all these warm feelings to remember on the cold nights when she was all alone.

Payne came up beside her. "They're good people."

"Family." The word sounded magical. "Do you ever think about having one?"

"A family? Sure."

However, from what Payne had observed, family life didn't fit well with undercover assignments. The very nature of his work meant keeping secrets. His job meant he couldn't share, couldn't be completely open—not even with a spouse. The divorce rate among law enforcement personnel was way higher than the norm.

Additionally, Payne was nearly thirty-six, too old to change his ways. His best chance at having a family had been long ago with Eden, and his job had destroyed that precious possibility.

He watched as she mingled with the others. Teasing, she exchanged barbs with Junior. Gracefully, she roughhoused with Junior's kids. Eden appeared to be in her element, sparkling and glowing. She reveled in the give and take, the sharing of unconditional love.

Uncle Frank stepped up beside him. "She'll make some man a good wife."

"Yes," Payne readily agreed.

"Maybe you," Frank said, shamelessly meddling. "Her son is at the age when he needs a father."

"A stepfather," Payne corrected. Eden's son had a father—a faceless man she'd met in Denver. It was a fact that couldn't be changed.

"You can make kids of your own." Frank winked. "The making part isn't so hard to do."

"It's the raising part that worries me."

"Amen to that, *professore*."

The doorbell pealed again and twin cousins, Spike and Mike, stormed into the burgeoning Borelli household. One of the twins, Spike, was still dressed in his cop's uniform, and he seemed to study Payne with suspicion in his eyes.

Payne knew it was time to go. The danger of exposure grew more likely with each new person who joined the throng. But how could he drag Eden away from here? She was the belle of the ball—a Cinderella who wasn't anxious for the clock to strike midnight.

He couldn't blame her for grabbing a little pleasure, indulging in laughter. Her move to Denver must have felt like exile. Eden had enough room in her heart to embrace a large, extended family.

As Payne watched Eden moving among the family, helping her aunt Camille serve the cannolis, he wanted to give her this warmth. He wished he could have seen her when she was pregnant. Her home in Denver, he imagined, would be charming—filled with plants and carefully dusted souvenirs. He wondered if she'd saved anything from their time together.

The crowd moved into the living room in a straggling herd. This reunion could go on all night. Aunt Camille was threatening to haul out the old photo albums.

Abruptly, Eden put an end to the party. "I'm so sorry. We need to be on our way."

Amid a chorus of protests, she insisted. And Payne backed her up until they made it out the door and into the Nissan. As he drove into the night, Eden was hanging out of the passenger side window, blowing kisses and waving.

Rounding the corner, she sank back into her seat. In the dim interior light of the car, he could see her beaming contentedly. "I wish Josh had been here. All these cousins, and he doesn't know a single one of them."

"You could manage a visit," Payne said.

"Oh, sure. You saw what happened tonight. That was an impromptu get-together. If I came here on a planned trip, word would get back to Chicago."

"And then what?"

"And then, my grandfather would get involved." She shook her head. "I couldn't do that to the Borellis. They have a decent life here, and Gus Verone would poison it."

Payne didn't argue. Though her grandfather wasn't directly responsible for Eddy's murder or the current violence surrounding the Verones, it had sprung from seeds he'd planted long ago. "Tell me about your home in Denver," he said.

"I own a little house in the city. It's small, but it suits me."

"A yard? Any pets?"

"A little garden," she said, "where I grow fresh herbs for cooking. And we have five goldfish. The shiniest one with the biggest tail is named Peter."

After Peter Maggio, he assumed. She'd relegated him to the position of fish. At least he had a shiny tail. "What else? Do you have bookshelves? What kind of pictures on the wall?"

"It's nothing special. You'll get to see the place yourself when we get to Denver."

Or not. Until this business was settled, he couldn't allow her to return to her home address. The feds would have her house under surveillance. Payne didn't point out that fact. It seemed unnecessarily cruel to tell her that she might be on the verge of losing everything.

"Let me ask you a question," she said. "At Aunt Camille's, why did you use the name Peter Maggio?"

"That's my undercover identity. I have a driver's license and credit card."

"Kind of strange," she said. "I thought you'd retire that name when you supposedly died."

"Being deceased is the best cover of all," he said. Nobody expected a corpse to use a credit card. "I guess I could've changed to a different alias, but I had a sentimental attachment to Peter Maggio. When I used that name... Well, I was happy then."

He hadn't meant to say that much. Foolishly, he'd let down his guard. There was no reason in hell that she should care about Pete Maggio and his happiness or lack thereof. She'd gone on with her life, gotten pregnant, bought a house and raised a son. "Why didn't you ever get married and start a family of your own?"

"I have Josh," she said.

"When we were together, you wanted lots of kids. At least four."

"Things change."

"But you'd make a terrific mother for a huge family. You love to cook. You obviously enjoy being surrounded by family."

"All true," she said.

"So, what changed for you?"

"The man I loved was dead."

Eden's breath caught in her chest. She hadn't meant to tell him.

A profound quiet descended upon her as she stared straight ahead into the darkness beyond the headlights. During these twelve years, she'd established a life and functioned on a satisfactory level. But she was never far from grief. At first, she thought of Peter Maggio every single day. She felt his presence in the sunset and heard his voice in the whispering wind. She'd cried. She'd cursed. Even the incredible blessing of childbirth had been tinged with sadness because she believed her baby would never know his father.

With the passage of time, the ache had grown less painful, but she never fully recovered. She tried to date, but no other man was capable of matching her lost lover whose memory—burnished with despair and polished by her tears—became perfect. "Maybe now that I know you're alive, I can finally put the ghost of Peter Maggio to rest."

IN A MOTEL at the west edge of St. Louis, Payne focused again on his investigation, looking for the vital clue that would link Danny-O with the faction of the Verones who were trying to take over the crime business.

He set up his computer and prepared to study the mini-cam video he'd taken of the funeral.

Eden sat yoga-style in the center of the bed, ready to view the computer screen. After her shower, she hadn't changed into silky lingerie. Her cotton nightshirt under a terrycloth robe was the opposite of sexy. But damn cute.

His instinct was to wrap his arm around her shoulder and give her a companionable hug, but Payne held back. He didn't want to get too close. There were strange emotional undercurrents flowing between them, and he didn't dare to open the floodgates.

"I need to play the video of your brother's funeral," he said. "It's okay if you don't want to watch."

"Maybe I can help. I know a lot of these people and I might notice odd reactions."

"Your impressions will be useful," he said. His hope was that, in the video, he might glimpse some familiar faces of his own. Other agents. Other law enforcement people.

Payne was certain that Danny-O wasn't working alone. At the very least, Luke Borman was with him. And someone near the top of the food chain had given Danny-O access to top secret testimonies and files.

"You're looking for your friends, the feds," she said. "Tell me why a federal agent would get involved with my family's business."

"A big payoff." Payne remembered the seductive pull of a crime family. The money was lucrative, but the greater appeal was power. Twelve years ago, when he walked down the street as a bona fide member of the Verones, he was respected and feared. He had the best table at every restaurant. Ordinary people rushed to do his bidding.

"Is there a lot of money at stake?" Eden asked. "From what I understand, the lucrative parts of my grandfather's businesses were dismantled twelve years ago."

"It's been a long time," Payne reminded her. "I haven't kept track of the details, but there's been a rise in criminal activity formerly associated with the Verone family."

"Like what?" she asked.

"Bookmaking, porn, illegal gambling and usurious loans. All hard to trace. All hard to prove in a court of law. All profitable."

"Victimless crimes," Eden said. "Don't get me wrong. I don't approve of porn or gambling, but I believe it's up to the individual whether or not they place a bet on a football game."

"If the crimes went no further than petty indiscretions, the feds would look the other way," Payne said. "But it never stops there."

The first taste was always easy. A simple bet. Accepting a friendly gift. Telling a little white lie. The next bite went deeper. Then deeper. Until finally, the whole cake was consumed. "The problems come when the guy who doesn't pay off on his football bet gets a leg broken. Porn slips into prostitution. A loan ends up costing somebody his house and his business. These are crimes of intimidation. Somebody who owes the Verones will do anything—anything!— to appease the family."

She winced. "It's still painful to think of my grandfather like this."

"He might be innocent," Payne said. "As far as our federal records show, there haven't been any assaults or crimes that could be directly traced to Gus. He's largely cruising on his past reputation."

"And losing control?" she questioned.

"Yes."

"The sharks are circling," she said. "Gus isn't as strong as he used to be. Especially now that Eddy is gone. Somebody else in the family thinks they can take over from him."

"And those are the people we're after."

Payne booted up the computer program and sat back to watch. The display flashed on the screen without sound. This camera had been placed at the front of the church, looking up the center aisle. The sanctuary of St. Catherine's loomed huge and eerie, full of shadows. He watched an array of strangely familiar faces as people took their places in the old oak pews.

"That's Robert Ciari," Eden said. "The woman with him is his wife and those must be his daughters."

Payne recognized the dramatically beautiful woman who came next. Angela Benedict. Though she walked beside her husband, Nicky, they weren't touching. Angela had presence, a dark dignity. She nodded, unsmiling, to people on either side of the aisle.

"She looks like a queen," Eden said.

"A powerful woman." But Payne still couldn't imagine the men in the Verone family accepting a female boss.

Several other people filed into the church. Payne recognized one of the men. He stopped the video. "Damn it!"

"It's one of the twins," Eden said. "Spike and Mike, the Borelli twins. Do you think it's the cop?"

Payne immediately turned off the computer. Alarms were going off inside his head, but he tried not to overreact. "What do you know about Spike Borelli?"

"Practically nothing," she said. "I think his real name is Steve but they call him Spike because his brother's name is Mike and they're twins. They come from a big family. Ten kids, I think.''

Possibly, Spike had attended the funeral for reasons that had nothing to do with nefarious connections between law enforcement and the Verone family. On the other hand, Spike might be a link.

Unfortunately, these were questions that couldn't be easily answered through his mentor in Las Vegas. Payne needed someone inside the local law enforcement scene for verification. He sat down in front of the computer to look up a phone number.

''What are you doing?'' Eden asked.

''I know an agent stationed in St. Louis. His name is Samuels. He's a computer expert who was once at Quantico. I'm going to call him to see if he can fill in this blank.''

Using his secured cell phone, Payne punched in the numbers. ''Samuels?''

''Who's this?''

''Payne Magnuson.''

There was unreadable silence on the other end of the phone. It would have been handy if there was a code word or a signal that would let him know Samuels was on his side. Payne had to rely on his instincts. With deadly calm, he said, ''I need your help.''

''Shoot.''

''I'm interested in a St. Louis cop, Steve Borelli. Ever heard of him?''

''No,'' Samuels said.

''I need for you to access his files and tell me if there's anything suspicious about him. Any hint he might be connected to the Verones.''

''I'm at home, Payne. I'd need to go back to the office. Meet me there.''

Nice try, Samuels! ''I'm not in the area,'' Payne lied. ''Use your home computer.''

"I want to help you," Samuels said. His voice was calm, almost a monotone. "The best advice I can give is for you to turn yourself in. I'll arrange it. I can guarantee—"

"Don't make promises you can't keep."

Payne was ready to disconnect the call. He'd been mistaken when he thought this computer jockey would take a risk on his behalf. Samuels wasn't that kind.

"Payne!" His voice raised. "Why did you call me?"

"I believed you were somebody I could trust. Was I wrong?"

Again, there was silence on the other end of the phone. Payne ended the call.

He turned to Eden who perched on the edge of the double bed, biting at her fingernails. "Get dressed," he said. "We've got to move on."

"What's going on?"

"I can't get information on Steve Borelli, so I'm going to assume he's working with the Verones. Cousin Steve knows what kind of car we're driving. He knows we planned to stop for the night. He could've followed us to this motel."

"I can't believe it." Eden shook her head. "Spike Borelli is Camille's nephew, and he's associated with the Verones. She'll be so disappointed. This will kill her."

"No, Eden. This is going to kill us. We've got to get out of here. Fast."

Chapter Seven

Until they were beyond the suburbs of St. Louis, Eden held her breath, constantly turning to check through the rear window of the Nissan to see if they were being tailed. As before, they avoided the interstate highways where they might be picked up by the state patrol or local police.

Gradually, the city lights became less frequent. Residences grew farther apart and then were separated by acres of fenced farmland. The rolling fields of Missouri, divided by thickets and trees, spread endlessly in the bright moonlight. Though only ten o'clock at night, their little Nissan was the sole vehicle on many roads. To Eden's mind, their presence was far too obvious. Their headlights were visible from miles away.

Too easily, she imagined snipers in the bushes, helicopters zeroing in and other vehicles in hot pursuit with nowhere for their Nissan to hide. She felt vulnerable. And guilty, too. This danger was directly attributable to her insistence that they stop to visit with the Borellis. She could understand how Junior Borelli would send flowers to the funeral, but the fact that Spike Borelli—the nephew of Camille—had actually attended the service implied a much closer connection to the Verones. "I'm sorry, Payne."

"Forgeddabouddit," he said. "I probably did more damage with that call to Samuels."

"I still feel bad." She glanced through the rear window again. "And I don't like driving out here on these deserted back roads. There's no concealment."

"We could disguise the car as a cow or a tractor," he suggested. "Then we'd blend in to the background."

"Very funny."

"Don't worry, Eden. We'll be okay."

But she knew a disaster when she saw one. Before now, the bad guys had no idea which direction they'd take across the Midwest to Denver. Or they might have believed her phone call to Angela which placed them in Iowa.

Now, their location was pinpointed. The search could concentrate on southern Missouri, then Kansas—hundreds of miles of wide, open prairie. "What's your plan?"

"Keep going."

"That's it? That's the whole plan?"

"Basically."

"All night?" she asked.

"Until tomorrow morning when we can rent another car. Don't worry about me. All-nighters are no problem. I've done stakeouts that lasted for days."

"Well, that's very macho of you," she said. "But it really isn't necessary. I'll take a turn with the driving."

"No," he said.

Taken aback by his flat refusal, she peered at him. In the reflected light from the dashboard, she saw resolute stubbornness in the set of his jaw. Why? Surely his reluctance to let her drive wasn't a trust issue. At this point, it was clear they both wanted the same thing: To get to Denver in one piece. So, what was his problem? "Do you doubt my ability to handle a car?"

"Not a bit."

His mouth clamped shut. He didn't intend to offer any explanation, but she wasn't about to let him off the hook so easily. "Then why?"

"I don't mind driving."

"That isn't an explanation, Payne. Why won't you let me get behind the wheel?"

"It's a thing I have." His voice sounded sheepish and therefore sincere. "I can't stand riding in a car with somebody else driving."

In spite of her heightened anxiety, she grinned. "Don't tell me the big, bad, undercover agent has a little phobia?"

"It's a control thing." He visibly winced. "I shouldn't have said that. You're going to blow it all out of proportion."

"It's not a big deal, Payne. Your need for control doesn't exactly come as a big surprise."

To be honest, she found that trait appealing. A lot of guys were so busy being sensitive that they forgot how to stand on their own two feet. She preferred a man who unapologetically took charge.

Still, she couldn't pass up this opportunity to tease him. "Were you always this way? Did your kindergarten teacher's report say 'Does not play well with others?'"

"I get along just fine. As long as I'm boss."

"Must be hard sometimes," she said. "Don't all you feds have partners?"

"Not undercover," he said. "Good undercover agents are usually loners. According to assessments, I fit that profile."

Again, not a shocker. She'd known he was a guy who liked his own company. And Eden was a woman who enjoyed a boisterous crowd. Obviously, they were not a good match socially. It might be all for the best that they'd never had a chance at a long-term relationship.

They rode in companionable silence until she ventured, "I liked when you were treating me like a partner. Back in the motel room. When we were watching the computer video."

"Did you notice anything else on the tape?"

"Like what?"

"Interaction. Who was the boss?"

Eden knew exactly what he was talking about. From childhood, she'd learned the signs that told her who she ought to respect, who was dangerous and who was friendly. There were subtle nonverbal indications of deference to the leaders. A nod of the head. A glancing away. "My first impression was that Angela and Nicky aren't getting along too well as husband and wife. It's also interesting that their boys—both of whom are in college—weren't at the funeral. It shows a lack of respect for my grandparents."

"I hadn't thought of that. Good point."

She continued, "We didn't watch long enough to see Eddy's wife. I'd like to take a look at her."

"Why?"

"It doesn't seem like they had a good marriage, either. All these years and no kids." She wasn't sure why, but that might be a clue. "By the way, why did we have to go back to St. Catherine's to pick up the cameras? Why didn't you set them up to transmit directly to your computer?"

"You can do that?"

"I can't," she said. "But anybody who knows computers could set up a remote transmission. Josh and his little friends have mini-cams to broadcast to each other."

"I'm not good with technology," he said.

"Another confession," she teased. "I'm learning all your deep, dark secrets."

"Not even close." He reached over and gave her a friendly pat on the shoulder. "For right now, I'd suggest that you curl up and take a nap. When we get to Kansas City, we'll ditch the Nissan, and you can use your Susan Anthony identity to rent a different vehicle. Then we'll take a motel room and rest before the last leg of the trip to Denver."

That sounded more like a plan, but she had no intention of sleeping. If Payne intended to drive all night, she'd keep him company so he wouldn't get drowsy and fly off the road into a cornfield.

Eden twisted around until she was comfortable in her bucket seat and started talking. First, about Josh, her son, the light of her life. She gave Payne the full story from birth to preschool to grade school. The next challenge: junior high. Though it seemed like she was rambling on and on, Payne asked alert questions that showed he was listening.

His attention gratified her. He'd be glad for all these details when she finally told him that he was Josh's father. And when would that be? Soon, she thought. Maybe tomorrow after they were rested.

And what would be his response? He really couldn't be angry. It wasn't as if she'd purposely chosen to exclude him. He'd probably want a relationship with Josh; Payne was the sort of responsible man who'd never turn his back on his own son. Would he want split custody? And what about his relationship with her?

After a couple of hours and giant coffees from a convenience store, she drifted into other topics. Freely associating, she jumped from past to future and back again.

Payne stayed along on the conversational roller coaster, even telling his own stories and filling in the blanks of his life. He liked working at Quantico and researching undercover assignments more than going into the field himself. He'd purchased mountain land in Virginia and planned to build a vacation cabin there.

"Do you like the mountains?" she asked.

"Very much. I like the peace and quiet."

"Have you ever thought about living in Colorado?"

"I wouldn't mind," he said.

As the night wore on, she began to believe in his theory that everything happened for a reason. They'd been flung together on this long cross-country trip. And the reason? So they might have a second chance. Their old relationship might take root and blossom anew. If that were true, she felt lucky, indeed. Twice blessed. It might be perfect if she fell in love again with Josh's father.

IT WAS ELEVEN O'CLOCK on the following morning when Payne collapsed across the bed in the Comanche Motel outside Lawrence, Kansas. They'd rented another car in Kansas City and proceeded to here. Though he'd wanted to continue, his eyes were burning and his body felt stiff, as if he'd been encased in cement. He couldn't go one more mile.

Running back and forth from the car, Eden unloaded her own suitcase and the remains of lasagne and cannolis packed by Aunt Camille. "Do you know why this motel is named Comanche?" she asked in a bright, educational tone.

"Indian tribe," he murmured.

"You'd think so," she said. "But it's actually named for a horse named Comanche, the only creature to survive at Little Big Horn. I'm reading this out of one of those brochures I picked up in the motel office. Apparently, the stuffed horse is at a museum somewhere around here."

"Swell." Behind his closed eyelids, he saw the endless ribbon of highways, the racing fence posts, the broken middle line stretching into infinity.

"According to the brochures, this whole area has a bloody history," she said. "This is where Quantrill's Raiders massacred all those people in the Civil War. This would be a good code word, you know."

"What?"

"If I ever need to warn you about danger, I'll say: Comanche. And you'll think, Little Big Horn."

He was vaguely aware that she was untying the laces on his shoes and pulling them off his feet. "Gotta sleep now," he muttered.

"At least take off your jacket, Payne."

Without opening his eyes, he sat up and dragged his arms out of his jacket sleeves. His numb fingers fumbled with the buttons on his shirt.

"Good," she encouraged. "I'm pulling down the bed-spread. You just get comfy."

How could she still be standing? She hadn't slept, either. Maybe she had. A lot of her verbal musings on the road sounded like she'd been talking from an altered state.

He felt his face crack as his mouth curved in a spontaneous smile. In an obscure way, last night had been fun. He liked listening to the alto melody of her voice as she wove her stories. Like Scheherazade—if that fabled storyteller had been a soccer mom—Eden had a thousand and one tales. Some were sad. Some ended with a moral. Others with a grin. All were, in some way, charming. If he'd been twelve years younger, he would've taken her in his arms right now and showed her how much he appreciated her.

"I unpacked Aunt Camille's lasagne," she called out. "Do you want some? There's a microwave in the kitchenette."

Payne didn't think he could summon the energy to chew. "No."

Tearing off the rest of his clothes, he crawled between the sheets and fell into a deep, dreamless sleep.

Hours passed. The inside of his head went from wet cotton to mush to loamy soil where thoughts might grow. He waited for coherence, an answer to questions unasked. Tattered images from irrelevant dreams blew across his mental landscape like discarded newspapers. A conclusion was forming. Something to do with Samuels the computer expert and Luke Borman and Danny-O. If only Payne could catch hold and...

"Payne? Are you awake?"

He smelled lasagne. Suddenly hungry, he licked his lips.

"I made coffee," she said. "And I got some soda from the machine."

"Coffee?" Blindly, he groped toward the bedside table.

"Aha," she said. "There are those amazing catlike reflexes of a super undercover agent."

He pried open one eyelid to glare at her. She was on the other double bed, wearing her nightshirt and looking spunky. "What time is it?"

"Five in the evening," she said. "You wanted to be wakened so we could drive at night."

His fist curled around the cardboard coffee cup, and he dosed himself with caffeine before checking her out again. Through the thin cotton of her nightshirt, he saw the peak of her nipples. Very sexy.

Under the covers, he had a morning erection though it was nearly dusk. And, he realized, he was naked. Had he undressed last night or had she pulled off his clothes? And, if she had removed his clothing, had he made the natural and expected moves? For sure, he wouldn't forget if they'd made love. He pushed himself up to a sitting position against the pillows.

She pointed to the container of steaming lasagne. "You should eat. *Mangi.*"

"You don't look tired," he observed. "You're all dewy and fresh. No bags under the eyes."

"Makeup," she said. "It does wonders."

Payne began putting two and two together. She was wearing makeup but not dressed. She pushed food at him when she knew that the way to a man's heart was through his stomach. "Are you seducing me?"

"That's kind of a stretch."

But she didn't deny her motives. He patted the edge of the bed beside him. "Come over here."

Her hazel eyes flashed coquettishly. "Why should I?"

He took another sip of coffee. "I could beat around the bush and make up clever little enticements, but I think we're both too old for playing those games."

"Too old?"

"Mature," he said. "That's a compliment."

"Maybe. If you were looking to hire me as a house-keeper."

"Do you want the truth?" he asked. "Can you take it?"

"Give it to me straight."

If Payne had been wide awake and thinking alertly, he would have been more clever. But there was very little boundary between his dreams and his consciousness. "I want you to sit beside me on the bed and feed me. Then, I want to make love to you. For twelve years, you've been my fantasy woman. Now, I want the reality. I want you, Eden Miller."

She bolted to her feet.

Quite possibly, he'd just made a giant error in judgment.

She stood for a moment between the two double beds. She might slap him. She might dump coffee over his head. But she couldn't fault him for lack of honesty.

With the winsome grace of a feather drifting on dying winds, she lowered herself to the edge of the bed beside him. Her sultry hazel eyes confronted him with his own blunt honesty. Wordlessly, she accepted his proposition.

As she reached for the container of lasagne, her slender arms formed a beautiful arch. Never before had he thought of a woman's elbow as sexy, but she continued to surprise and reward him with unexpected charm in the simplest acts. She loaded a plastic fork. "Taste."

Dutifully, he opened his mouth and accepted the moz-zarella-laden pasta, thick and rich. Almost better as a left-over. "Good."

The texture of the lasagne aroused the juices in his mouth. When he swallowed, the needed nourishment gave him a surge of energy.

Another bite. A sip of soda to wash it down.

Since both of her hands were occupied with feeding him, Payne took advantage. He rested his palm on her firm thigh.

Her satiny skin gleamed in the light from the bedside lamp.

His fingertips eased higher, sliding under her nightshirt. When he reached the angle of her hip and spread his fingers to span her buttocks, he made a pleasant discovery. "You're not wearing panties."

"So? You're not wearing anything at all."

"Doesn't seem fair." He took the container of lasagne from her and set it on the table. "Let's get rid of the nightshirt."

She raised her arms above her head, and he lifted the soft cotton material, slowly revealing her hips, her belly button, her rib cage, her rounded breasts with dusky nipples. He beheld her with a sort of reverence. For twelve years, he had imagined this moment. Her body had undergone a few changes. The curve of her waist was more emphatic. Her breasts were heavier and even more enticing.

He threw the nightshirt across the bed and looked up to her face.

"Disappointed?" she asked. "As you pointed out, I'm older."

His hands rested on her flat stomach. Was it possible that she'd had a child? "When you were younger, you were...ethereal. Like a sea sprite. The flicker of sunlight on water." He cupped her breasts. "Now, the light has become you. There's a glow from within. You're a beautiful woman."

When she gifted him with a radiant smile, Payne knew he'd said the right thing. Even though there weren't enough words in his vocabulary to describe the way he was feeling, he'd pleased her and he was proud of himself for doing so. "That was poetic, wasn't it?"

"Very." She leaned forward to rest both hands on his chest. "Your body is different, too. There's a lot more hair."

"I'm a man," he said. "That's what happens to us."

"I like it." She bent down and nestled her cheek against his chest hair. Her streaked chestnut hair tickled his chin and he could smell the fragrance of her shampoo. She growled, "All this fur."

He slid down on the pillows, pulling her along with him, fitting her body against his. With incredible suppleness, she molded herself to him. Her thigh rubbed his erection, and he shuddered at the resulting jolt of electricity. It would take every shred of his willpower to hold off on his own climax until she was thoroughly satisfied. "Slowly," he cautioned.

"You're in charge," she said.

Willfully, Eden abandoned herself to his skillful touch. She closed her eyes and reveled in his tenderness which quickly grew to a wonderful ferocity. He yanked her across the bed. She lay on her back, and he rose above. His strength overpowered her, and she offered no resistance. Instead, she arched toward him, needing the touch of his flesh against hers. When he sought her lips, she allowed his tongue to force through her teeth and plunder the inside of her mouth.

Her entire body tingled with unbearable, delightful sensation as he fondled her breast and tweaked her taut nipple. She felt hot and needy. Desperately, she wanted him inside her. At the same time, she wished these erotic caresses might continue forever and ever and ever. Had it been this good before? Had she been so overwhelmed by his sheer male energy?

Anxious for fulfillment, she stroked his hardness. "Can't go slow."

He was groping across the bed. "Where are my pants? In my wallet. A condom."

A rational thread stitched through her unconscious passion. She might become pregnant again. It had happened once before with Payne and resulted in her son. "We don't need a condom," she said.

It wasn't a lie. She wanted another child.

"You're sure?" he asked.

"Yes." She pulled him toward her. "I want you. Now."

He poised above her. With maddening slowness, he entered her. With his first hard thrusts, he drove her to the brink. She trembled, reaching fulfillment.

Her soft moans of sheer pleasure did not end his controlled campaign of passion. He continued, unabated. She climaxed again and again until she was drained, exhausted by ecstasy.

Shuddering, he exploded within her.

They lay side by side, gasping and astounded by the most natural act imaginable. She wanted to speak, to tell him how fulfilled she felt. But her tongue wouldn't move. A perfect languor weighted her limbs.

She imagined his seed within her body, seeking to fertilize and propagate. Another child. She would love to be pregnant with his child. This time, he would stay with her. He would hold her hand in the delivery room.

Was it the right moment to tell him about Josh? In her mind, she searched for the right phrase, but she couldn't think clearly. What if he got angry? Or sad? It was better to wait. She didn't want to ruin their spectacular reunion.

"Hungry," he said. He grabbed for the remnants of the lasagne and began shoveling. "You want some?"

"I had some earlier." Watching him eat amused her. "There are also cannolis in the kitchenette."

He finished off the lasagne and bounded from the bed. Naked and unselfconscious, he strode across the motel room to the kitchenette. Gorgeous butt! His body amazed her.

He rejoined her on the bed to munch on his cannoli. First, he sucked out the cream. Then, he ate the outer pastry. When he leaned over and kissed her, he tasted sugary. "We should be going."

"Probably." She stroked the line of his jaw.

"On the other hand," he said, "Danny-O seems to have studied my psychological profile and knows my M.O., method of operation."

Where was he going with this logic? "And?"

"He'd expect me to be on the move. Completely dedicated to making fast progress across the country. Might be better to deviate from my usual single-minded attitude."

"What does that mean?"

He turned toward her. Gently, he took her hand and guided it down his body so she could feel his renewed erection. "I want to stay here all night. With you."

She couldn't think of a single objection.

Chapter Eight

Nightfall extinguished the hint of daylight that streaked between the imperfectly closed curtains in the Comanche Motel room. The digital clock on the table between the two double beds read: 9:28.

According to Eden's calculations, her initial physical contact with Payne had been at approximately half past five, which was four hours ago—four unbelievable, fantastic hours during which they'd made love again and again. And yet again. It had been the best afternoon of her life. She rolled to her side and rose up on her elbow to gaze down at Payne who lay flat on his back. The habitual tension in his face had calmed. His forehead smoothed, leaving only a trace of worry lines. A contented smile relaxed his jawline causing him to look years younger. Though his eyelids were closed, he wasn't sleeping. His hand crept toward her and tenderly fondled her breast.

Bemused, she caught hold of his questing fingers and held them. Eden wasn't sure she could survive another outburst of passion. Moments ago, when she'd gone to the bathroom, her legs trembled so much that she could barely walk. Marvelously exhausted, she felt weak as a newborn, well-suckled kitten.

His eyes snapped open. He was far too alert. "I could go again."

"Not now," she said firmly. "Honestly, Payne, I don't remember you like this at all. So insatiable."

"You love it," he said.

If she'd been a proper lady, she might have objected. But Eden was a woman with natural appetites that hadn't been satisfied in many years. "You're so right. Your lovemaking is better than Aunt Camille's cannolis. Better than fettuccine Alfredo."

"I want you to cook for me again," he said. "I want to see you in the kitchen wearing an apron and nothing else."

"With all those simmering sauces?" She brushed her lips across his knuckles. "Not going to happen."

"What would you make for me?"

"Something spicy," she said. She felt completely relaxed with him. Their passion had knocked down the barriers of mistrust. "I could name a dish after you. Payne's penne with meatballs."

"Do you make up your own recipes?"

"Sometimes. I've been playing around with culinary fusion."

"Fusion sounds dangerous," he teased. "Like something that might explode in my face."

She'd had her share of explosions in the kitchen—disasters when she experimented with new types of cuisines. "Fusion is the mixing of two ethnic types of cooking. I'm an Italian living in Denver where there's a lot of great Mexican food. So I'm fusing the two. My favorite is enchilada parmesan with Italian sausage and sour cream."

"Oh yeah," he said. "What's another one?"

"Angel hair pasta with tiny bits of jalapeña and guacamole on the side." The caterer she worked for had used that recipe for a side dish at a wedding, and it was a hit. "Once I tried chocolate mole on linguini. Not delicious."

"Do you try out these recipes on your son?"

"Not often. Josh doesn't like being my lab rat, not even when he's very well-fed."

If it wasn't a hamburger, her son didn't like it. Eden looked down at Payne and smiled. It would be so much fun to cook for him, to surprise him with a fantastic dinner. The perfect wine. Candlelight.

She wanted to take him home with her. To feed him every day. And make love every night. Apart from the fact that he hadn't offered to be her constant food taster, there was one more hurdle between them. Josh.

Until now, she hadn't felt safe telling Payne about their son, and she was still reluctant, unable to get over her fear that he would reject them both. But how could he? After these hours of intimacy, they'd reached a new level of trust. She broached the topic. "It's funny that you mentioned Josh. I was just thinking about him. I'm sure he's going to like you."

"What's not to like? I'm a fed. I carry a gun. I'm a cool guy." He sat up on the bed, rising to her eye level. "I know what's going on in your head, Eden. You're thinking about tomorrow. And the tomorrow after that. You're wondering how our relationship will affect your son."

Wordlessly, she nodded. He'd read her mind.

"The future," he said, "needs to stay in the future. While I'm a fugitive agent, I can't make promises. Do you understand?"

"Unfortunately, yes."

"First, I've got to deal with our immediate problems and eliminate every threat. Then, we can start thinking about all those tomorrows."

She accepted his reasoning. Until they were sure of survival, long-term commitments would not be discussed. But what if something terrible happened to him? Or to her? It was important that he know about Josh. "Payne, there's something I need to—"

"Hush." He placed a finger across her lips. "Later, we'll talk. Right now, I'm starving. We killed off all the lasagne and cannolis, right?"

"Right."

Payne rose from the bed, naked. He stretched and yawned like a gorgeous male animal. And he took her breath away. She was fascinated by his musculature, by the way his chest hair trailed down his torso.

"I'm going out to grab some burgers," he said. "Any requests?"

"Be careful," she said. Though she was hungry, her only certain need was for him to come back to her in one piece.

After he kissed her goodbye and went out the door, Eden stretched out on the sheets. For a moment, she contemplated taking a shower but then decided she enjoyed being wrapped in the musky scent of their spent passion. She liked the happy exhaustion, the tender ache of her body, the subtle heat that swelled through her veins.

A longing sigh escaped her lips. Payne had only been gone a moment, and she missed him already. This investigation needed to be completed soon so they could make plans for the future. More than ever, she wanted to solve the mystery of her brother's murder. The killer, of course, was not in question. Danny Oliphant had pulled the trigger.

The question was: Why? Who was he working for? What did he hope to gain?

Time to look for clues. After slipping into her nightshirt, she hooked up Payne's laptop and prepared to watch the tapes of Eddy's funeral. The positioning of the camera was fortunate because she wasn't forced to confront the coffin which she knew would be blanketed with grief, memory and fragrant white flowers.

Junior Borelli said he'd sent flowers which—at the time—struck her as a thoughtful gesture. Was there a more sinister connection? Junior ran a car lot, and the Verones had done their share of trafficking in stolen vehicles.

Eden shook her head. Even if his car lot had occasionally benefited from his distant connection to the Verones, Junior

GET FREE BOOKS and a FREE GIFT WHEN YOU PLAY THE...

Just scratch off the silver box with a coin. Then check below to see the gifts you get!

SLOT MACHINE GAME!

YES! I have scratched off the silver box. Please send me the 2 free Harlequin Intrigue® books and gift for which I qualify. I understand I am under no obligation to purchase any books, as explained on the back of this card.

181 HDL DRR4
(H-I-01/03)

381 HDL DRRN

FIRST NAME _____ LAST NAME _____

ADDRESS _____

APT.# _____ CITY _____

STATE/PROV. _____ ZIP/POSTAL CODE _____

7	7	7	Worth TWO FREE BOOKS plus a BONUS Mystery Gift!
🍒	🍒	🍒	Worth TWO FREE BOOKS!
♣	♣	♣	Worth ONE FREE BOOK!
🔔	🔔	🍒	TRY AGAIN!

Visit us online at www.eHarlequin.com

DETACH AND MAIL CARD TODAY!

The Harlequin Reader Service® — Here's how it works:

Accepting your 2 free books and gift places you under no obligation to buy anything. You may keep the books and gift and return the shipping statement marked "cancel." If you do not cancel, about a month later we'll send you 4 additional books and bill you just $3.99 each in the U.S., or $4.74 each in Canada, plus 25¢ shipping & handling per book and applicable taxes if any.* That's the complete price and — compared to cover prices of $4.75 each in the U.S. and $5.75 each in Canada — it's quite a bargain! You may cancel at any time, but if you choose to continue, every month we'll send you 4 more books, which you may either purchase at the discount price or return to us and cancel your subscription.

*Terms and prices subject to change without notice. Sales tax applicable in N.Y. Canadian residents will be charged applicable provincial taxes and GST.

was utterly settled in the St. Louis area. He had a family and ties to the community. She didn't suspect Junior.

His cousin Spike, the cop who had attended the funeral, was another matter. Watching the tape for the second time, she tried to figure out who was the companion of the Borelli cousin. As far as Eden could tell, Spike Borelli walked down the center aisle of the church alone, but he chose a pew near Robert Ciari and his family.

As she watched, other family members paraded into the church. Their expressions were somber and respectful as befit the funeral of a young man, dead before his time. She remembered from her youth, there was always a black dress in her closet, ready for another tragic death in her large extended family.

Her life as a soccer mom was so very different. Her son didn't even own a black suit. In Denver, they seldom attended funerals. Why would they? She and Josh had no family and only a few select friends. Though she regretted the isolation, it was far better than constant sorrow. She'd done the right thing in tearing her son away from the clutches of Gus Verone.

On the computer screen, she watched her grandmother Sophia walking stiffly into the church. She glanced neither right nor left. Her dry eyes stared straight ahead.

Conflicting emotions wrenched Eden's heart. Though her grandmother had betrayed her before the funeral, Sophia had also saved her. Twelve years ago, when Eden made her escape, Sophia protected her, lying to her husband and friends, keeping Eden's secret. Sophia understood. Though she herself was trapped, she knew that Eden would find a better life away from the family.

Behind her was Gus, the patriarch. His thick white hair was perfectly combed. His expensively tailored black suit fit his broad shoulders perfectly. He was still a handsome man. Much as Eden wanted to blame and despise him, she couldn't deny a certain fondness for her grandfather. As he marched toward the altar, Eden watched the reactions of the other mourners. Did anyone look away? Did their eyes shift with guilty knowledge?

Eden focused on the voluptuous Angela Benedict who was seated near the front pews. Her gaze cast downward in proper deference and respect, but as soon as Gus passed, Angela sat up straight. She held a small gold compact in her hand to check her appearance. *Strange.* They'd been in the ladies' room only moments before this video was taken.

Tapping on the computer keys, Eden froze the picture, then zoomed in for a close-up of Angela. Though the image was grainy, it was obvious why she needed a touch-up. Black mascara streaked her cheeks. She'd been weeping copiously.

"My God," Eden whispered. "Angela meant what she said about missing Eddy."

Though Eden's heart was touched by her cousin's display of sorrow, she had to consider another possibility. Maybe Angela cried from the guilt that came because she'd ordered Eddy's murder.

Eden went back to the action. Nicky, Angela's husband, reached over and snapped her compact closed with a brusque gesture. He looked angry.

The Benedicts were definitely not a happy couple.

The last mourner to come down the aisle was Eddy's wife. Leaning heavily on the arm of someone Eden didn't know, she seemed disoriented, almost drugged. Was she regretting her decision not to have children? Eddy's wife was a wild card; Eden knew very little about her.

She was, however, beginning to get a feel for Angela, and it was important to know more. Impulsively, Eden dug into her purse for her cell phone and the business card Angela had given her. As long as she kept the call brief, it couldn't be traced to her cell phone signal.

The phone rang only once before Angela answered in

her husky voice. In the background, Eden heard Bruce Springsteen's music. Springsteen had been Eddy's favorite.

"It's Eden," she said.

"You lied when you said you were in Iowa," Angela said. "Where are you?"

"I wanted to talk about Eddy," Eden said. "We'd been apart so long, I hardly knew him. Was he happy? How was his marriage?"

"Not so good. He deserved better than that sow he married." Angela didn't mince words. "Eddy deserved a lot better than her."

"Why? What did she do to him?"

"Spent his money too fast. Never took care of their house or Eddy. She'd rather go shopping than be with him. He was lonely."

Eden had known this conversation might be painful. She felt a stab of guilt. Eddy had been lonely, and she wasn't there to comfort him. His only sister had abandoned him. "I miss him," Eden said. "And I believe you do, too."

"Of course I miss him. His murder was a tragedy. And you know what's even sadder? The guy who killed him is your boyfriend. That fed."

"We both know that's a lie," Eden said. "You and I, we both know who pulled the trigger. And it wasn't Peter Maggio."

"You think you're smart," Angela challenged.

"I'm right," Eden responded. "The man who killed my brother is called Danny-O."

"I'm warning you right now," Angela said. "Get away from that fed who broke your heart. He'll bring you nothing but trouble. He's dangerous."

"I'm right, aren't I? It was Danny-O who murdered Eddy in cold blood."

After a telling silence, Angela said, "Where are you right now?"

Eden disconnected the call and sat on the edge of the bed,

staring at her cell phone. She had one answer. Angela hadn't denied that Danny-O was the murderer. She knew the truth. But was she responsible? Had she been the one who ordered the hit on Eddy?

When Payne returned with the burgers, fries and milk shakes, Eden bounced off the bed to greet him, eager to talk about her suspicions. "Angela is involved in this. She knows about Danny-O."

"And how do you know this?" He went to the kitchenette and set the paper bags of food on the little table.

"I called her."

He looked up sharply. "When?"

"Just now."

"I wish you hadn't done that," he said as he unwrapped a burger. "I'd rather take this investigation a step at a time. Logical steps."

She frowned as she grabbed a sandwich of her own. Though she probably should have consulted with him, she wasn't going to apologize for her impulse. "Want to hear about my conversation?"

"Might as well," Payne said.

She recounted word-for-word, then waited expectantly for his response. "Well?"

"Well." He finished chewing and swallowed. "I think we knew before that Angela was a major player in this game. Now she knows that we know."

"How can we find out if she's the one in charge?" Eden asked.

"Nine times out of ten, crimes are solved by following the money. Your cousin Angela drives a mighty expensive black Corvette. A brand-new car with temporary tags."

"It was bought just a few days ago. Right after Eddy's murder."

"What does that suggest?" Payne asked.

"A payoff." Eden enjoyed the way they were working

together, exchanging ideas. "Somebody else could be paying for her silence."

"It's a possibility," he said.

"Disgusting," Eden pronounced. "She'd sell out my brother for a new car. Greedy witch."

"Greed is only one possible motivation," he said philosophically. "There's also the desire for power. Or the need to take care of her loved ones. Revenge is another good motive. And sex, of course."

"How sex?" she asked.

"Angela might be turned on by the man with the biggest bankroll. A lot of women are that way."

"Not me," Eden disagreed. "I've never been aroused by flashy cars or fancy gifts."

"So, my baby don't care for rings or other expensive things." He grinned. "What attracts you?"

"I don't know. Nothing in particular."

"Come on, Eden. What floats your boat?"

She thought for a moment. She wanted a decent guy with a sense of humor and intelligence. But there was more—much more that she needed. He had to be sure of his masculinity. Had to be strong. Had to be good-looking. Had to be…Payne. "You attract me."

"Me?"

"'fraid so." No other man exerted this elemental magnetic pull on her senses. Nobody else had ever come close. Payne was, in her mind, the very essence of attraction. "I wonder why."

"I know the answer." Payne finished off his first burger and reached for another. His protein level had been severely depleted by their hours of lovemaking. He needed fuel.

"Why?" she demanded.

With her head cocked to one side and her thick chestnut hair falling across her forehead, he thought she was adorable. Eden Miller might not be the fantasy woman he'd imagined for all these years, but she fulfilled him in many ways. He liked her womanly body, her erotic responsiveness and the constant surprise of her feisty temperament.

"Payne?" Impatiently, she tapped her fingernails on the tabletop. "Why do you think you're so attractive to me?"

"Because there's nothing more appealing to a woman than a man who…appreciates her."

He'd almost said "a man who loves her." But he wasn't ready to make that declaration.

"Appreciation," she repeated. "That's not quite right. I mean, my son's soccer coach appreciates me when I bring orange slices to the games."

"As soon as I finish this burger and make a phone call, I'm going to show you exactly how you should be appreciated." He sucked his chocolate milk shake through a straw. The cold thick liquid melted on his tongue. "I'll start with your toes and work my way up your entire beautiful body."

Her smile enticed him. The facets of her hazel eyes sparkled with mysterious depth. No matter how much she protested that she'd had enough, he knew that Eden was enjoying their banquet of lovemaking as much as he was.

As he polished off his last burger, she ducked into the bathroom, saying she wanted to clean up. He heard the sound of the shower being turned on. Most definitely, he wanted to join her and lather her slender body with soap.

But first, Payne needed to contact his mentor. The man went by several different aliases, including Hawk, Cougar and Hammer. Payne called him Skip. He was in his sixties, a former U.S. Marine, a Vietnam veteran who had gone to work for the FBI as a trainer in undercover operations. His methods were unconventional—more focused on instinct than technology. He'd taught Payne how to think, how to keep his temper in check and how to survive. Currently living in Vegas with a brainy and beautiful former showgirl, Skip was supposedly retired.

Payne dialed, hung up and waited for the call back to his cell phone. The response came quickly.

"Hello, Skip," Payne said.

"Where the hell are you, buddy?"

"Kansas."

"You're in a lot of trouble." Skip's voice was gravelly, more like a growl than human speech. "If I didn't trust you like a son, I'd believe the story Danny-O and Borman are putting out."

"How's Borman doing?" Payne felt no guilt for the shooting in that Brooklyn restaurant, but he'd be glad if Borman survived.

"He's out of the hospital," Skip said. "The docs removed a couple yards of intestines, but you didn't hit any major organs with your body shot. Borman's worst injury was a sprained ankle when he hit the floor."

"Good," Payne said. "What else do you hear?"

"The spin on your cross-country drive is that you kidnapped Eden Miller, and you're using her to extort Gus Verone."

Frustration knotted in his belly. There was nothing worse than being accused and not given a chance to defend yourself. He waited for Skip to continue. In the background, Payne could hear the raucous dinging of Las Vegas slot machines.

"Here's an interesting twist," Skip said. "Eddy Verone didn't take that trip to New York by himself. He was accompanied by a couple of foot soldiers, his wife, Robert Ciari and Angela Benedict."

"What was the reason for the trip?" Payne asked.

"Business and pleasure. A couple of high-level meetings with the New York families which any semi-alert federal agent might take to mean that the Verones were getting back to criminal business under Eddy's leadership."

"I'm assuming Danny-O was assigned to surveillance."

"A-plus," Skip said. "Here's an interesting piece. You

said Luke Borman claimed to be waiting for his girlfriend at the restaurant.''

"That's right."

"That girlfriend was one of the Verone women."

"Angela," Payne said.

"Not so fast, buddy. Borman might've been dating Eddy's wife who was just about as faithful as an alley cat in heat." His rumbling laugh sounded like a cement mixer in overdrive. "The ladies in this family aren't crystal pure."

"Not all the ladies in the family," Payne said, thinking of Eden. "I'm worried about Eden. Is it safe to drop her off with her son and leave them both in Colorado?"

"I trust my man with the safe house. But there's a net out there, and it's drawing tight. Be careful. I wouldn't want Eden and her son to end up in the custody of Danny-O."

"Thanks, Skip, I'll talk to you tomorrow."

Payne disconnected the call.

As if from faraway, he heard the thrumming of the shower in the motel bathroom. The sound eased his tension as he thought of Eden standing naked in the shower with droplets glistening on her full breasts.

He began unbuttoning his shirt. Later, he'd worry about the Verone family intrigues and the federal agents who were working the angles. Tonight, there was another priority. Tonight, he had promised Eden that he would appreciate her, and he meant to be true to his word.

AT FOUR O'CLOCK in the morning, they were back on the road again with Payne behind the wheel of the fourth car they'd driven on this journey. Few streetlights interrupted the dark as they drove by abandoned farmhouses with plows and swingsets rusting in overgrown yards. There were occasional small towns, nearly identical with their storefronts, post offices and gas stations.

Staring through the moonlight across the treeless open spaces, Payne imagined he could see the curve of the earth on the horizon beneath an infinite canopy of stars. A desolate landscape. Yet, he was not alone.

In the passenger seat beside him, Eden had slipped into sleep. She curled into a ball, using his leather jacket as a blanket pulled up to her chin. Her hands fisted at the edge of his jacket.

He wanted to soothe her, to give her the peace and stability she desperately sought. After spending the night making love to her, he wanted to give her everything she ever wanted. She was fantastic. Unbelievable. If there had been only the two of them, he wouldn't have hesitated to make plans for a future with her—maybe nothing so permanent as marriage but a definite promise that they would live together after this investigation.

There was, however, her son to consider. Though Josh sounded like a good kid, Payne wasn't sure he was ready to become the father of another man's child. He'd spent his life as a bachelor. An instant family seemed like a radical adjustment.

In the distance, he saw the lights of a city which had to be Topeka. If he turned now, he could pick up Interstate 70 with its higher speed limit and straightforward route. He was tempted. This slow, tedious progress on back routes had begun to seem excessively cautious. This particular economy sedan had been rented in Kansas City using Eden's alter-identity as Susan Anthony. There was no way this car could be linked to them—no way there could be an APB for this license plate.

He took the turn and aimed toward the highway. When he merged onto I-70, Eden stirred. She peeked up. "Where are we?"

"Just past Topeka."

"On the highway? Is it safe?"

"I think so." With a feeling of exhilaration, he accelerated to pass a rumbling semi-truck. The little economy sedan was eating up the miles. "I don't think we're in serious danger of being discovered until we get near Denver."

"I thought it was risky," she said. "There's only one Interstate that leads from Kansas City to Denver."

"I'll get off soon," he promised.

They drove in silence for a while, staring through the windshield. Eden sighed. "So many truckers."

"Knights of the highway."

"That's a romantic image. I like to think of all these big rigs being on a quest, driving in all weather." She yawned. "I've always been fond of teamsters."

Payne grinned as he reconciled the idea of delicate little Eden hanging out with burly truck drivers. She'd be able to hold her own, would probably end up bossing them around.

The night had begun to thin as dawn streaked the skies behind them. The expanse of sheltering stars turned to a faint purple slate. No clouds meant no rain, which could be interpreted as a positive sign. Yet, as a state highway patrol car slipped past them, Payne worried. If they were stopped, the game was over. It might be smart to get off this highway. "We'll exit at Abilene."

"That's a famous cowboy town," she said. "I read about it in one of those motel brochures. Abilene is the end of the Chisholm Trail. Cattle were driven here from Texas and shipped east by railroad."

"Didn't know that," he said. "I don't think of Kansas as being part of the wild west."

"But it is," she said. "With Dodge City and Abilene. Wyatt Earp and bandits."

A second police vehicle cruised up beside them and kept pace for several miles, enough time to look through the window. The morning light was enough to give a clear view. Payne's senses prickled. Two patrol cars in a brief stretch seemed ominous. He was beginning to think he'd made a bad mistake in following this route.

"So," Eden said, "you've had some quiet time to think about the investigation. Any new conclusions?"

"Last night I talked to my mentor and he had some new information."

"Tell."

She tossed his jacket into the back seat. Today, she was dressed for action, wearing jeans and sneakers and a blouse under a loden sweater that made her hazel eyes look green. Casual and pretty, she looked like a soccer mom on her way to practice instead of a fugitive on the run.

Payne told her about the people accompanying Eddy on his fatal New York trip, and the clue that one of the women—either Angela or Eddy's wife—was having an affair with Borman.

"I'm betting on Eddy's wife," Eden said. "Angela is too smart to be unfaithful to Nicky. No matter how bad their marriage."

"You might be right."

Payne noticed in the rearview mirror that another car was following them. Headlights dimmed as the sky grew lighter. Another vehicle shouldn't be anything to worry about. They were on a highway, which meant traffic.

"What's wrong?" she asked. "You seem distracted."

"Nothing," he said.

But she turned in her seat and looked out the rear window. "Are they following us?"

"I doubt it. I mean, what are the odds? This is a huge countryside. Finding us out here would be like picking a needle out of a haystack."

Payne thought of the net drawing tight. Without signalling, he took the exit at Abilene. The other car stayed on their tail.

Chapter Nine

Eden's chatty morning attitude dried up faster than dew on the prairie where the morning wind whipped swirls in grassy rolling fields of green. Her throat felt suddenly parched. Someone was following them.

Payne had taken the first off-ramp that led to the outskirts of Abilene. The rural farming landscape became more hard-edged and rocky. Stacked stone walls marked the boundaries at the side of the road.

"Make a quick turn," she said. "See if he follows you."

"Can't," Payne replied as he checked in the rearview mirror. "I don't know the area. We might get stuck at a dead end."

Literally. "But we can't really know if this guy is following us or if he just happened to take the same exit off the highway."

"We'll know soon enough."

This wasn't fair! Last night, she and Payne had shared something fantastic. At the very least, their lovemaking had to be called a grand passion.

Not fair at all! She'd started to believe again that life might be beautiful, to hope that she might have a real future, a real family. Her son would know his father—a good man even though he was wearing his shoulder holster this morning.

Unfair! Her fragile dreams would be squashed before she had a chance to explore the myriad possibilities of a relationship. "How did they find us?"

"Luck and technology," he said. "A couple of police cars passed us on the highway. They have descriptions of us. Or photos."

"How?"

"Photos transmitted via fax machines to every cop on this stretch of highway. The patrolmen could identify us, then report their suspicions to local feds. It's our bad luck that there isn't much else going on and the weather is clear enough that these guys could see into our car."

"Why haven't they pulled us over?"

"My guess," he said, "is that we've been reported as being armed and dangerous. The feds are proceeding with caution."

The landscape along the two-lane road transformed to a more urban character as they approached town. Payne kept to the main route, leading past gas stations, cafes, motels and strip malls.

The black sedan stayed behind them. Though Eden peered hard, she couldn't see the driver through the tinted windows of the vehicle. A fed car, she thought. Big, powerful, dangerous and relentless. When Payne took a left turn toward the central business district of Abilene, Eden stared through the rear window. She held her breath, watching and waiting to see what the sedan would do. *Please don't let him turn.*

But he did. The ominous faceless pursuit continued through two more turns. The sedan was there, following from a few cars back. Any question of coincidence vanished from her mind. "They're definitely tailing us, Payne. I'm going to need a gun."

"No way."

"Hey! If I'm being treated like somebody who's armed and dangerous, I ought to have a weapon."

"As far as the feds are concerned, you're a hostage. If you start shooting at them, they won't buy that story, Patty Hearst. Trust me on this one. I know procedure."

"But I—"

"No gun." He shot her a glance that was immutable. He wouldn't change his mind. "I don't want you involved in a shoot-out. If bullets start flying, hit the ground and stay there."

She grasped his arm, pleading. "I can't stand idly by while you get gunned down. You've already died on me once, Payne. I won't let it happen again."

"It won't," he promised.

Remembering the agony of mourning his first demise, she'd almost prefer to die herself. But there was Josh to consider. She couldn't leave him motherless. There had to be another solution. "How can we both get out of this without being dead?"

"We could surrender," he said. "I'd be arrested. There's always a chance that the system would work the way it's supposed to, and the bad guys would get caught in their own web of lies."

What happened if the system failed? Eden already knew the answer. Payne would be in jail, and she'd be at the mercy of her grandfather and the new boss of the Verone family—whoever that might be. "Give me another option."

"Not a shoot-out," he said firmly. "We'll abandon the car and make a run for it."

They were driving through a warehouse area crisscrossed with bumpy train tracks. Perhaps he was planning another race with a speeding locomotive, darting across the tracks and leaving the feds behind.

But she doubted that strategy would work in this situation. It was morning, nearing rush hour, under clear skies. Even if they eluded this car, it would be difficult to disappear. How many routes led into or out of Abilene? How could they vanish in miles and miles of open fields?

Payne took another left and aimed their little rental car toward the downtown area. "Get ready to run," he said. "Anything you want to take with you, put in your pockets."

As he drove, he slipped into his leather jacket.

Traffic at the lights slowed to stop and start as they approached the business district. By zigzagging through the lanes, Payne gained some distance. He managed to get three cars between them and the black sedan.

Eden rested her hand on the door handle, ready to bolt. Her adrenaline keyed to a higher level, and she could feel her heart beating faster.

At a stoplight, Payne turned off the car engine. "Now. Follow me and keep low."

Almost as quickly as she opened the passenger door, he'd come around to her side. They darted between the stopped vehicles, bunched at the traffic jam he'd created.

Payne grabbed her hand, yanking her forward as they hit the sidewalk. Pedestrians stared as Payne and Eden ran past them, dodging around the corner of a building. Down the street, they sprinted at top speed.

At the corner, she glanced over her shoulder. From almost a block away, she saw the pursuers. Men in black windbreakers that likely said FBI in bold white letters across the back. Did they have guns?

Of course, the feds were armed!

They raced down another street, then turned, then doubled back. Payne seemed to know where he was going. Two more streets. They were back at the warehouses near the train yard.

When she looked back again, she saw no one, but she could feel them getting closer. In her mind, she heard the echo of running feet. Her shoulders twitched. She could feel unseen hands clawing at her.

Payne jogged across the tracks. "Be careful where you step, Eden."

"Right." Gasping for breath, she looked down at her feet, being careful not to stumble.

He barely seemed winded. His gun was in his hand. Calm and in control, Payne seemed to be in his natural element.

They reached a switching yard for trains with several parallel tracks and many trains. Payne led her down a narrow corridor between boxcars. These were dirty old freight trains, not gleaming Amtrak trains with dining cars and sleeping cabins. The stink of oil and soot clogged her nostrils. There was another odor, too. Stockyards were nearby.

Payne came to a halt, and she paused. Her lungs heaved, couldn't get enough air. She was dizzy, completely disoriented. Hazy spots danced at the edge of her peripheral vision.

"Come on," Payne urged. He pointed to a ladder on the side of an old boxcar. "Climb up here."

"You've got to be joking."

"Do it."

He lifted her up to grasp the rungs, and Eden climbed. The rusty metal scraped her palms. When she reached the top, she sprawled flat.

Payne lay beside her. He raised his head to look around. "I'm getting my bearings," he whispered. "Okay. I know where we go next."

Against the regular noise of the city, she heard shouts in the train yard. They were searching.

How could they escape? Did Payne mean to run across the top of the freight cars? She couldn't do it. These things were tall and scary. She couldn't make a leap from one to another.

"Down the ladder," he said.

She balked. "What are we doing?"

"There's a train getting ready to leave. We're going to hop a ride."

"That's crazy. I'm not a Hollywood stuntwoman."

"You're right." On top of the boxcar, he turned on his side and gazed into her eyes. "This might be where we part ways. You don't have to come with me."

She exhaled a shuddering breath. The panic she'd held at bay caught up to her. "I'm scared."

"It's going to be okay. These are the feds. Not the Verones." His voice was tender. "They think you're a hostage. They won't hurt you."

For an instant, she considered taking his advice. She wasn't a fugitive. Eden had spent her life as a law-abiding citizen, following the rules and rejecting her past. She wanted to believe Mr. Policeman was her friend, and elected officials didn't lie and good would always win in the end.

But she knew better. She would rather trust her fate to Payne. "I'm coming with you."

He gave her a quick kiss. "I'm glad."

They climbed down from the boxcar. This time, he went first and caught her at the bottom.

She followed him on a circuitous route, slipping between engines, oilcars, refrigerated cars and freight cars. They climbed across the ties and tracks. Shouts seemed to come from all directions, but she saw no one.

Beside a freight car that had once been painted red but had long since faded to gray, Payne climbed on the couplings between the cars then stepped onto a small platform where there was a door. He tried the handle. "Locked," he muttered.

He slammed his shoulder against it. The door into the freight car didn't budge.

The train lurched. It was about to pull away.

He reached down for her. When she clasped his hand,

he pulled her onto the small platform beside him. The mass of metal, wood and freight creaked and groaned.

Again, Payne flung himself against the locked door. Nothing happened.

"Hurry," she whispered.

"Not so fast," came a shout.

She looked down and saw a man wearing a black windbreaker. A fed. With both hands, he aimed his pistol at them. In a matter-of-fact monotone, he said, "Gotcha, Payne."

"Samuels," Payne said. "I should have known when you wouldn't help me. You're in this with Danny-O."

"That's correct." Except for the gun, he looked like an accountant.

"Why?" Payne demanded. "When I knew you at Quantico, you were a good agent."

"Then why did they ship me to St. Louis? You wouldn't understand, Payne. You've always been a star. I'm just another computer geek."

"It was you," Payne said. "You're the one who gave Danny-O access to those top secret files."

"Correct, again." A tiny smile touched the corner of his mouth. "And now, I'm going to be a very rich man."

Eden knew this man, Samuels, was the enemy. Why would he confess to them, unless he meant to—

"Step down from the train," he said.

"So you can get a better shot?" Payne shielded her with his body. "It's not too late to change your mind, Samuels. If you testify against Danny-O, you'll get a deal. Protective custody."

For a few seconds, he considered. Then he shook his head. "I already made my choice."

"You know it's wrong," Payne said.

With a ferocious jolt, the train started to move.

"Hey," Samuels yelled. "Get off there."

She heard two shots from his gun and felt the thuds as the bullets burrowed into the wall behind them.

Payne returned fire. Samuels went down.

Quickly, Payne turned and blasted the door handle behind them. He pulled her inside.

The dark interior of the freight car was filled with rubber tires, stacked one on top of another almost to the ceiling.

Flattened against the side of the car, Payne held her close. She could feel his heartbeat, only slightly accelerated. This was the way he lived! Close to danger, he was always on the run, undercover, using a gun.

A wave of revulsion swept over her. Eden didn't want this life for herself. And especially not for her son.

PAYNE COULDN'T REMEMBER another time when he'd so thoroughly botched an undercover operation. He never should've taken the highway, putting them at risk of being discovered. He should've known the cops would be watching, should've known they'd have photographs transmitted over fax machines to every cop on their route. What the hell had he been thinking?

Now their situation was even worse. He'd shot another agent—another nail in the coffin Danny-O was constructing for him. Payne knew the search would intensify. Federal agents would be instructed to shoot first and ask questions later.

It didn't seem possible to make things right. He and Eden were stuck on a slow-moving freight train headed to God-knowswhere, Kansas. Soon the other feds would figure out how they'd escaped from Abilene. They'd stop the trains. They'd search.

Leaning against the side of the boxcar, he thunked the back of his skull against the wall. Stupid, stupid, stupid. The old freight car rattled and rumbled like an earthquake on wheels. The floor shifted beneath his feet. He'd been too cocksure of himself, had underestimated the enemy.

Sure, he was out of practice in field work, but why had he made so damn many mistakes?

The answer came through the dark with a flash of clarity. On this operation, he had a partner. Eden.

Usually, Payne worked alone. His focus was undivided. Now, he was distracted by his need to protect her, to care for her. If he hadn't hooked up with Eden, he would've stayed in the Chicago area, tracking down leads at their source. He might have had this confusion solved, if it hadn't been for Eden.

Yet, he wouldn't have it any other way. Rediscovering this amazing woman made everything worthwhile. It was up to him to regain focus and save them both.

"Payne." Eden clung to him. "Do you think you killed that man? Samuels?"

"I hope not."

"This may sound strange, given my background and all, but I've never actually seen someone get shot." Her voice trembled. "It was terrible."

When he gave her a comforting squeeze, she felt stiff in his arms. The last thing he needed was for her to go into shock. "Pull yourself together, Eden."

"But you might have killed him. Aren't you even a little bit concerned?"

"For what?" he said bitterly. "The salvation of my immortal soul?"

"I wouldn't put it quite like that," she said. "But yes."

"Honey, when I start worrying about the condition of my soul, it's time to retire."

"I can't believe you're joking about this." Though he couldn't see her expression in the dark of the boxcar, he heard the condemnation in her voice when she continued, "Taking another man's life is a serious matter."

Later, he would repent. Later, he would agonize—as he always did—about the violence his job required. Late at night, he remembered the faces of every person he'd harmed in the line of duty. The injured, the dead and those he had betrayed. They haunted him. Their accusing presence was one of the reasons he left the field and arranged to teach at Quantico. There were too damned many ghosts, too many regrets.

And yet, Payne knew in his heart that his cause was just. The violence was necessary. "Tell me this, Eden. Would it have been better to stand down and let Samuels shoot us? Both of us?"

For a moment, she said nothing. They both knew he was right. There had been no choice but to return fire in self-defense.

In an outburst, she said, "You have to quit this job. I can't stand it."

"It's who I am," he said. He'd never been anything but a federal agent. Graduating college early, he'd breezed through law school and signed up, becoming one of the youngest agents ever hired by the Bureau. "It's all I ever wanted to do."

"Well, you've got to change."

"Why?"

"Because you have a son," she said.

Her words hung between them, suspended amid the rattling and roaring of the train. "Explain."

"Josh is your son. When I left Chicago, when I thought you were dead, I was pregnant with your son."

Payne's mind went blank. His heart wrenched. A shudder spread through his body and shivered across his flesh. But he wasn't cold. He was waking from a deep hibernation, shaking off the prickling pins and needles of temporary paralysis. He inhaled a deep breath, and fresh oxygen whooshed through him, expanding. It felt like he was about to explode, like his skin would peel away from his flesh transforming him from the inside out.

He was a father. He had no solid reason to be proud, but he was…a father. The realization knitted through his consciousness, drawing his fragmented self back together. He accepted her statement without doubt or question. On a cellular level, he must have known.

In the dark of the boxcar, he felt a smile crawl across his face. Being a father changed everything. "Eden, why did you pick this moment to tell me?"

"Because I'm afraid." But her voice sounded strong and defiant. "I thought we might be killed, and you deserve to know before you die."

"No more negative thoughts." He rubbed his hands up and down on her arms. "We're going to make it."

"How can you be so sure?"

"Because I've got to meet my son."

The rest of Payne's life spread before him like a map with a straightforward shining arrow marking the route to his future. He would clear himself in this investigation and devote the rest of his days to being a good, loving father.

He'd missed so much already. Nearly twelve years of his son's life.

"We've got to get off this train," he said. "The feds are going to guess this was our escape. They'll come after us."

"You're right," she said. "And how are we going to get off?"

"We'll jump."

He knew this feat was easier said than done. But they had no choice. Through the dark, he started climbing over stacks of rubber tires toward the sliding door in the center of the car.

"What are you doing?" Eden demanded.

"We can't jump from the platform outside the door to this car. We'd be squashed by the train. So we have to go out the side. Follow me."

"I can't even see you," she snarled.

He fished around in the pocket of his leather jacket and found a small laser beam flashlight. The dim illumination wasn't much better than total darkness. He turned it on and passed it back to her. "Keep up with me, Eden. We have to move fast."

Totally in focus, he charged forward. He'd been going at this investigation all wrong. He'd spent too much time running and hiding when he should have been on the offensive, taking the initiative.

It was unfortunate that he had to shoot Samuels. The computer geek would have made a powerful witness against Danny-O. Apparently, Samuels had been involved from the start. Resentful about his transfer to St. Louis, Samuels had joined with Danny-O and provided him with top secret information, probably hacking into the FBI files with fake clearances.

But Samuels was out of the picture. Payne needed to find another link between Danny-O and the Verone family. He needed proof of their conspiracy to murder Eddy.

At the side of the boxcar, he found the sliding door and shot off the lock. He shoved the heavy door open three feet, wide enough for them to jump.

The landscape rushed past. Green fields stretched toward clumps of trees. Few houses. When he looked straight down, the railroad ties blurred.

Eden peeked over his shoulder. "We can't do this. We'll break every bone in our bodies."

"Got a better plan?"

"No."

He looked down at her lovely face. Her chestnut hair tossed in the wind. She was the mother of his child. Alone, she'd raised him. "You can do this," he said. "You're the bravest woman I've ever known."

The train whistle sounded a long mournful wail, a signal that they were approaching a town. With any luck, the engine would slow down. "Get ready," he said.

"Wait a minute, Payne. How do we do this?"

"You might not believe this, but I've never jumped off a speeding locomotive."

Over the rumble of the train, he heard her mutter. "Gosh, Payne, I thought you were a superhero."

"Sarcasm," he said as he jostled against her. "That's good. You're getting back to normal."

"Just tell me how we're going to get off this thing."

He looked down at the sloping land beyond the tracks. "It's important to jump out—like a long jump in track. You want to be far enough away to clear the tracks. When you hit the ground, tuck and roll."

"We're slowing down," she said. "I can feel it."

Though they might be stopping to take on more cargo, he doubted it. More likely, they were going to be stopped so the feds could search the train.

On the plus side, they were losing speed. The whistle sounded again. The wheels squealed against the steel tracks. "I'm going to jump."

"What about me?"

If she didn't jump, it would be okay. The feds had no reason to harm her. If they took her into custody, Payne would find a way to protect her from the inside. He'd call Skip. He'd collect every favor owed to him during the course of his long career. From this moment forward, his life would be all about taking care of Eden and their son, Josh.

He held her upper arms. Balancing against the sway of the train, he kissed her hard on the mouth, tasting the sweet honey of her lips. "I'm glad you told me about our son. You've made me a happy man."

Turning away from her, he leapt from the train.

IF SHE'D HAD half a brain, Eden would've stayed in the boxcar. But there wasn't time to make rational decisions. She saw Payne tumbling and threw herself after him.

After her long jump, the earth came up fast. She crashed hard, rolling head over heels. Momentum ruled. Her body somersaulted out of control.

When she stopped, she lay flat on her back staring up at a whirling kaleidoscope of sky and clouds. Though aware of bruises, she didn't really feel the pain—too shocked by her impetuous leap to understand what had happened to her.

Slowly, she lifted one arm, then the other. They seemed to be in working order with nothing broken. She pushed herself to a sitting posture and tested her legs. She was functional. Everything was going to be okay.

She saw Payne striding toward her through the grass. His jeans were smeared with mud. His face was likewise streaked. He squatted down beside her. "Are you all right?"

Still a bit dazed, she nodded. "I think so."

"Then let's move it."

He stood, hitched up his belt and shrugged his shoulders inside his leather bomber jacket. When he put on his aviator sunglasses and scanned the horizon, he looked every inch the hero—tough, resilient and incredibly handsome with his thick, black hair and chiseled features.

There seemed to be a new sense of purpose in his stance. He radiated energy and vitality. "What's different about you?"

He held out his hand to help her to her feet, and when she was standing beside him, he pulled her close and said, "I'm tired of being chased and threatened. That's over."

She applauded the sentiment but doubted he could back up such a statement. They were, after all, stranded in the middle of a deserted grass field in Kansas with no visible means of escape.

"Don't get me wrong, Payne. I'm all in favor of positive thinking, but—" She winced as he hugged her closer. There was a serious ache in her hip. "How do you plan to avoid being threatened?"

"Strike first. As of this moment, I'm after them. The feds. The Verones. All of them." He pointed toward a barn in the distance. "We'll go that way."

Holding her hand, he set off at a relatively easy pace which was a good thing because, with every step she took, Eden discovered another bruise. Her joints felt like they were rubbing bone against bone. Her shoulders were stiff. Even her butt was sore.

As she moved, her muscles loosened. Though she'd sustained no permanent damage, her body felt battered as though she'd gone ten rounds with the heavyweight champ of the world. Right now, it was all she could do to walk in a semi-straight line.

He encouraged her. "You're doing great. Come on, Eden. We're going to make it."

"And how can you be so sure?" she asked.

Instead of answering, he posed a question. "In all the world, what's the most dangerous predator?"

She thought for a moment. Lions or tigers? Maybe some kind of poisonous snake? Or a hawk? Then, she had the answer. "A shark."

"The most dangerous predator is man." When he met her gaze, she saw his fierce resolve. "And I am that predator, that hunter."

The most dangerous man in the world? Eden shuddered. She did not feel reassured.

Chapter Ten

Eden leaned against the barn door, arms folded beneath her breasts. At the moment, she wasn't terribly fond of this newly macho incarnation of Payne who was saddling up a black-and-white spotted horse as if he knew what he was doing.

"This is stealing," she said.

"Borrowing," he corrected. "When we're done with the horses, we'll hop off, give them a slap on the rump and they'll find their way back home."

"How can you be so sure?"

"I grew up in Wisconsin. I know something about horses."

As far as she knew, growing up in Wisconsin was no particular qualification for handling livestock. For twelve years, she'd lived in Denver—home to the annual National Western Stock Show and dozens of rodeos—but that certainly didn't make her an expert on farm creatures. "Payne, this is ridiculous. Please let me hot-wire the truck that's just sitting out there."

"Grand theft auto," he said. "Very nice."

"Well, this is—" She flapped her hands angrily. "This is grand theft animal."

"We're *borrowing* the horses. Not stealing the truck."

"Please," she said.

"Forgeddaboudit."

She paced stiffly on the barn floor. Her body still ached from her punishing leap from the train. Now, he expected her to bounce around on horseback. "How far are we going?"

"Less than twenty miles."

He'd made arrangements on his cell phone with his mysterious mentor who pinpointed their location in central Kansas using global satellite technology. The plan was for them to rendezvous with a private pilot at Marion Lake and complete their journey by plane. She liked that part. Flying the rest of the way to Denver seemed like a very pleasant way to evade their pursuers.

Finishing with the saddle, he motioned to her. "Come on. I'll help you up."

"I'm warning you, Payne. I've only been on horseback three times in my whole life. And one of those was a painted pony on a carousel."

"It's not hard. I'll be right here with you."

Following his instructions, she reached for the saddle horn and jammed her toe into the dangling stirrup. Payne gave her a boost. She swung her leg wide and straddled. There she sat. On top of a large wide animal that smelled like hay. "Oh. My. God."

"You're going to be all right," he assured her as he easily mounted his own chestnut horse. "Take the reins and tug lightly in the direction you want to go."

Somewhere she'd heard that animals can smell fear, so Eden told herself she wasn't scared, wasn't scared, wasn't scared. She reached forward and patted the black mane that was scratchy and rough as...well, rough as horsehair. "How do I make him go?"

"Tap your heels against the flanks."

"Shouldn't I say giddyup? Maybe I should know his name. Do they all answer to Trigger or something?"

"Don't worry about it," he said. "We were damn lucky

to find a farmhouse with nobody home. We can't hang around to ask the horse's name.''

''Because we're stealing,'' she said emphatically.

''Head 'em up, move it out, cowgirl.''

With a jolt, they were on their way. Her black-and-white horse fell into step behind Payne's more spirited stallion. They left the barn and crossed the farmyard, heading across country rather than toward the road.

Eden balanced herself, trying to adjust to the rocking motion of her horse's gait. Her buttocks were already sore. It felt like she was too high off the ground. Longingly, she gazed toward the truck.

In a field of high grass, Payne turned back toward her. When he grinned, she felt a romantic little shiver. He looked good in the saddle. What was it about cowboys? The union of man and horse seemed so natural and sexy.

''Are you okay?'' he asked.

She might have told him that he was hot, but she was still too annoyed to toss any compliments in his direction. ''If I fall off this thing, you're in deep trouble.''

''We don't have time to walk twenty miles,'' he said. ''I'm going to speed up. Hold on with your knees and don't lose the reins.''

Abruptly, their pace sped up. Her horse started running. She went up and down on his back like a yo-yo on a short string. ''Ow. Ow. Ow.''

''Don't fight it,'' Payne advised. ''Get into the motion. Relax. Be one with the horse.''

''Ow. Ow. How about I make you one with my fist? Ow.''

Before she knew what was going on, they had reached a line of cottonwood trees beside a stream. They stopped. Her horse immediately dropped its head to nibble at a wildflower.

''Should the horse be eating that?'' she asked.

''It's fine. You're doing fine.''

"Payne, how do you know where we're going?"

"Dead reckoning. Our general direction is southeast. I figured we could avoid some fences by following the stream."

He was always so logical and smart. She felt her pique begin to fade. Payne really did look dashing on horseback with his long legs spread wide and broad shoulders in perfect balance. She wished she could ride with him on his horse, snuggled against his chest. With a sigh, she said, "You'd make a studly cowboy."

"Yeah? Maybe I ought to get a stallion to ride around and impress you."

"Or not," she said. "A horse is a rather large accessory. And don't they eat a lot?"

"Do you think Josh would like horses?"

It was the first time since the train that he'd mentioned their son. Earlier, his interest in Josh had taken the form of polite inquiries and comments. Now, Payne removed his sunglasses and looked directly at her. His gaze was intense; he really wanted to know about his son.

She could see how much he cared and that pleased her, but she also felt protective and a little reticent about revealing too much. She still wasn't sure how she'd handle this complicated triangle. It didn't seem right to spring a father on Josh, especially when she didn't know if she and Payne had a future. "We need to talk about Josh."

"Our son," he said. There was more than a hint of possessiveness in his voice. "Yes, we need to talk. The first thing I want to say is I'm sorry."

"For what?"

"Everything." He edged closer to her on his horse. "I'm sorry you had to go through childbirth alone and to raise our son by yourself. And I deeply regret that I've missed so much of his life. His first step. His first word. My God, Eden, he's almost old enough to start shaving."

Too late for bonding. That early developmental phase

had passed. The best Payne could hope for with Josh was friendship that might blossom into a deeper relationship. "I'm sorry, too," she said.

"Have you got a photograph of Josh?"

When they'd fled from the car, she had barely enough time to grab the essentials. Digging into the pocket of her jeans, she pulled out her wallet. Behind her fake driver's license in the name of Susan Anthony, she kept the most recent school photo of her son. She removed it and handed it out toward Payne.

He took the small picture and studied it carefully, memorizing the features of his son. Payne's voice was husky when he said, "The kid has my coloring."

"Black hair and dark eyes." In the quiet shelter of the trees beside a stream, she watched Payne struggling with his emotions. And her heart melted. "I wish you'd had the chance to know Josh when he was a little boy."

"Fate." He spat the word. "There's no one to blame. You did the right thing, getting yourself and our child away from the influence of your family."

Sometimes, she wondered if running away had been such a smart move. She'd denied her son the loving embrace of a family—not an admirable lineage but a family nonetheless. Also, if she'd stayed in Chicago, Payne could have found her easily. Josh would've known his father from an early age.

Payne tucked the photograph into his shirt pocket. "I'm keeping this."

"Okay."

He checked his wristwatch. "We better speed up. We're supposed to meet the pilot in less than two hours."

Keeping to the trees, they proceeded at a steady clip. Eden was beginning to feel more comfortable on horseback. This wasn't really difficult. Her only challenge was to hold the reins and not fall off. Through the leafy branches of gnarled trees, she gazed out at greening fields of early spring. The blue sky overhead had turned hazy and had begun to fill with scudding wisps of cloud.

After a ways, they came to a road and followed it until they came upon a sign indicating the route number which Payne checked against written instructions. "We're headed in the right direction," he said. "There's a wildlife refuge up here. We cross that and we're almost to the lake."

"Seems like a long way." She ran her fingers through the rough mane of her horse. "Are you sure these ponies can find their way back to their barn?"

"If not, somebody will return them," Payne said. "They're branded."

The thought of a flaming iron searing into the flesh of this gentle creature seemed utterly barbaric. She scratched the short hairs on her horse's neck. "Poor baby!"

"Are you getting attached to that animal?"

"Of course not, but if I owned a horse, I'd never brand him or make him sleep outside. And I would definitely use conditioner on the mane."

Off the road again, Payne urged his horse to a gallop, and Eden followed. Holding tight with her knees and leaning forward, she kept from bouncing too much in the hard leather saddle. An exhilarating wind swept across her face and through her hair. She laughed out loud. This was great! Not hard at all! She felt like a totally professional cowgirl.

Through a back gate, they entered the wildlife preserve. The uncultivated land was hilly and overgrown with abundant weeds and wildflowers. At the top of a rise, Payne pulled up short. "Whoa!"

She stopped beside him.

They looked down on a herd of buffalo. There must have been over a hundred. The huge, woolly creatures grazed calmly, not noticing them.

The spectacle amazed her. "What are they doing here?"

"It's their land," he said. "The buffalo were here way before we came west."

"I know. But not since long ago. Did we fall through a time warp?"

"I'd like that," Payne said. He would've preferred a simpler time, riding west with his lady to meet their son. Gladly, he would've traded modern conveniences for safety and security. In another time, the only threat would be the elements.

He looked up and scanned the skies overhead. The lowering clouds had begun to thicken which was good luck for them. If the feds sent out a chopper to search, they'd have to go low and couldn't see as far. On the other hand, the small plane that was supposed to pick them up might have a difficult landing.

A drop of moisture splattered on his forehead. "Rain. Let's get past this herd. Follow me."

"As if I had a choice," she muttered. "My horse is a sweetie-pie. Not a leader."

He stayed at the far edge of the herd, moving at a steady gait to avoid spooking these primitive animals. Up close, the bison were massive with little mean eyes. Payne detoured wide to keep a safe distance between them and the herd. Though he had no experience with buffalo, he'd heard they were bad-tempered beasts—short on brains, long on bulk. It was a description that might also apply to some of the thugs who worked for the Verones.

Looking up, Payne saw the jagged flash of lightning before he heard the thunderclap, louder than cannon fire. Static energy charged the atmosphere around them, and Payne glanced toward the herd of buffalo, about a hundred yards away. Several of them quit grazing and milled nervously. Not a good sign.

Another ferocious boom shattered the humid air.

Eden pulled up beside him. "It's not safe for us to be out here in lightning."

Nowhere was safe. Mentally, he weighed the immediate danger pressing down upon them. If they dismounted and walked, they'd be a less likely target for a thunderbolt. But if they missed their rendezvous with the plane, they'd be stuck in central Kansas. "Ride faster."

The sky crackled and roared.

The buffalo started moving toward them. Suddenly, as if they operated with one mind, they bunched together and charged toward him and Eden. Stampede!

Payne dug his heels into his horse's flanks. They had to get out of the way or be trampled to death.

Beside him, her horse burst into a gallop. Eden leaned forward and hung on. Her hair streamed behind her like a ragged flag. She screamed as her horse made a skittish turn toward the buffalo herd.

"No," she yelled. "Payne, help me!"

He whirled on his horse and tore after her. She wasn't far from him, but he couldn't reach her. Eden looked weak. If she fell from her mount, it could be fatal.

Her pinto stopped and reared back. The horse's forefeet pawed the air.

Payne yelled, "Hang on, Eden."

"I can't. I'm slipping."

The buffalo surged toward them in a rumbling, relentless wave of hoof and sinew. Closer and closer.

Payne was beside her. He grabbed the reins from her hand. "Hold on tight."

There was no way they could outrun the herd. The huge animals were almost on top of them. Up close, they were unbelievably big. Payne edged his horse next to hers, flank to flank. They had to stand their ground.

Another ear-splitting jolt of thunder sounded. The direction of the stampede shifted. Most of the buffalo turned away from them. Several stopped cold, staring at Payne and Eden.

Raindrops splattered his face and bare head. Payne urged his horse forward. Slowly.

"What are you doing?" she said.

"Retreating."

As their horses walked through the pelting rain, several buffalo lumbered toward them.

"Give me back my reins," she said. "I want to go faster."

"Not yet." He kept a careful watch on one giant bison who looked like he wanted a fight. If this animal charged, it would be no contest. This beast was as big as a truck.

They eased by, slowly. He handed back her reins. "Are you sure you can ride?"

"Just get me away from here."

He urged his horse forward, and Eden's pinto followed. They speeded up. Directly ahead was a barbed wire fence. If Payne had been alone, he might have attempted a jump. With Eden, he didn't dare.

"Faster," he called to her. "Ride fast along the fence line."

They headed due south, leaving the herd behind. As they crested a hill, Payne looked back over his shoulder. The last buffalo turned away from them. "We made it," he said.

Through the downpour, Payne continued riding until they reached a grove of overarching trees. He pulled up short. Eden stopped beside him. She was drenched, gasping. Before he could stop her, she'd dragged her leg over the saddle and clumsily slid off the horse, crumpling to the earth in a heap.

He dismounted and caught the reins of both horses. He knelt beside her, and she collapsed against him.

Sobbing, she said, "I can't go any farther. I don't have the strength."

"You're doing great," he assured her.

"I thought we were dead for sure." She trembled from head to toe. Trying to lift her arm to embrace him, she gave up on the effort and sat there in a puddle of exhaustion. "I can't ride anymore."

He wiped the face of his wristwatch and checked the time. Forty-five minutes until they were scheduled to meet the private plane. Though he figured they were near Marion Lake, he didn't know the geography and the obstacles. They had to keep moving. "Eden, are you sure you can't ride?"

When she lifted her head to look up at him, Payne was struck first by the ashen hue of her complexion. Her hair streamed wetly across her forehead. The hollows of her eyes were smeared by running mascara. With an effort, she wiped the rain from her face. Her hazel eyes flashed—still fiery in spite of thunder, rain and fatigue. "I can try to ride," she said. "I won't give up."

He didn't have the heart to shove her back onto her horse. There had to be another way. "You can ride with me."

After some maneuvering, Payne was back in the saddle. Eden's horse was following, attached by a lead rope, while Eden herself sat in front of him. With one hand, he guided his horse. The other arm was wrapped snugly around her trembling body. She seemed ill, stressed, worn to the bitter end of her endurance.

Payne knew she needed rest and gentle nurturing. But he couldn't stop riding until they made it to the lake. The private plane was their best hope for escape.

"About Josh," she said.

"Don't try to talk. Save your strength."

"This is important." She shuddered with each breath, chilled by the rain. "I need a promise from you."

"Anything," he said. And he meant it. He would do whatever she asked when it came to their son.

"You can't tell him," she said. "When you meet, you can't tell him you're his father. Not until I say it's the right time."

Payne hadn't planned to announce himself with a fanfare.

He might not be the world's most sensitive man, but he knew better. "I promise," he said.

"Good." She relaxed a little.

Soon enough, Payne would greet Josh and welcome him with the entitlement he deserved. Son. My son.

HUDDLED WITH EDEN and the horses in a clump of trees at the southern tip of Lake Marion, Payne glanced up through the dripping wet leaves. Though the rain still drizzled, the dark gray clouds had begun to break apart. The weather wasn't too severe for a small plane landing.

He wasn't sure what to expect from this pilot. When Payne had called his mentor and apprised him of the situation with the train, Skip arranged for this pickup using his network of contacts—guys, like Payne, who would do anything for Skip without asking too many questions. But who would he send? It might be a mercenary daredevil or a wealthy guy with his own fleet of aircraft or a Midwestern farmer with a crop duster.

Payne checked his wristwatch. The pilot was already ten minutes late. If he ran half an hour past schedule, Payne would use his cell phone to contact Skip for updated info. The worst-case scenario was that the feds had closed down all airspace over this area so they could pursue their misguided manhunt.

In his arms, Eden leaned away from his chest and looked up at him. She looked exhausted. Her complexion was drained of color except for two feverish red spots on her cheeks. She murmured, "It smells good after a rain. Clean."

"Are you warm enough?"

She nodded. "I'm okay."

With her damp hair pushed back, her hazel eyes shone brightly as if washed clean by the downpour. Gently, he asked, "Do you like this kind of weather? Are you a rainy day woman?"

"I am. Rain wakes you up. And then, there's the best part when you go inside and dry off in front of a fireplace. Maybe have a warm drink, like cocoa."

"Or brandy."

"Oh yes, brandy. Rich, liquid fire. And when we got all warm and cozy, I'd slide my hand inside your shirt. And we'd share our warmth while the drumming rain splashed against the windowpanes."

He smiled, becoming aroused in spite of the chill. "You've got a strong imagination, Eden."

"It's all I had," she said.

"What do you mean?"

Her shimmering eyes regarded him steadily. "I thought you were dead, Payne. And I didn't want to be with any other man. So, I kept you alive in my imagination."

Her loyalty touched his heart, especially now that he knew she'd been true to him. There had been no other man. He was the father of her child. "Even though we were apart, we shared a lot. I kept you alive in my memory. You were always my fantasy woman."

"In a way, we're lucky," she said. "Not many people experience such a perfect model of young love."

But she sounded unhappy. "What's wrong, Eden?"

"I was thinking of my brother. His marriage sounds like it was awful, but they must have been in love once upon a time."

"Do you still believe that Eddy's wife was the one who was having an affair with Luke Borman?"

She reached into her jacket pocket and pulled out her cell phone. "I could call Angela and ask."

Payne didn't much care for these communications with her cousin. He didn't like for Eden to be exposed in any way. Yet, Angela Benedict was a definite source of information. "Make the call."

Eden checked Angela's business card and punched in the

number. She snuggled against Payne's chest, waiting while the cell phone rang. Once. Twice.

Her eyelids felt heavy. She was near falling asleep. It might not be smart to talk to her cousin when she was drowsy, not alert, not—

"Hello?" Angela said.

"It's Eden. I know about the affair."

"How did you find out?" Angela sounded frightened. "Did Eddy tell you?"

Why was she talking about Eddy? "My brother and I hadn't spoken in twelve years," Eden said.

"Not that it matters to you," Angela said, "but I really loved him. We became lovers when Nicky was in prison. When he got out, I broke it off. But I couldn't stay away."

She was talking about a long time ago. Obviously, this had nothing to do with Luke Borman. Eden concluded, "You had a love affair with my brother."

"It wasn't right. But we were happy. So damn happy."

"I'm glad." At least Eddy had had a moment in the sun. "Take care of yourself, Angela."

Eden disconnected the call and looked up at Payne. With a sigh, she reported, "Angela Benedict and my brother were in love."

"Then she wasn't the one who ordered the hit on Eddy."

"I don't think so," Eden said.

"We'd better take a closer look at Robert Ciari. He was in Brooklyn with Eddy before he died. Logically, he's the one who should take over the family business."

Before he could check his wristwatch again, Payne heard the drone of an airplane engine. Down the hill from where they sat was an unmanned airfield—a minimally maintained strip of tarmac beside a locked shack and a Day-Glo orange windsock blowing toward the south.

A single engine Piper Cub swooped through the clouds and lit on the asphalt.

Payne rose to his feet, helping Eden up with him. "Can you walk?" he asked.

"I'm stiff, but I can manage."

He turned the horses loose and headed down the hill where a pilot had already climbed down from the cockpit and stood waving. He was a tall, skinny guy in a fringed leather jacket and a cowboy hat. His long white hair hung loose to his shoulders, and he reminded Payne of old daguerreotype photos of Buffalo Bill Cody's Wild West Show.

Half-carrying Eden, Payne hurried toward the plane.

"Howdy, kids," the cowboy drawled. "Get your tails on board. It's time to fly."

Payne helped Eden into the rear of the small plane, fastened her seat belt and tucked her in with a thermal blanket. He sat in the co-pilot position. By the time he'd turned to face the front windshield, the pilot had already begun to taxi on the short runway.

Payne slipped on a set of earphones with a built-in microphone for talking to the pilot over the drone of the propellor. With a quick whoosh and a hop, they were airborne, punching a hole in the sky toward more stable weather at a higher altitude. Up here, the sun shone steadily across a field of cottony clouds as they headed west.

After days on the run, it felt good to sit back and let someone else worry about the transportation. Because this wild man pilot from the old west had been sent by Skip, Payne trusted him implicitly in spite of the slightly bizarre interior of the cockpit. If the inside of an airplane could be called eccentric, this one qualified. The seats were upholstered in zebra skin print. A faded photograph of a woman in an old-fashioned two-piece bathing suit was taped above the throttle. The pilot's yoke of the Piper Cub was lined with something that looked like a dead raccoon. A matching yoke was on the dashboard in front of the co-pilot.

"Dual controls," Payne said, speaking into the intercom microphone. "Do you use this plane for teaching?"

"Sometimes," the old-timer said. "Mostly, it's handy to have the co-pilot yoke and pedals in case of pilot emergency. I've had a few problems with the old ticker."

"Heart attack?"

"Quadruple bypass. If I grab my chest and start wheezing, you just take over the controls."

"Right."

The half-baked plan didn't exactly inspire confidence. Payne knew the basics of flying but didn't have his pilot's license.

He pointed to an egg timer attached with Velcro beside his head. "What's this?"

"Glad you mentioned it, son. Keep an eye on the sands. When they run out, it's time to switch to the auxiliary fuel tank."

Not exactly state of the art, but Payne wasn't complaining. "What should I call you?"

"Cody. Like Buffalo Bill. He's not a relation, but I always wished he was."

Payne introduced himself. He leaned around the edge of his seat to check on Eden who clutched the thermal blanket under her chin. As they bounced across a current of air, her expressive eyes showed a hint of panic. She shouted toward the pilot. "I'm Eden Miller."

Cody turned away from the windshield to look directly at her. "Pleased to meet you, Miss. Right now, you look a bit like a drowned rat, but I'll bet you clean up real pretty."

Gesturing wildly, she pointed toward the windshield of the single engine plane. "Don't you need to keep your eyes on the…on the road?"

"No roads in the sky," he said. He indicated another headset in the back. "Put that on."

Payne helped her slip on the earphones and headset and

hooked her into the intercom so they could all hear each other without yelling.

Cody offered her reassurance. "Don't you worry, Eden. I'm going to get you where you're going."

"Okay." She sounded slightly doubtful. "Thank you."

"Don't mention it," Cody said.

Payne knew this pilot wouldn't expect thanks or even an explanation. There was a code among men like them. When called upon, they did what was needed. They honored each other's requests.

To Cody, he said, "Nice little plane you've got here."

"I call her Sylvia after my first wife." He reached forward with a long, bony finger and tapped the woman in the photograph. "Both the Piper Cub and my late wife were always a little temperamental. I use her to race around on my ranch in Oklahoma—the plane, that is. The wife is long gone. She was a southern gal."

Cody launched into a long story about first seeing Sylvia on a beach in the Florida Keys while he was fighting to land a giant swordfish. His fanciful tale was a cross between *Old Man and the Sea* and *Gone with the Wind.* Cody concluded, "I landed them both."

Payne sensed that with very little provocation, Cody would ramble for hours. Now might be a good time to ascertain some solid information. "What's our route?"

"West," Cody said. "I don't much care for filing flight plans, so I'm going to stay low, far away from cities. We'll only need to stop once near Pueblo in Colorado for fuel. Does that suit your purpose?"

"Excellent plan."

"Excuse me," Eden said. "When do you think we'll reach our destination?"

"I'm hoping we'll make it before nightfall," Cody said, "but that's pushing it. We've got maybe five or six hours to go."

"Why are you worried about nightfall?" Eden asked. "Is it dangerous to land in the dark?"

"Depends on the landing area."

The little plane bucked again, and she let out a little squeak. "Have you ever been in a plane crash, Cody?"

"Hell, yes. There was the time I was flying in the Tetons and I came face-to-face with a bald eagle. That old bird was half the size of this plane. I swear he was. And we danced with each other in the clouds. Had to make an emergency landing on a jagged peak that busted off my wings. Then there was the freak snowstorm in Sonoma when I—"

"We won't crash today," Payne said. He reached back toward Eden and rested his hand on her knee. "The weather is clearing, and there are no eagles in sight."

"That's right," Cody said. "Nothing to worry about, young lady."

Nothing but a nationwide manhunt from the FBI and a vendetta from the Verones. Still, Payne reassured her, "We're going to make it."

If it meant sprouting wings and carrying her to their destination, he would make sure she stayed safe. Crash landings were not an option; they had too much to live for.

Chapter Eleven

After flying for five hours with Cody, Eden would never again consider air travel to be a luxury. In this small plane, a simple turn meant tilting and sliding. The atmosphere above the clouds was often turbulent resulting in constant bouncing on her already aching posterior. Plus, she had ample time to worry about the decidedly weird character of their pilot. Among the bizarre objects decorating the rear of "Sylvia" the Piper Cub were postcards, bolo ties, several strands of Mardi Gras beads and shrunken heads which she could only hope were plastic. Through the headset, she listened as Cody talked nonstop on subjects that ranged from running with the bulls in Pamplona to a private audience with Albert Einstein.

Either Cody was a bona fide nutball or a genius. Definitely, he wasn't the kind of man she encountered in her daily life as a soccer mom in Denver. Her world was different now. From the moment she hooked up with Payne Magnuson, her life had been transformed into an adventure—exciting, daring and ultimately dangerous. Eden doubted she could maintain this level of adrenaline rush when she was back together with Josh, returning to her primary identity as his mother.

While listening to Cody's stories, she'd eaten a tuna fish sandwich with too much mayo and had a few sips of water

Though she discovered beer in a cooler, Payne advised against drinking for a very good reason. There was no bathroom on this tiny plane. By the time they landed for fuel near Pueblo, Eden thought her bladder would explode.

After the fueling stop, she took her turn in the co-pilot seat which was a major improvement in terms of the view. The orange-and-pink sunset streaked the skies above the front range of the Rockies. In the small plane, they merged into the light and air as though they had become part of a fantastic universal painting. Her awe-filled observations were, however, short-lived. Too soon, she learned that Cody was seventy-three years old. What happened to the plane if he keeled over? She quickly traded places with Payne, wanting him to be in the co-pilot seat in case of emergency.

As they neared the end of their ride, the old cowboy went quiet, and she sensed an air of fragility about him. "Cody? Are you feeling okay?"

"I'm concentrating," he said. "I don't much care for landing in the dark."

"I can bring us down," Payne offered. "I'm not a certified pilot, but I—"

"Hold your horses, sonny. Sylvia is my lady and she don't much cotton to amateurs."

Eden inched forward to a position between the pilot and co-pilot seats. She peered through the windshield at the disappearing sunlight. Stars twinkled in the skies around them. The mountains loomed below in giant shadows dotted with occasional sprinkles of light. She saw nothing resembling an airfield.

Though she'd heard Cody and Payne discussing the landing with someone on the ground, she had no idea where they were. "Are we close?"

"We'll be landing real soon," Cody promised. "You'd best sit in the back and put on that seat belt."

Soon, she'd be seeing Josh again, hugging him and hearing his eleven year old voice that sometimes slipped into a scratchy lower register. Her eagerness to be with him was tempered with a fair amount of anxiety. There would be much to explain. Not only would she need to eventually introduce him to Payne—his real father who was supposed to be dead—but she couldn't possibly explain their current situation without telling her son about his true heritage.

Though she'd considered elaborate lies about why she was being pursued, Eden recognized that the time had come for the truth. Josh was the last direct descendant of Gus Verone. Her son needed to know.

As if on cue, Payne turned in the co-pilot seat and gazed directly at her. "Everything is going to be all right," he said.

"I hope so."

"We're together," he said. "That's the main thing. Together, you and I can lick the world."

Eden wished she could be so certain.

She sat back, fastened her seat belt and closed her eyes. The rapid-fire conversation between Payne, Cody and someone on the ground worried her, so she took off the earphones and listened instead to the drone of the engine. *Everything was going to be all right.* She desperately wanted to believe in the glowing positive, but there were so many doubts. So many perils yet to overcome.

As they made their descent, her stomach dropped. It felt like they were coming down too fast, plummeting toward the earth. Dread sliced through her. She kept her eyelids squeezed tightly shut. If they were going to crash, there was nothing she could do to stop it.

She felt the fixed wheels hit the ground and bounce. The jolt rattled her teeth. Another hop and a thud. Then they skidded. And stopped.

She felt Payne's hand on her knee.

The engine went silent, and the absence of noise was deafening.

"We're here," he said. "We made it."

Eden exhaled the breath she'd been holding and opened her eyes. The sight of Payne's face still amazed her. The depths of his eyes, filled with concern, drew her toward him. In his presence, she felt safe. "We're here," she said.

"Don't know why you sound so surprised," Cody grumbled. "I had everything under control."

She unfastened her seat belt, leaned forward and kissed the grizzled cheek of the old cowboy. "Thank you."

When she turned to Payne, her kiss was less perfunctory. Her lips pressed firmly against his, tasting the possibility of a future.

"Somebody's coming toward us," Cody said. "A kid."

"Josh," she said.

Through the windshield, she looked out at a vacant stretch of tarmac with a few lights outlining the edges of this unmanned landing strip. Outside the door of a small shack stood her son with his fists stuffed into the pockets of his loose-fitting jeans. His skinny shoulders slouched forward inside his brown-and-white parka. Even at a distance, she sensed his confusion. He wanted to come toward her, but he was trying to be cool. God, how she loved him! She'd do anything to protect her son. For a long time, Josh was all she had. He was her entire life.

"He looks like me," Payne said.

In some part of her mind, Eden wanted to deny the resemblance, to keep Josh all for herself. "You promised not to say anything to him about your relationship."

"I won't," he said. "Not until it's the right time."

Payne opened the hatch door of the Piper Cub and climbed out. Then he helped her down. As soon as her feet touched the tarmac, her son abandoned his attempt at coolness and charged toward her. Her heart rejoiced as she gathered him into a fierce hug. They'd only been apart for a few days, but it felt like a lifetime. Had he grown? Impossible! He was already as tall as she was.

Tears of happiness spilled down her cheeks. "I missed you, Josh. Oh, it's good to see you."

He stepped back and dashed away his own tears with the sleeve of his parka. "Are you okay, Mom?"

"Now I am." She turned toward Payne and pulled him closer. "This is Payne Magnuson. He's been helping me."

In the lights from the plane and the unmanned runway, she watched as her son shook hands with his father for the first time. Their profiles were similar though Payne's features were chiseled by maturity and Josh's face was smooth and unformed. The color and shape of their eyes were almost identical.

The lights on the airstrip went out, and the Colorado night surrounded them. In the flickering starlight, Eden could see the outline of jagged pines on one side of the runway.

Another man came toward them. His stride was brisk, and there was something about his manner that made her uneasy.

"We haven't got much time," he said.

The words sent a chill through Eden. They weren't out of danger. Not yet.

INSIDE THE sprawling but rustic mountain home which had been used as a safe house, Payne couldn't take his eyes off Josh. The physical resemblance was clear as could be. And there was something more—a similarity that went deeper than the color of their eyes and hair. Payne saw his son from the inside out. He recognized Josh's protective attitude toward his mother. Beneath his son's boyish playfulness was an incisive intelligence—not the kind of smarts that came with book learning but an intuition. Payne knew. He, too, had that sense of wariness until he decided who was an enemy and who was a friend.

Payne's attention turned toward the FBI agent who had introduced himself as Chuck Sonderberg. Blond and tall with a leathery tan, Chuck looked like a skier—an impression that was confirmed by a few discarded lift tickets on the table by the door. He crossed the room toward Payne. "We need to talk," he said.

Payne followed him into the front room by the gas fireplace while Josh took his mother and Cody into the kitchen. Keeping his voice low, Payne said, "You've taken a big risk by helping us. I can never repay you."

"We want the same thing," Chuck said. His voice had a plain Midwestern flavor. "We both want to put the cap on dishonest agents like Danny-O. I only met that guy once and didn't like him. When Skipper called, I knew who was in the right."

Payne nodded. Chuck Sonderberg was a man of principle. "Give me an update."

"You're in big trouble, Payne. You've shot two agents. Luke Borman in Brooklyn. Samuels in Abilene."

Payne braced himself for bad news. He already knew that Borman's injuries were not life-threatening. "How is Samuels?"

"Dead."

A coldness whipped through Payne. Icy fingers squeezed the air from his lungs as he absorbed this painful fact. He had taken another man's life.

Only once before in his long career had he committed murder. Twelve years ago in Chicago during the shoot-out with the Verones, bullets had been flying. When the smoke cleared, three men were dead. Though Payne could never be certain that he was the one who'd done the killing, he accepted the life-long burden of guilt.

"Samuels's death wasn't your fault," Chuck said. "He was in the Abilene hospital. After the operation when he was coming out from anesthetic, he started talking about plots and payoffs. His rambling sounded enough like a confession to get some attention. Before they could take his statement, somebody sneaked into his hospital room and shot him in the head. An execution. Gangland style.''

Payne's guilt froze into a glacial rage. ''Danny-O.''

''Or somebody working with him,'' Chuck agreed. ''My money is on the Verones. In either case, the story is that you're behind Samuels's murder. Right now, my friend, you are public enemy number one for the Bureau.''

With the entire network of the FBI looking for him, escape seemed impossible. ''Are there more men like you? Other agents who believe I've been framed?''

''Some,'' Chuck said.

''But we can't be sure of who.'' With this level of conspiracy, there was no certain way of telling who he could trust. He'd sure as hell been wrong about Samuels.

''Frankly,'' Chuck said, ''your best chance for making it out of this situation alive is to go to Vegas and let Skipper handle the politics. Sooner or later, one of these other agents is going to confess.''

''Why should they?'' Payne asked, tight-lipped. ''They're in line for payoffs. The execution-style murder of Samuels shows the consequence of betrayal.''

''But they're still federal agents,'' Chuck said. ''Just like you and me. When they first joined, their motivations were positive and their ideals were high. I can't believe there's not one of them who won't reconnect with honesty.''

Payne's view was far more cynical. He'd seen how one corrupt act led to another and another until the route back to the truth was an impossible labyrinth. He'd seen agents absorbed into their undercover identities, seduced by money and power. ''What else do we know about the Verones? You said they might be behind the murder of Samuels. Is there evidence that anyone in the family has left Chicago?''

''Most of the major players are still in Chicago,'' Chuck said. ''Do you know Nicky Benedict?''

Angela's husband who'd been in jail. ''Yes.''

"He's still on parole and not supposed to leave Illinois. The same holds for Titty Ameche."

"That's good news," Payne said.

"And here comes the bad. Gus Verone and his wife, Sophia, boarded a plane for Denver yesterday."

The arrival of the family patriarch wasn't something Payne wanted to hear about, but there it was. Big as life and twice as ugly. He was sure that Gus hadn't come to Denver alone. He'd brought foot soldiers who would fan out and search.

Still, Payne reminded himself, Gus wasn't the real danger. The faction of the Verone family who had arranged the murder of Eden's brother were far more deadly. They were the ones who had made a pact with Danny-O. They were the real enemy.

"What about Robert Ciari?" Payne thought of the former football player whose offspring had all been daughters. After Eden's last phone call to Angela, Robert Ciari was the most likely villain.

"He's travelling with Gus," Chuck said. "The next move is your decision, but I'd advise you to get to Vegas where Skipper can circle the wagons and protect you."

"What about Eden and Josh?" Payne asked. Whoever killed Eddy might also want to harm them. "Are they safe at this house?"

"Negative. I've already had a couple of guys calling and sniffing around. It's only a matter of time before somebody comes up here."

Chuck paced. He frowned. He was the kind of guy who needed action to get his brain moving, a habit that Payne found completely understandable. He was beginning to like Chuck.

"How about this," Chuck said. "It's possible that I could arrange for Josh and Eden to be taken into protective custody."

"Not with the FBI," Payne said. "Not with Danny-O on the loose."

"We could use another branch of the government to protect them. Secret Service. Or Special Ops. The Skipper could make the connections."

The plan made sense, but Payne didn't want to trust the welfare of his son and Eden to anyone else. He wanted to take care of them himself. "I should talk to Eden. This isn't my decision."

"Move fast," Chuck suggested. "The noose is drawing tight."

Payne didn't want to hang himself. Worse, he didn't want the slightest breath of danger to affect Eden or Josh. He watched as they came into the dining room, carrying trays of sandwiches and drinks. Cody was telling a rambling story to Josh who listened politely. Eden's gaze cast across the adjoining rooms and hooked him.

When they'd made love, her eyes had been hot, sexy and welcoming. In danger, she reacted with spunk and guts. Her attitude now seemed reserved. She was vigilant as a mother bear watching over her cub.

Payne made his decision. "I'll take off for Vegas at first light with Cody."

"Why wait until morning?" Chuck asked.

Payne didn't want to complain about Cody's piloting skills. After all, the old man had plucked them out of a field in Kansas and delivered them safely here. But night flying wasn't Cody's forte. They'd almost crashed on the mountain airstrip. "Dawn is soon enough."

"What about Eden and Josh?" Chuck asked "Will they go with you?"

"That decision is up to her."

AFTER THE OTHERS had gone to bed, Eden quietly descended the staircase inside the cabin. There were three large bedrooms on the second floor which meant the four males shared two and she had her own space. If circumstances had been different, she would have invited Payne to join her, but she didn't dare make love to him while her son was in the next bedroom. Josh was old enough to know what happened when a man and a woman slept together, and she wasn't yet ready to tell him about his father.

She pushed up the sleeve of her borrowed parka and checked her wristwatch. Exactly eleven o'clock. That was the time Payne had whispered to her. And she'd agreed to meet him.

But now, she had second thoughts. It seemed wrong to be sneaking out to see Payne, her boyfriend, while her son was nearby. In an odd way, she felt like she was betraying the memory of Josh's father. But, of course, that made no sense. Payne was both father and boyfriend. He was no longer a memory; he was real.

Her fingers rested on the doorknob. She could still run back up the stairs, dive under the comforter and avoid seeing him alone. But Eden wasn't a coward.

Hesitantly, she stepped outside. In the moonlight, she followed the downhill path toward the garage, their appointed meeting place. Her stride was less than graceful. After today's exertions, her muscles ached, and her bottom felt like one big bruise.

Through the surrounding conifers, she saw the light of another cabin on the opposite side of the canyon. The whispering breeze harmonized with a rippling stream at the bottom of the hill. She zipped her parka all the way up so the wind couldn't sneak down her collar. Though it was cold, the arid climate of Colorado never felt as icy as when she was growing up in Chicago.

"Eden."

She saw him. He leaned against the rough bark of a pine at the edge of the path. In his worn leather bomber jacket with the collar turned up, he seemed utterly calm and collected. Last night, she would've flown into his arms. But things were different now; she had to think first about her son.

She stopped in front of Payne, keeping a safe distance between them. "I haven't told Josh," she said, "about his grandfather."

"He's in Denver," Payne said. "Gus and your grandmother came to Denver last night. And guess who was with them? Your cousin, Robert Ciari."

She gritted her teeth. Though she'd half-expected this news, she dreaded hearing it. "He's coming after us. Stalking us."

"He wants to see his grandson," Payne said.

"And drag him into a life of danger," she said bitterly.

"That's not his intention. I'm sure Gus would do everything in his power to protect you and Josh."

"Like he protected my brother? You might have noticed that the men in my family have a tendency to die young." She didn't understand why Payne was taking her grandfather's side. "What's going on here? It sounds like you're defending Gus."

"Maybe I understand him better than I did before." Payne shrugged. "It's only natural to want a connection with your family."

"Are you trying to lay a guilt trip on me?" She couldn't believe his attitude. Hiding her son from his grandfather, an acknowledged monster, was no cause for regret. Payne's suggestion to the contrary ticked her off. "Keeping Josh away from the Verones has been my mission in life."

"What about me?" Payne pushed away from the sheltering tree and took a step toward her. "When do we tell Josh about me?"

She gazed up into his face. His jaw was clenched hard as these granite mountains. In the dark shadows beneath his brow, she saw a flicker of light, the glimmer of an unshed tear. He wasn't crying. Tough guys like Payne never wept.

But he was hurting. "Payne, I'm sorry. It must be hell for you to be so close to your son and yet—"

"It's like I don't exist," he said. "As if the moment of his conception never happened."

She wasn't going to be pressured into speaking too soon to Josh. Such emotional matters had to be handled carefully. "I'm sorry," she repeated. "You have to be patient."

"I'm his father, Eden."

In spite of her steely resolve to protect Josh, her heart wrenched. "I can't tell him. Not yet."

"Twelve years ago, if I had known you were pregnant, I would have done the right thing. I would have married you."

"You always were a stand-up kind of guy," she said. "A straight arrow."

He gently rested one hand on her shoulder. With the other, he tilted her chin up so she had to look directly into his eyes. "I would have married you because I loved you with all my heart. You were the girl of my dreams."

She stepped forward. Her arms slid inside his jacket, and she buried her face against his warm chest. Melting in his embrace, her eyelids closed. Her ears tuned to the steady beating of his heart, and she inhaled his musky scent.

He lightly stroked her back, and her physical aches faded. Being close to him was better than a full-body massage. Still, she clung to her resolve. "I can't tell him yet."

She wished that he'd say it was all right, that he understood. But it didn't seem that such reassurances were coming.

"We might not have much time," he said. "Tomorrow morning at dawn, I'm taking off with Cody to go to Vegas. There are people there I trust."

She drew the obvious conclusion. "You're leaving me."

"It's your decision, Eden. You and Josh can come with me to Vegas. Or you can go into protective custody."

"What does that mean?"

"A branch of law enforcement, probably the Secret Service, can arrange for you and Josh to stay in a safe house. You'd be guarded."

"It sounds like jail," she said. The idea of taking her son into a protection program appalled her. "This isn't fair. I've never broken any laws. I've never done anything wrong, except being born into the wrong family."

She felt exhausted, tired of fighting the same old battles, facing the same fate. No matter how far she ran, she could never escape her heritage. The curse of being a Verone was always with her, threatening her tenuous grasp on security. "What should I do?"

He nuzzled the top of her head. "This is your decision, Eden. Come with me to Vegas. Or go into protective custody. Your call."

Accepting the protection of the feds would probably be the safest decision. But how could she be sure? "What about Danny-O? If we're in custody, couldn't he find us?"

"Possibly," Payne said. "But it's a slim chance. The federal marshalls are good at protecting important witnesses."

"I'm a witness?" She hadn't considered that aspect. Eden leaned away from him and stared up. "I don't understand. Do I have to go to court?"

"It's possible," he said.

"But why?"

"That's the way the system works." He gently brushed her hair off her forehead. "There have been crimes committed. The perpetrators will be charged. You might be called to give testimony."

"About what?"

"Your brother's murder. And the conspiracy to put out a hit on him. My self-defense shooting of Samuels in the Abilene train yard."

"I can talk about Samuels," she said. "But I won't testify against my family. I might hate the Verones, but I could never be the instrument of their downfall."

"I understand," Payne said. "What about the protective custody? Should I arrange for it?"

"No way."

A smile hitched the corner of his mouth. "Then I guess you and Josh are coming with me to Vegas."

Eden smiled back. "I guess so."

"Good choice."

He held her more tightly. His mouth slanted against hers, and he kissed her hard, setting off a chain reaction of fireworks inside her body until she was buzzing all over. For a moment, she reveled in the mindless pleasure of pure sensation.

Payne broke off their kiss and loosened his grasp. "We should go back to the cabin and try to get some sleep before dawn."

"Right." She never wanted to leave this man, never wanted to be apart from him again.

"I don't suppose," he whispered, "that I could join you in the private bedroom."

"As much as I'd like to say yes…not tonight."

He gave her one last hug before they started up the hill to the cabin. Eden hiked slowly. The stiffness in her bruised body had returned, and her legs felt weak. Tired, she was very, very tired.

As they approached the cabin, a light went on in one of the first floor rooms. Immediately, Payne stepped in front of her. His gun was in his hand. "Let me go first. In case this is somebody who shouldn't be here."

Before she had time to consider his words, he'd opened the door and slipped inside. Soundlessly, Payne crossed the front room toward the open door where a light was shining. After he glanced inside, he motioned to Eden.

She looked inside the room and saw Josh, sitting at a computer in his pajamas. She gestured for Payne to stay outside the room as she entered. "Hey, Josh. Shouldn't you be in bed?"

"I couldn't sleep," he said. "Mom, there's something I need to ask you about."

She pulled up a wooden chair beside the desk and sat. "What's bothering you, Josh?"

His fingers darted across the keyboard, then he leaned back and pointed to the flat screen of the computer. It was a photograph of Eden, aged eighteen, with long hair down to her shoulders, grinning as if she didn't have a care in the world. "That's you," Josh said.

"How did you find that picture?"

"Don't tell Chuck, but I was messing around with his computer after he was working. There was all this really awesome FBI stuff. And I found this file about a crime family in Chicago." He turned in the swivel chair and stared directly at her. "Is it you in the picture?"

This wasn't exactly the way she would have chosen to tell her son about his heritage, but she couldn't lie to him when confronted with this direct evidence. "It's me. That photograph was taken a long time ago. Before you were born."

"It says your name is Candace Verone."

"That's correct."

"But you're Eden Miller," he said.

She took his hand. "When I found out I was pregnant, I didn't want you to be brought up in the Verone family. So, I ran away to Denver, changed my name to Eden Miller and started the best part of my life being your mom."

"But you're really Candace Verone, the granddaughter of Gus Verone. He's the boss of this crime family."

She nodded. "How much of this file have you read?"

"A whole bunch," he said. "So, who am I?"

Eden sighed, wishing she didn't have to say these words.

"You are the great-grandson of Gus Verone, the male heir to the family name."

Josh bobbed his head. A grin curved his mouth and his eyebrows lifted. He gave a thumbs-up. "Way cool."

Chapter Twelve

His palms were sweating inside his black leather gloves as Danny-O trotted along the narrow-graded gravel road leading toward a rustic two-story cabin in Colorado. Three other agents accompanied him. All were locals from the Colorado Bureau—unwilling recruits who couldn't believe their co-worker, Chuck Sonderberg, would be involved with the renegade Payne Magnuson.

In sight of the cabin, Danny-O drew his gun. With any luck, he could pick off Payne and his fiery little girlfriend before they had a chance to shoot off their mouths and make the situation worse. Danny-O's position had become tenuous. The murder of Agent Samuels in Abilene raised doubts about the investigation. Under anesthetic, Samuels babbled about a conspiracy which caused Payne's supporters in the Bureau to pose the obvious question: If Samuels was in cahoots with Payne and the Verones, why did Payne shoot him in the train yard?

Danny-O had done some fast talking about how there was no honor among thieves and how Samuels might have threatened Payne earlier with his intention to confess.

Though Danny-O's superiors agreed that Payne needed to be taken into custody, they were now unconvinced about his culpability. They cited his outstanding reputation and career. Danny-O countered with a logic of his own: If Payne had nothing to hide, why didn't he turn himself in?

And so, the manhunt continued, but with less enthusiasm. There was a subtle but unmistakable tide change, and Danny-O couldn't allow Payne to live long enough to point an accusing finger in his direction.

It would all be over soon enough. The people who had been baby-sitting for Eden's brat had identified Chuck Sonderberg as the agent who picked up the kid. And Chuck had access to this handy mountain hideaway to use as a safe house. Danny-O had to believe Payne was in the cabin, hiding behind log walls. Soon, they'd come face-to-face. Soon, Payne Magnuson would be dead.

After climbing the hill leading up to the cabin, Danny-O paused to catch his breath in the high altitude. He was tense. In addition to the ongoing headache from his concussion, he'd developed a constant tension at his nape, literally a pain in the neck.

The midmorning sun glared across the rugged mountain terrain. It was warmer than he would've expected for early spring in Colorado. He squinted against the sunlight. The expanse of wide open space irritated him. Danny-O was a city cat, comfortable on the pavement between canyons of man-made skyscrapers. After he collected his payoffs from the Verones, he intended to buy a penthouse in Manhattan.

One of the local agents joined him. "Put the gun away, man."

The hell he would. "This is a raid. We need to be ready."

"If you ask me, we're wasting our time. Chuck Sonderberg is a good guy."

"Let me remind you. Payne Magnuson has already shot two agents." Danny-O stared hard at the local agent who looked comfortable in hiking boots and a windbreaker while Danny-O was wearing trousers and a suit coat over his Kevlar vest. He ordered, "Draw your sidearm."

Reluctantly, the Colorado agent obeyed. "This is all wrong. Magnuson is a legend. He wouldn't—"

"I was there," Danny-O interrupted. "I saw the legendary Payne Magnuson kill Eddy Verone in cold blood. Then he shot Luke Borman—a guy who was like a brother to me."

"Sorry, man."

"Yeah, you should be. Real damn sorry." By mentioning the injury to Borman, Danny-O had invoked the most powerful motivation for members of the law enforcement community; an attack on any one of them was a personal affront. "Payne is armed and dangerous. Never forget that fact."

Danny-O peered through the conifer forest. Damn, it was bright. The sunlight fell like rain. He could see that the other two agents were ready to enter the cabin through the back door. At Danny-O's signal, the two groups moved simultaneously.

The local guy got to the door first. He twisted the handle to open it. Danny-O charged inside. "FBI! Freeze!"

He heard his words echoed by the other agents coming through the rear. His gaze swept the front room. He spotted a blond woman sitting in front of the fireplace.

"What's the meaning of this?" she demanded.

"Get your hands up." Fury surged through Danny-O. He was sweating beneath his Kevlar vest. His neck throbbed. "Where's Payne?"

"Take it easy." The local agent spoke in an infuriatingly calm voice. "This is Chuck's sister."

"Where's Payne?" Danny-O yelled. He was losing it. His self-control was on the ragged edge. This should have been the end of the road. "Where the hell is he?"

With hands raised, a blond man stepped into the room. "What are you guys doing? Is this a joke?"

"Hey, Chuck," said the local agent. "We've got some kind of misunderstanding here."

"No way," Danny-O roared. Gun in hand, he mounted the staircase. Upstairs, he crashed open each door and searched each bedroom. No one was up here.

They were too late. Damn it! Tension knifed between his shoulder blades and ripped upward to the base of his skull. The stitches from his concussion pulsed in agony. He was too damn late.

From downstairs, he heard low-key conversation. The local jerks were probably apologizing to Chuck Sonderberg for the inconvenience. What about Danny-O's inconvenience? None of this should have happened. Payne should have been killed in Brooklyn.

Danny-O rubbed his eyes. He had to rein himself in, had to get a grip. If he wanted to be believed, he couldn't present himself as a raging maniac.

With shaking hands, he pulled the cell phone from his pocket and punched in the phone number for his Verone contact. In a low voice, he said, "We missed them in Colorado."

"We know where they're headed."

Not possible. The best intelligence of the FBI had come up empty-handed. The Verones couldn't do better. "Where?"

"Vegas."

"How do you know?"

"Let's just say we have a friend on the inside."

That didn't make sense. Danny-O was the friend on the inside. He was the boss. He was the man. Nobody else was an inside contact. "Who?"

"Meet us in Vegas."

The phone went dead in his hand. Danny cursed under his breath. He didn't like this new direction.

SITTING IN THE REAR of the Piper Cub beside Eden, Payne slipped off his headphones with attached microphone. The drone of the single engine surrounded him like a tingling swarm of bees. He glanced toward the front of the plane where Cody and Josh were busy flying and swapping stories, then he quickly removed Eden's headphones and microphone. Before she could object, he leaned close to her and whispered, "I want you."

"Stop it," she hissed.

He held her head. His tongue traced the shell-like ridges of her ear. "Eden, you taste sweeter than tiramisu."

"Not now, Payne." She snatched the headset from his hands and stuck it back onto her head. If he spoke to her again, his words would be broadcast through the microphones to Cody and Josh.

He made another grab for the headset. She dug her elbow into his rib cage and bared her teeth in a silent snarl. Because they hadn't told Josh about their relationship—past or present—she insisted that they avoid kissing or tenderly touching. She wouldn't even let him hold her hand.

"Great," Payne muttered as he put on his headset again. If this was what family life was like, he wasn't sure he wanted to sign on.

He leaned back in his seat. Actually, there was little reason for complaint. Everything had gone well today. They'd taken off at dawn and had maintained a cruising speed of around a hundred and fifty kilometers an hour which would have been faster if there hadn't been four passengers, adding extra weight to the small plane. After a refueling stop at a godforsaken little airstrip, Payne figured they'd reach Slippery Spring Airfield northwest of Las Vegas at about one o'clock in the afternoon, half an hour from now. In Vegas, Skip would arrange for their protection. Nothing to worry about, but he still felt edgy. Riding with him in this Piper Cub were the two most precious people in his world—Eden and his son.

He glanced over at her, again. Their forced distance

while being physically so close was frustrating and, at the same time, incredibly tempting. He measured the distance to her lips. His gaze caressed the perfect line of her ivory throat, and he marvelled at the delicacy of her chin, her cheekbones and her lovely liquid eyes. Her silky hair begged to be stroked. He leaned closer to her again, hoping to smell her clean fragrance through the chilly atmosphere in the rear of the small plane.

Seat-belted beside her, Payne felt himself becoming aroused. Forbidden desire—it tasted fantastic and sweet. Tonight, in Las Vegas when they were safe, he would make love to her, thoroughly and completely. He would shower her with romance.

"Hey, Mom." Josh leaned around the co-pilot's seat to peek into the rear of the plane. "There's no such thing as aliens. Right?"

"I don't know," Eden said quickly. Even though she was speaking through the headset, her voice sounded breathy, and Payne wondered if she'd been sharing his passionate thoughts.

"I'm telling you the truth," Cody drawled in his raspy voice. "I've seen the little alien critters at Roswell, New Mexico."

"Are they green?" Josh asked sarcastically. "Do they glow in the dark?"

"Not the ones I saw. They were short, but their arms were long like apes. Mostly though, they looked like humans. How else are they going to fit in if they don't look like us?"

Josh glanced back at his mother, then he rolled his eyes. "Why would aliens come to Earth?"

"And they had six fingers," Cody said. "That's the best way you can spot an alien. Six fingers on each hand. They're here to study us humans."

"To take over the world?" Josh asked.

"Nope. These guys are scientists, just making a study. Interplanetary anthropologists."

Josh repeated the words to himself, rolling the syllables around in his mouth. "Mom, do you believe that? Interplanetary anthropologists?"

"It's a good story," Eden said.

"God's truth." Without pausing for breath, Cody launched into a tale of being chased by a U.F.O. in his Piper Cub. He concluded by reaching forward to pat the dashboard near the gyro. "This is a good little aircraft. Good old Sylvia. She gave those aliens the slip."

"Or maybe not," Josh teased. "Maybe you're an alien."

"Maybe I am." Cody echoed the boy's joking tone. "Maybe I had my sixth finger cut off."

For all Payne knew about Cody, he could be an alien. Though he'd been sent by Skip and had given no cause for mistrust, the old man hid his real background in a series of outrageous stories. He might be linked to Danny-O or to the Verones. Not likely, Payne thought, but it was his nature to doubt everyone. Healthy paranoia was the trait that kept him alive in undercover situations. He had to stay on his toes, to explore every suspicion. Damn it, he just couldn't believe that everything was going so smoothly.

Josh spoke up again. "Looks like the moon down there on the ground. Mom, can you see it?"

Eden turned her head to look through the porthole window in the rear. "Desert," she said.

"I wish we could fly over Lake Mead," Payne said, "But there's too much government surveillance around Hoover Dam."

Eden asked, "Why do I see patches of green down there?"

"It's the season," Payne said. "When the snows melt in the mountains, the water washes down here through gullies and ravines. Water brings life. For a little while, the desert blooms."

"Have you ever lived in a desert?" Josh asked.

Payne was startled by his question. Though Josh had been chatty with Cody and his mother, the boy avoided talking to him. Payne grabbed this opportunity. "I never lived in a desert, Josh. I grew up in Wisconsin where it's lush and green with a lot of rolling hills."

"Not as pretty as Colorado," Josh said. "Have you ever been to Chicago?"

"I've lived there, too."

Eden cast a warning glance in Payne's direction as if to say: Don't encourage him.

After last night's revelation of his heritage when Josh announced that it was cool to be related to the Verones and wanted to know all about his exciting criminal relations, his mother had issued a moratorium on discussion of family. There would be no glamorous, mythic tales of the Verones.

"My grandfather," Josh announced, "lives in Chicago."

Eden cut in, "That's enough, Josh."

"Well, he does. And you grew up there. Why can't you tell me about it?"

"Another time," she said.

Her tone was stern, but she was no match for a stubborn eleven-year-old. "It's not fair," Josh whined through the communicating headset. "You lied to me."

"Life isn't always fair," Payne said.

"What do you know about it?" Josh demanded. "You're a fed. You just take orders."

"And I give orders," Payne said, squelching an urge to snarl. "Here comes an order right now. Change seats with me, Josh. We're getting close to landing."

"That's right," Cody confirmed. "We're about twenty minutes out, and I need Payne up here as co-pilot."

The boy's skinny arms wrapped around his chest. He slouched deeper into the co-pilot's seat. His tone was petulant. "I wanna stay right here."

"Please, Josh," his mother started in. "You need to listen to what Payne is saying."

"He's not the boss of me."

A growl rumbled deep inside Payne's chest. The kid was pushing his buttons. Apparently, being a father wasn't always a bed of roses. "Move your little butt, Josh. Now."

"Make me."

There wasn't room in the Piper Cub for a wrestling match, but Josh's bad attitude could not be allowed to go unchecked. Though Payne didn't know beans about being a father, the FBI had taught him how to establish chain of command. There was only one Alpha male on this plane, and that leader was Payne.

He unfastened his seat belt, reached forward and clamped his fingers around the boy's upper arm. Payne tightened his grip enough to exert pressure but not enough to hurt. "Look at me, Josh."

"No way."

Payne constricted his grip.

Josh wriggled in his seat. He didn't like being held down.

"Look at me," Payne repeated.

When his son obeyed, Payne didn't have to fake the controlled fury in his voice. "This isn't a video game, Josh. I have safety concerns that require me to be in the co-pilot's seat during landing. You will do what I tell you. Trade places. Now."

The boy's dark eyes stared up at him with pure resentment. His complexion flushed red. His mouth twisted in a scowl. But he unfastened his seat belt. He took off his headset and microphone. Still looking at Payne, he mouthed his words so his mother wouldn't hear, "I hate you."

Payne's instinct was to snap back with an equally cruel response, but he restrained himself. He was the adult. He needed to behave like a grown-up and not be drawn into name-calling with his son. His son? My God, what was Payne getting himself into? How could he jump into the middle of this parenting game and expect to survive? The rules of engagement were simple when you faced a declared adversary. How the hell should he handle Josh? Payne wanted to love the kid, but Josh clearly hated his guts.

In the co-pilot seat, Payne fastened his seat belt and put on the headset. "Okay, Cody. How far are we from Slippery Spring Airfield?"

"Just a couple of clicks. I ought to check in to let them know we're making an approach."

This morning before they left Colorado, Skip had advised using the small airfield at Slippery Spring northwest of Las Vegas. He'd made arrangements to hangar the plane and to have them met by a vehicle.

Using his air-to-ground communications, Cody ran through the basic approach information and received terse responses from the airfield. Everything was going perfectly. Too perfect, Payne thought as he sighted the runways in the desert. He took out his cell phone and put in a call to Skip for confirmation.

The voice of his former mentor was uncharacteristically agitated. "Where the hell are you? I've been trying to reach you."

Payne's cell phone had been in his pocket. Wearing his headset on the plane, he hadn't been able to hear the ring. "I'm here now. What's up?"

"Where are you?"

"Making a final approach at Slippery Spring."

"Abort," Skip barked. "You've got a welcoming party, and they're not carrying a birthday cake."

Payne turned to Cody. "Pull up. We can't land here."

The old man was slow to react. He shook his head in confusion. "I'm on approach. I'm all set for landing."

There wasn't time to argue or explain. Payne reached across and flipped the switch to change the control of the aircraft to the co-pilot side. He held the yoke. Though he wasn't certified and his piloting skills were rusty, Payne knew what to do. He eased back on the yoke, leveling their descent. They were close enough to the airstrip that Payne could see human figures and cars. There was some sort of stir, people running.

He pulled back, and they swooped again into the skies. Safely airborne, he gave Cody a nod. "Sorry, sir. I had information that we were flying into an ambush. There wasn't time to—"

"It's okay," Cody said. "I'm taking back the controls. You talk to Skip and find us a safe place to land." He tapped the fuel gauge. "We're riding on empty."

Payne felt Eden's hand clawing at his shoulder. Her voice was loud enough that he could hear her without the microphone. "What's going on?"

"It's okay," he said. "We caught the problem in time. Sit down and fasten your belt."

"Why didn't we land there?" she asked.

"Josh," Payne snapped. "Take care of your mother."

Eden spoke through the communication microphone. "For your information, I do not need caretaking. I want to be told what's wrong."

"Don't have time," Payne said. "Sit down."

He took off his headset so he couldn't hear the conversation on the plane while he got instructions from Skip on a new landing site at a vast ranch with a private landing strip. Payne relayed the coordinates and description to Cody who swung the Piper Cub around.

"You know," Cody said, "our flight can be traced on radar. Whoever was waiting for us at Slippery Spring will know exactly where we're headed."

"We'll have to hit the ground running," Payne said. "You can stay at the ranch. I'll take Eden and the boy."

"You got it," Cody said. He pointed toward a tiny ribbon of tarmac beside a scraggly rock formation. "There's our landing."

When Payne tuned in to the microphone conversation, he heard only silence from Eden and Josh. Swell! In a matter of moments, he'd managed to alienate both of them. Fortunately, there wasn't time for him to worry about how his lack of sensitivity and parenting skills had failed. Payne had a larger concern.

The landing party at Slippery Spring Airfield meant they'd been betrayed by someone inside Skip's cadre of loyal followers. They couldn't trust anyone.

WHEN THEY TOUCHED DOWN at the private airstrip outside a desert version of an antebellum mansion, Eden's emotions were in chaos. They were in danger, and she was scared about the obvious threat. But she also felt anger at Payne for dismissing her and for the domineering manner he'd used with Josh. And then there was Josh. His bratty behavior embarrassed her. At the same time, she was concerned about him.

Sorting through the clutter inside her head would take time—a luxury she didn't have. She clasped her son's hand and squeezed, hoping to reassure him.

He squeezed back. But when she looked at him, his expression was unreadable. "Mom? Are you okay?"

She should have been the one asking that question. Eden was the mother, the caretaker. She had to pull herself together. "Are you?"

"Sure."

She wanted to ask if he was frightened. Or if he was angry with her for not defending him. Was he ready to apologize for his obnoxious attitude toward Payne? Eden studied her son's face, but she couldn't tell what he was thinking or feeling. Damn it, he was just like his father!

The plane taxied into a whitewashed barn and the wide double doors closed behind them. Before she had a chance to think, Payne ordered her and Josh to follow him out of the plane. When her feet touched the solid ground, Eden realized she was shaking. Her level of confusion made the situation seem unreal, especially when a handsome white-haired man came toward them. He was a movie actor. Though she couldn't recall his name, she'd seen him a million times on the screen. And now, he was shaking her hand. This wasn't really happening. Obviously, Eden was dreaming.

They were herded into a limo by a tall blond woman who had a fabulous tan and a figure to die for. She introduced herself as Melissa, and she sat beside Eden in the back of the black limousine with tinted windows. As the limo took off, she patted Eden's hand. "You look like you could use a drink."

"Just water," Eden croaked.

Melissa reached into a bar and handed out bottled water to Eden, Josh and Payne, who barely glanced up from his cell phone conversation. "I know what you really need," she said to Eden. "And, don't worry. We're only fifteen minutes away from a rest room. You're going to be staying on the strip."

"Cool," Josh said. He glued his face to the limo window, staring at the skyline that seemed to come nearer and nearer. "Look, Mom! It's a pyramid."

"Well, of course." Eden took a swallow of water. Could this situation become any more bizarre? She and her son and his unacknowledged father were on the run from the combined forces of the FBI and various thugs from her family. They were approaching a pyramid, a gambling mecca in the middle of the desert. Their hostess, Melissa, was gorgeous enough to be a showgirl. And they were riding in a limo that probably belonged to a movie star.

An inappropriate giggle tickled in the back of Eden's throat. What was a nice soccer mom like her doing in the middle of this chaos? She ought to be home in her kitchen baking lasagne. To Melissa, she said, "I've never been to Las Vegas."

"Relax and enjoy the ride." As she gestured grandly, her diamond tennis bracelet sparkled. "The main thing about Vegas is not to take anything too seriously. It's all for show."

When Melissa grinned, the crow's feet around her eyes deepened, and Eden wondered about the age of this leggy blonde. She could have been anywhere from thirty to fifty. Not that her age mattered. Melissa was incredibly attractive—radiant with the confidence that came from a woman who had lived well.

"Were you a showgirl?" As soon as Eden spoke, she regretted her blunt words. "I'm sorry, Melissa. That's none of my business."

"It's okay." She grinned. "I'm not ashamed of being a showgirl. In my day, I kicked up my heels and danced all night."

"I've never done that," Eden said. She went straight from Catholic school to honor student in college to pregnant. "I had my son when I was only twenty."

"I've got four kids," Melissa said. "Just because you're a mother doesn't mean you're dead. While you're in town, let's you and me have a little fun. Let me show you the town. And don't you worry about expenses. My hubby will foot the bill."

"Your husband?"

"Skip," she said.

Eden glanced toward Payne who was still on the cell phone. She was fairly certain that he'd veto any plans for a girls' night out with Melissa. They were—as he kept telling her—in danger.

But Eden looked Melissa straight in the eye and said, "Thank you. I would very much like to have you show me the town."

Chapter Thirteen

On the eighteenth floor of a deluxe Las Vegas hotel, Eden stretched out on the queen-size bed in her own private room. Finally, she had a couple of moments to herself. The door to her bedroom opened into a huge, luxurious sitting room which was designed for high rollers and contained sofas, table and chairs and a black marble Jacuzzi below the window. In this sitting room, Payne's mysterious mentor had posted three guards—burly men with Las Vegas tans and shoulder holsters under their lightweight sports coats. On the opposite side of the sitting room, Josh also had a bedroom to himself which—much to his delight—had a computer and his own private television.

Flat on her back, Eden stared up at the glittering chandelier-style light fixture on the ceiling. She tried to relax. Her physical stiffness and bruising had begun to fade, but her mental state was vividly troubled. She wasn't sure what was going on with the investigation and the betrayal of their arrival at Slippery Spring Airfield. Payne wasn't confiding in her anymore. Instead, he huddled with his mysterious mentor and left her completely out of the loop.

She'd show him, she'd teach him a lesson about how valuable she was in the investigation. From the bedside table, Eden grabbed her cell phone and plugged in the numbers. When Angela answered, Eden said simply, "It's me."

"Give me your cell number," Angela said. "My caller ID isn't working, and I need to be able to call you back."

Not yet, Eden thought. Though these brief conversations were making her feel more friendly toward her cousin, she hadn't forgotten that Angela set her up. "Do you know the guy they call Danny-O."

"*Basta*! I hate that redheaded devil."

"Who's his contact in the family?" Eden asked.

"I can't talk to you about this," Angela said. "Not while you're with the feds."

"But I'm not," she protested. "All I want is for me and my son to be safe."

"Really?"

Angela's disdain was clear in the tone of her voice. On her end of the call, there was some kind of commotion, people shouting and bells ringing. Eden listened hard to the background noise, and she recognized the sounds. A casino! "You're in Vegas. Who's with you?"

"First, tell me where you are," Angela said. "If you really want to be safe, you'll come back to the family."

"Is Robert with you?"

"Robert Ciari? Yeah, he's here. Thank God, he left his boring wife and kids at home."

"Who else?" Eden asked.

"Why don't you meet us," Angela said. "I can set it up."

Eden pressed the disconnect button on her cell phone. Angela was here. That meant there would be others, a whole cadre of Verones.

She should have expected this. Lying back on the bed, Eden wondered why she wasn't more distressed about the nearness of her family. Instead, she felt a strange apathy. What will be, will be.

Of course, she wanted to know who was responsible for her brother's murder. And she desperately longed for this chase to be over. But another issue had taken precedence in her mind.

Until the moment she saw Payne in St. Catherine's basement, Eden felt like she'd never really lived. Sheltered as a young woman and alienated by her heritage, she'd never been a teenaged rebel. A good girl, she concentrated on her studies at school. There had never been any man in her life except for Payne, and he'd been torn from her when she was only twenty, thrusting her into the role of a bereaved young woman with no close friends. Then she'd been a single mother, devoted to her son.

Now that Josh was almost a teenager who didn't seem to require her constant and vigilant care, her identity as a mom was slipping. So, who was she?

Her gaze drifted down from the ceiling to a marble-topped dresser where she'd placed the gold box with a black bow that had been delivered to her bedroom. Inside was an incredible black-and-silver sequined dress with a halter top and low back. The dress was the most sophisticated, fantastic creation Eden had ever seen up close. Though there was no card with the box, it must have come from Melissa who promised a girls' night out.

Eden hadn't yet dared to try on the dress, but she had slipped her feet into the matching high-heeled sandals that were impractical for anything except the tango...as if she knew how to perform that exotic dance.

There was a knock at her door. "Come in," she called out.

Payne stepped inside and closed the door behind him. "Nice little place you've got here."

"Pretty snazzy." She sat up on the raised platform of the bed and gestured toward the polished marble and mirrors. "It feels like I ought to be a harem girl."

"Only if I can be your sheik." He joined her on the bed and leaned forward for a kiss.

"No kissing," she said. "Not until you tell me what's going on. What happened at Slippery Spring Airfield?"

"The guys waiting for us were sent by the Verones. Vegas guys. Friends of your family."

"But the Verones are here," she said. "Angela is here."

"Did you call her?"

Archly, she said, "I'm not completely ineffective when it comes to this investigation."

"What did you learn?"

"Just that she's here. And so is Robert Ciari."

Calmly, he accepted her information, but he didn't thank her. His expression was annoyingly stern. "In the future, when you call Angela, I want to know."

"You don't have to treat me like a child, Payne."

"Believe me, I don't think of you as a child. You're a full-grown, very attractive woman."

In an instant, his gaze switched from disapproval to red-hot lust. She might have been complimented if she hadn't felt so irritable and left out. Determined to turn his attention away from sex and onto the investigation, she said, "Tell me more about what happened at Slippery Spring."

Rising from the bed, he went to the built-in refrigerator where he took out a bottle of water. "We should count ourselves lucky that our welcoming party was Verones instead of feds. If the FBI had been waiting, they could have tracked our route to landing and would have known exactly where we were."

"Are we safe now?"

"Seems like it," he said. "This hotel is owned by Skip's friends. The security people, the dealers and the pit bosses are keeping an eye on you, me and Josh. As long as we stay in this hotel, we ought to be all right."

"Even from the feds? Can't they bust in here and close everything down?"

Payne laughed as he screwed the top off his bottled water and took a sip. "You've been reading too many Elliot Ness comic books. Las Vegas is a wealthy and powerful place. It would take a direct order of Congress to close down a casino."

"But they could search," she said.

"And we'd be spirited out of here. The hotel is huge."

Sitting in the middle of the bed, she curled her feet under her bottom. Her gaze shifted toward the box with the sequined dress. "Would it be safe for me to leave this room?"

"Yes," he said simply. "You and I could go out for dinner. Downstairs, there's a five-star gourmet restaurant with candlelight and a string quartet."

His invitation appealed to her. Twelve years ago, she and Payne had never had much of a courtship. She'd missed out on the romance of being treated like a desirable and beautiful lady.

Yet, she had doubts—the same reservations that arose when she thought of putting on the glamorous sequined dress in that box. When she was twenty, she might have enjoyed being swept off her feet. But her life was different now. She was a mother. Responsible. Practical. Totally unsweepable. "We could take Josh. It would do him good to eat something other than fast food hamburgers."

Payne sank into a brocaded chair. His dark eyes regarded her steadily. "Are you telling me that you want to take Josh out on the town in Las Vegas?"

"Maybe."

"Okay, I guess we need to talk about Josh. I didn't handle the situation on the plane very well. Twisting his little arm wasn't the best way to deal with a disagreement."

"Payne, it's going to take time for you to build a relationship with Josh. Developing trust doesn't happen overnight."

"I want to tell him, Eden. I want him to know that I'm his father."

"Not yet. He's been through enough trauma."

"Oh, yeah." His voice dripped with sarcasm. "The kid is real traumatized."

"Maybe he's not showing the signs, but—"

"When you told him he was related to a crime family, he thought it was cool. Is it really going to be more damaging for him to know I'm his father?"

"Possibly. I can't say for certain."

Though she was closer to Josh than anyone on earth, Eden couldn't tell if he was covering his real feelings with adolescent bravado. She suspected that was the case. Josh didn't want to admit that being a Verone frightened him or disgusted him. Therefore, he pretended that it was okay.

Accepting Payne as a father was a more immediate and difficult problem. Though she'd been careful not to introduce Payne as her boyfriend, her son already resented him. This sort of behavior had happened before when she went on dates. Josh reacted with hostility toward anyone who might usurp his mother's affection.

"There has to be a good way to put you and Josh together," she said. "A counselor could help."

"A shrink." Settling back in his chair, Payne took another swallow of his water. He had nothing against psychology. In profiling and his undercover work, he'd been trained in practical psychological principles and found them useful. In the long term, he expected he and Josh would need some counseling. But right now? "There isn't time."

"Why not?" she asked. "Are you planning to disappear again?"

"I didn't plan it the first time," he said.

But bad things happened. Payne knew they were in the middle of a tense situation that could take off in any given direction. He might be arrested by the feds. He might be killed by the Verones.

Tomorrow, if all went as Skip planned, Payne would come face-to-face with Danny-O. The simmering cauldron of conspiracy and intrigue was about to come to a full boil.

Before any sort of unexpected disaster struck, Payne wanted his son to know his identity. He needed for Josh to understand that he hadn't been abandoned. It had never been Payne's choice to live apart from his only child. "Let me tell him."

"Not tonight," she said.

"When?"

"I'll know when the time is right," she said.

Though it went against his better judgment, Payne bowed to her verdict. Eden ought to know what was best for the kid.

He rose from the brocade chair and strolled across her palatial bedroom. His gaze rested on the gold box with a black ribbon. He knew what was inside. He'd selected the dress with Melissa's help, and he wanted to see Eden draped in sparkles. If only for one night, he hoped to treat her like a princess.

"About this evening," he said. "Let me take you to dinner alone. We can talk more about our son."

"An evening of argument? How special!"

When he looked toward her, Eden's gaze slipped away. She seemed to be avoiding him. Damn it, why? He stood ready to give her an enchanted evening she would never forget. "I'll pick you up at nine o'clock."

"I don't think so." Her chin jutted at a stubborn angle. "I'm really tired."

He recognized this ploy. She was playing hard to get, wanted him to beg. Well, that wasn't going to happen. With exaggerated nonchalance, he headed toward the door. "If you change your mind—"

"I'll see you tomorrow morning, Payne."

He turned away from her. He'd never enjoyed the games that women played when dating, but this time he would accept the challenge. He wasn't giving up. Tonight, when she fell into his arms, the conquest would be even more sweet.

IN HER FABULOUS DRESS, Eden breezed into the sitting room where Melissa and Josh and their bodyguards were waiting. Though she felt a bit like a gawky child dressed up in her mother's clothes, she struck a dramatic pose.

"Wow," Josh said. "Mom, you look awesome."

"Absolutely lovely," Melissa agreed. She turned to the bodyguards who smiled and nodded.

"Really?" Eden had fussed with her makeup for half an hour. "I thought the lipstick might be too dark."

"For evening, you can go more dramatic," Melissa said. "And your eyes are fabulous."

"Shiny," Josh said. "Like diamonds."

Delighted, she laughed. She truly did feel pretty and had already begun to regret not accepting the dinner invitation from Payne. She wanted him to see her all dolled up. But she'd rejected him. It was not the smartest move she'd ever made.

When Melissa called to make plans for a girls' night out, Eden had agreed in the hopes that she might salvage the evening.

After giving Josh a hug, Eden followed the former show-girl into the hallway. Together, they sashayed toward the elevator. Eden's delicate-looking sandals were surprisingly comfortable when she modified her bouncy athletic stride to a more feminine pace.

"Shouldn't we have a bodyguard?" Eden asked.

"Honey, this entire hotel is a bodyguard. At any given moment, there are ten different guys keeping a close eye on you and me."

They stepped inside the mirrored elevator where Eden caught a glimpse of them both. Melissa was a glittery, golden blonde. Eden was a dark-haired, smooth, sophisti-cated vision in silver. Together, they complemented each other. "Where are we headed, Melissa?"

"Second floor casino," she said. "We'll go directly to the high rollers' room. What do you like to play?"

"I'm not much of a gambler," Eden confessed. She'd visited Central City outside Denver and plugged a few nickels into slot machines, but that was the extent of her experience. "I know the basics of poker and blackjack. But that's about it."

"Blackjack it is." She held out a sequined bag on a drawstring. "And here's something to get you started."

"I can't take your money," Eden said.

"This comes from Skip, and he insists."

The elevator doors opened onto the flashing lights and clanging bells of a vast casino beneath vaulted cathedral ceilings and Romanesque architecture. Eden stepped forward. For a moment, she stood at the top of a grand red-carpeted staircase, staring down at the rows of slot machines.

"Do you hear that?" Melissa whispered. "It's the sound of jaws dropping. We look great."

It really did seem like people were staring at them. Eden straightened her shoulders. "This is weird for me. I'm not a sequin-wearing woman."

"It's all in the attitude," Melissa said as she directed her around a marble walkway that circled above the main casino area. "When I first came to Vegas, over twenty-five years ago, I was just another tall girl from Oregon. But I didn't know that. I felt like a star, and that's how people treated me."

"I wish I had a tenth of your confidence," Eden said.

"I've had my share of bad times, but I know how to bounce back." She paused, lightly touching Eden's shoulder. "From what I've heard, so do you."

"What have you heard?"

"Enough to know that you're strong and smart and able to land on your feet." She winked. "And you clean up real nice, Eden."

"Thanks."

Through the arched entryway into the high rollers' arena,

the *bing-bing-bing* of slot machines melted into the subtle rustle of shuffling cards and spinning roulette wheels. In this area, the decor was subtly more elegant. Women were dressed more like Eden and Melissa. Several of the men wore tuxedos.

"Nice," Eden murmured. Even the carpet beneath her feet felt more thick and plush.

Melissa smiled a greeting to several people. Everybody knew her. Eden felt like she was with the most popular girl at the party.

"Who would you like to be tonight?" Melissa asked.

Eden shrugged. "What do you mean?"

"A lot of people are going to want to meet you, and it might be best if I don't give out your real name."

"Susan Anthony," Eden said with a grin, remembering how Payne had been amused with her alias.

"Okay, Susan. And what do you do for a living?" Melissa nudged her with an elbow. "Think big."

"I'm in transportation," Eden said. Again, she thought of the escape from Chicago with Payne. "And I own a string of racehorses."

And that was exactly how Melissa introduced her to several people. Within minutes, Eden was beginning to believe her fabricated, adventurous identity. Beautiful, well-dressed people swirled around her. A cocktail waitress in a skimpy outfit brought her a mint julep, compliments of the man whose horse had won the Kentucky Derby two years ago. Oh my, if the car pool moms could see her now!

With Melissa at her side, Eden perched at a green felt table for a few games of blackjack. Using the chips in her sequined purse, she lost a few and then won a few more.

And then, across the room, she saw him. Payne wore a fitted tuxedo that emphasized his broad shoulders. His snowy white shirt glistened. His dark eyes smouldered with an intense sensual heat that focused only on her.

As he approached, the rest of the room faded in a glittering blur. Other sounds were muted by the clanging of her heart.

Payne stopped before her. Instead of saying Eden's name, he looked to Melissa and asked, "Would you introduce me to your charming friend?"

"You bet," Melissa said, playing along. "Susan Anthony, this is Payne Magnuson. Would you two please excuse me?"

Payne held Eden's hand in his and lifted her fingertips to his lips for a light kiss. All the while, he maintained eye contact, devouring her. Gesturing to the stool beside her, he asked, "Is this seat vacant?"

"Not if you sit there," she said. She felt a blush warming her cheeks.

"I'm honored, Susan."

As he perched beside her, Eden decided she liked this role-playing game. It was fun to think that the most handsome man in the high rollers' room had singled her out. "And what do you do for a living, Payne?"

"I'm a spy," he said, somewhat truthfully. "You?"

"A little of this. A little of that. I raise racehorses."

"I must take you riding," he said.

"You must." She pursed her lips to keep from giggling and added, "I understand there are some fabulous trails in central Kansas."

"Ah yes," he said. "Near the railroad."

They played a game of blackjack with the dealer, and Eden won.

"May I buy you a drink?" he asked.

"White wine," she said.

"Dom Perignon." He gestured to a cocktail waitress who raced off to do his bidding, then he turned back to Eden. His sardonic smile was totally sexy. "Do you come here often, Susan?"

She fluttered her lashes, flirting shamelessly. "I'd come more often if I could be sure you were here."

They played again. And she won, again. The stack of chips beside her had grown to a decent-size pile.

Their champagne arrived in crystal flutes. She clinked the edge with him and took a sip.

"I'd like very much to share dinner with you," he said. "Shall we leave the gaming tables?"

"Yes." She gathered up her chips, leaving one for the dealer as she'd seen Melissa do.

Payne offered his arm to escort her. "Nice tip," he said, "a hundred bucks."

"No, I only left one chip."

"A hundred bucks," he repeated.

Oh my God, she'd been playing with hundred dollar chips. That was definitely insane. She might have lost thousands of dollars in a few minutes. "Good thing for beginner's luck."

"For you, everything will be lucky tonight."

They entered a gorgeous ballroom with white linen draped tables around a dance floor. A twelve-piece orchestra played a swing tune.

The maître d' led them to a table beside the floor where they drank their champagne and watched for a moment. After consulting with her, Payne placed their order.

As the orchestra shifted to a slow tune, he asked, "Shall we dance?"

Eden wasn't sure how she'd manage in the high-heeled sandals. "I'm a little rusty. What with flying all over the country and raising my thoroughbreds, I don't have much time for dancing."

"Just follow my lead."

If Eden had been herself—a single mother, soccer mom with responsibilities—she would have refused, not daring to make a fool of herself. But tonight, she was an adventuress.

She allowed herself to be swept into Payne's arms. He held her close. Their bodies pressed snugly together. His hand at her waist guided her movements, and she didn't stumble once—not even when he dipped her backwards.

"You're incredible," he whispered.

"You're not so bad yourself," she said.

"And you're mine. Tonight will end with you in my bed."

He swirled her around the dance floor until they reached their table again. Recklessly, she had more champagne with their gourmet dinner of kiwi and mango, filet mignon and polished vegetables that looked like jewels. Though there wasn't a bite of pasta or mozzarella, the fare was delectable.

Throughout their meal, their conversation slid from her fantasy identity to real opinions on life, art and dreams. "Some days," she said, "are so hectic that I'd give anything for an hour of peace and quiet. And then, there are plenty of times when all I want is the sound of another human voice."

"It's easier to balance with two people," he said.

"How so?"

"Think about it," he said. "When you're by yourself, it's hard to hold up the whole load."

She nodded, envisioning her life as a balancing act where she held the laundry on her lap, drove her turn at carpool, raced to a catering job and signed bills with her free hand. "But if you add another person, doesn't that mean twice the chores?"

He shook his head. "First, you build a foundation—a carry-all with two handles. And you lift together."

She took another sip of champagne. "That's brilliant."

"One more dance."

When he offered his hand, she gladly accepted, confident that she could manage the most complicated tango in his arms. Being with Payne made everything easy.

When he led her to his hotel suite where he'd scattered fresh rose petals on the ivory satin sheets, Eden felt like an entire courtship had been played in one special night.

Slowly and sensuously, she slipped the tuxedo jacket from his shoulders. Her fingers unbuttoned his glistening white shirt. He was the only man for her. The best man. When he stripped her glittering dress from her body, she felt like the most beautiful woman on earth.

Chapter Fourteen

If last night had turned out to be his final hours on earth, Payne wouldn't have complained too much. In Eden's passionate embrace, he'd experienced a tender, fierce, perfect happiness. She fulfilled his every dream.

Before he left her sleeping in his bedroom suite, he placed a rose on the pillow beside her head. He considered leaving a note but didn't know what to say. How could he describe this crazy tumult of feelings? If he started writing, he'd scribble on for an eternity only to find there weren't words enough. Instead, he leaned down and gently kissed her smooth forehead.

Her nose crinkled. She was adorable. He kissed her again.

Still asleep, she batted him away with her hand as though he was nothing more than an annoying, stinging pest. That was him, all right. He chuckled quietly. He was the Mosquito of Love.

Being with her made him feel good. Young and free from care. He checked his wristwatch. Unfortunately, there was no more time for fun and games this morning.

After one last longing gaze, he tore himself from her orbit and went toward the door. In those few strides, his manner changed completely. He was on his way to meet with Danny-O.

Last night, Danny-O had arrived in Vegas and contacted Skip with an offer to meet…but only with Payne. Alone.

If Payne had been an idealist, he might have believed— like Chuck Sonderberg in Colorado—that Danny-O's conscience had caught up with him and he was ready to confess. Not likely. The correct procedure for an agent who'd stepped out of line was to report transgressions to his superiors, then to step back and await disciplinary action. But Danny-O requested a meet with Payne. Why?

Worst case scenario: Driven mad by the failure of his carefully orchestrated alliance with the Verones, Danny-O wanted vengeance at any cost. He wanted to meet Payne and kill him.

Though Payne was armed and prepared for that possibility, he didn't expect raging insanity. The way he figured, Danny-O had an ego bigger than the Golden Nugget Casino. He was trying to work an angle and wanted to meet with Payne to lay the groundwork for talking his way out of trouble.

In the hotel lobby, Payne strolled past a bank of slot machines that were being played even now, at eight o'clock in the morning.

He stepped outside under a neon canopy that would never be as bright as the splash of sunlight on the curb. A black limousine driven by a gray-haired chauffeur pulled up beside him.

Payne opened the door and climbed inside.

Danny-O sat in the middle of the bench seat in the rear. His red hair was neatly combed. Looking composed, he wore a dark gray suit, white shirt and striped necktie. His blue eyes were covered by sunglasses. "Thanks for meeting me, Payne."

Slamming the limo door with a solid thunk, Payne seated himself opposite Danny-O. There were only a few feet between them, and Payne measured the distance carefully. If this confrontation came down to a shoot-out, he'd aim his bullet for the direct center of his adversary's forehead because Danny-O was undoubtedly clever enough to be wearing a bullet-proof vest under that conservative white shirt.

"Here's the true story," Danny-O said. "I'm an ambitious guy. I wanted to get ahead, and when I heard on the street that the Verones were getting active again, I saw an opportunity for undercover work. I thought if I got inside, I could bring them down."

Payne didn't believe a word he was hearing, but he gave no sign of his opinion. He wanted two names from Danny-O: The new boss of the Verones, and the name of the person inside Skip's network who had betrayed them at Slippery Spring Airfield.

Danny-O grinned. Were his lips trembling? "I wanted to be like you. The legendary Payne Magnuson. The fed who successfully infiltrated the Verone family twelve years ago."

"A little touch of the blarney. Right, Danny?" This guy thought he could talk his way out of anything, including murder. "Is that why you killed Eddy Verone? To be like me?"

"It wasn't supposed to go down that way," Danny-O said. "I thought Eddy was drawing on me. I saw a gun. I shot back. Protecting myself."

With utter disbelief, Payne said, "You'd call your actions self-defense?"

"That's correct, sir."

Payne vividly recalled every detail of that restaurant in Brooklyn. He remembered the redolence of garlic and spices. In his mind, he saw the checkered tablecloths, the Chianti bottles, the faces of families eating dinner. He knew precisely what had happened in that restaurant. Danny-O and his cohort, Luke Borman, had set up the murder of Eddy Verone and had intended for Payne to be blamed, and killed himself. Too bad for them. Payne had escaped.

"It's not my job to judge," he said. He'd leave it to the

higher authorities and due process to give Danny-O what he deserved. "But I want my good name back."

"Absolutely," Danny-O said. "If I ever have to testify on this matter, I'll tell it the way I saw it. In the restaurant, Luke Borman was confused. For some reason, he was aiming at you. And you returned fire."

"What about Samuels in Abilene?" Payne asked.

"What did he tell you?"

No way would Payne reveal that Samuels had directly implicated Danny-O. To do so would put Eden in danger; she was a witness to Samuels' statements. "Nothing. He told me nothing."

Danny-O scowled in feigned disgust. "Samuels must have been working directly with the Verones. That's for sure why they killed him."

"Who killed him?" Payne asked. "Who gave the order?"

Danny-O removed his sunglasses. Though his blue eyes were watery and red-rimmed with exhaustion, he stared hard to convey the importance of what he was about to reveal. "You want me to tell you who's in charge of the Verone family, the name of the person who is taking over from old Gus. You want the results of my undercover investigation."

Investigation? Not hardly. Danny-O was on the take. He'd been promised big bucks. Payne had no doubt of that. "I want the name," he confirmed.

"Angela Benedict."

"A woman?" Though she'd been near the top of Payne's suspect list, he wasn't sure he believed Danny-O. "Are you telling me the Verones are going to let a woman be the boss?"

"It's exactly what I'm telling you. She's tough. She's strong. And she's running the show."

"Is that why she seduced Luke Borman?"

"That wasn't Angela. It was Eddy's wife." He brightened as a new idea occurred to him. "Hey, maybe that's why Borman was aiming at you. He was trying to impress his girlfriend."

Danny-O was slime of the lowest order. He was willing to throw suspicion on his partners to save his own sorry tail.

"One more question," Payne said. "The ambush at Slippery Spring Airfield. Who gave away our plans?"

"I don't know."

For the first time since he'd entered the limo, Payne sensed that Danny-O was telling the truth. Plus, his lack of knowledge fit with what Skip had said. The welcoming party at the airfield had been friends of the Verones.

Still, Payne tried one more time. "I need the name of that informant."

"I can't help you," Danny-O said. "Whoever it was talked directly to the Verones. Not to me."

Payne tapped on the window separating the rear of the limo from the driver. Soundlessly, the window went down. "Pull over," Payne ordered.

"Wait a minute," Danny said. "I told you what you wanted, now I need something from you."

"I don't do quid pro quo with traitors."

"If this comes to an investigation…" Danny-O was talking fast, breathing hard. He was scared. "Payne, you've got to stand up for me. You're the only one who understands what it's like to be undercover with these people. At least help me get into witness protection."

The limo parked at a curb at the edge of the old downtown Las Vegas. Payne nodded to the door. "Get out."

"With all due respect, sir, if I hadn't been involved, your girlfriend would be dead right now."

"Explain."

When Danny-O raised his hand to massage the back of his neck, Payne reached up to adjust his shirt collar. His fingers were inches away from the weapon in his shoulder holster.

"I held them back," Danny-O said. "They were ready to kill her right there at St. Catherine's. As soon as she walked in the door dressed like a nun. They were going to kill her under Gus's nose."

"But you wanted to use Eden to find me," Payne said. "Bad move, Danny-O. But I'm glad you did it."

"So, you owe me."

His reasoning was pure stupidity. Because Danny-O missed when he was trying to kill Payne, he wanted to take credit for saving his life. Desperately stupid. Disgusted, Payne didn't want to mess with this lowlife anymore. "Get out of the limo."

"Not until you swear you'll help me. Not until I have your word."

"Here's the only word you'll get from me: Traitor."

Danny-O reached for his gun, but Payne was faster. He held his pistol at arm's length. The bore was three inches away from Danny-O's forehead.

Calmly, Payne said, "You're a traitor to the ideals you swore to uphold as a federal officer. You've turned on your friends. Now you're trying to double-cross the Verones."

"Don't shoot, Payne. Please."

"I won't hurt you. I'll leave you to the mercy of the others you've betrayed." Payne's gunhand was unwavering. "For the last time. Get out of my sight."

Danny-O shoved open the limo door and staggered out onto the street.

Payne pulled the door closed and returned to his seat near the driver's window.

As the limo merged into traffic, a familiar voice came from the front seat. "Glad you didn't shoot him, Payne. Would have made one heck of a mess."

"Cody?"

"Don't worry. I've got a chauffeur's license as well as

being able to fly a plane. I had to get one the last time I was in New Orleans during Mardi Gras when—''

''How about if you chauffeur me to someplace where I can talk to Skip?''

''Sure thing. By the way, I taped your conversation. I guess, since Danny-O admitted that he was the one working the Verones, you're off the hook with the feds.''

''Almost,'' Payne said. But another important question remained unanswered. Who was the informant? Who told the Verones that the Piper Cub was landing at Slippery Spring Airfield?

If it wasn't Cody and wasn't Chuck Sonderberg in Colorado, there were very few choices. Melissa? Skip himself? Payne was beginning to draw a conclusion he didn't like. He knew that Eden had been secretly placing phone calls to her cousin. Was Eden the informant?

AFTER THEY'D FINISHED a room service lunch in the hotel suite, Eden and Josh settled down for a serious card game with the two bodyguards in their room. Though Josh wanted to learn poker, Eden insisted on playing go fish. Last night, after she learned she'd accidentally been playing with hundred dollar chips, she'd had enough gambling. *Last night. Ah, last night.*

She closed her eyes and remembered with a contented sigh. The spangles and champagne, dinner and dancing with a gallant, dashing, handsome man in a tuxedo. Last night, she was Cinderella, and Payne was her Prince Charming.

She'd talked to him on the phone about an hour ago, and he promised to come here as soon as he could. Every few minutes, her gaze strayed toward the hotel room door, eager to see him again.

''Mom! Have you got any sevens?''

She stared at the fan of cards in her hand. ''Go fish.''

''I want to go someplace this afternoon,'' Josh said. ''To

the hotel with a bird on the front. I looked on a map, and it's right next door to here.''

''And why do you want to go there?'' she asked.

''They've got bears.''

''Bears?'' He shrugged and concentrated on his cards, avoiding her gaze. Eden had seen that look before. He was hiding something from her.

''There was something on TV about it,'' he said. ''Can we go?''

''Maybe.'' Though she'd been assured that they were safe in this hotel, their protection might not extend to next door. Nonetheless, it seemed a shame to be in Las Vegas and not take in the sights.

When the phone rang, one of the bodyguards answered. To Eden, he announced, ''It's Payne. He's in the hotel. Should be here in a sec.''

Josh threw his cards on the table. His skinny shoulders slumped sulkily. He grumbled, ''Now I won't get to go anywhere.''

She reached toward her son. ''Honey, that's not true. Maybe Payne will come with us.''

''He doesn't care about me.'' Josh pushed away from the table and stalked toward his private bedroom. ''He just wants to be with you.''

As Josh slammed his door, the bodyguard opened the main door to the suite to admit Payne. Eden was torn. Her son needed her attention, but she wanted to be with Prince Charming. The mere sight of him flooded her with anticipation.

He sauntered toward her, leaned down and lightly kissed her lips. ''I have good news,'' he said.

For a moment, she weighed the alternatives. Good news from Payne versus dealing with a pouting adolescent. Payne won.

She smiled up at him. ''What's your news?''

With a nod toward her private bedroom, he grasped her

hand and tugged. Willingly, Eden rose to her feet. As she followed him, she felt lighter than air. The soles of her bare feet seemed to be walking inches above the carpet.

Of course, she wouldn't forget about Josh and his frustrations. But right now, she longed to indulge herself, to bathe herself in the warm sensual glow that enveloped her when she was with Payne.

Inside her bedroom with the door closed, he gathered her into his arms for a deep, breathtaking kiss. Excitement raced through her, churning her blood. She wanted to experience this sensation again and again, to be truly alive.

"Are you ready for the good news?" he asked.

She nodded, ready for almost anything he might suggest.

"I'm in the clear," he announced. "No more running from the feds."

She squeezed him in a tight embrace. They were one step closer to safety, to normalcy. "How did that happen?"

"I met with Danny-O this morning. He admitted that he killed your brother and was trying to pursue his own phony private undercover investigation of the Verones. His confession and Skip's contacts were enough to clear my name."

"Are you telling me that Danny-O suddenly saw the light and confessed?"

"Not formally," Payne conceded. "But I got the conversation on tape."

She knew how these things worked. When Danny-O offered information to Payne, he would expect something in return. "What did you promise Danny-O?"

"Nothing. I'm in charge now, Eden."

"I can't believe you met with that creep." Irritated, she took a step away from him. "I hate when you take risks. He could have killed you."

"It's my job," he said.

She wasn't entirely thrilled with his occupation, but that

discussion would wait for another day. "Why didn't you tell me you were going to meet Danny-O?"

"Because I knew you'd worry. Last night, I didn't want any negative thoughts to intrude on our special time together. I wanted everything to be perfect."

"And it was." If he'd told her last night, there might have been a shadow on her magical evening. "In the future, I don't want you to keep anything from me. I want you to be honest."

"Agreed," he said. "And you'll be honest with me."

"One hundred percent."

Fully dressed, he stretched out on her bed, which was still perfectly made since she didn't sleep there last night. He grinned. "I like your outfit."

She wore a striped T-shirt and khaki walking shorts with her ever-present cell phone tucked in the pocket. "A little less formal than last night."

"It's cute," he said, patting the space on the bed beside him. "Come here, cutie."

She lay down next to him. They were both on their sides, facing each other. Rather than sexual, their position felt comfortably intimate. "What happens next, Payne?"

"I need to go back east, to Chicago. From there, I can help run this investigation and find out what's really happening with your family." He paused. "I want you and Josh to come with me."

"To Chicago?" That seemed a little like jumping out of the frying pan into the fire. "Isn't that dangerous?"

"Not if you're with me. I'll make sure you're both in a safe house—a house that I'll come home to every night. Just like a regular working man."

Who was he kidding? There was nothing regular about living with bodyguards in a safe house. "What about school for Josh?"

"Until we're sure there's no danger, he'll have tutors."

"I don't like it, Payne. Sounds claustrophobic. He wouldn't have any friends. And what about soccer?"

"You won't be in a safe house forever," he assured her. "Only until the danger is over."

She didn't like the idea of being cooped up, constantly under threat. "Is it really that dangerous?"

"Could be. I don't take chances with the people I care about." Casually, he caressed her shoulder. His hand slid down her arm and he clasped her hand. "Danny-O told me who was trying to take over the Verone family business."

She tensed. A tight knot formed in the back of her throat. She was about to learn who—in her family—was responsible for Eddy's murder. She guessed, "It's Robert Ciari, isn't it?"

"It's Angela," he said.

"I don't believe it."

Agitated, she rolled off the bed and began pacing the room. She'd been confiding in Angela for days, had come to trust her as much as she relied on anyone in the Verone family circle. Either Eden had been a complete fool or Angela was a brilliant actress.

"Why couldn't it be Angela?" Payne asked.

"She wouldn't do that to her sons. She's not a total monster. Though at first, I thought she was."

Eden recalled her impression of Angela in the ladies' room at St. Catherine's. She'd seemed hard and cold. Since then, she'd seen Angela crying at Eddy's funeral. She'd heard that Angela was having an affair with her brother, that her own marriage was falling apart. "She's just a woman with problems. I feel sorry for her."

"What else have you been talking to Angela about?" he asked.

"Things," she said.

"While you were chatting about things, did you happen to mention that we'd be landing at Slippery Spring outside of Las Vegas?"

"No!" How could he think she was so stupid? "I never gave her any location, except when I lied about being in Iowa. And I kept our conversations short so she couldn't draw a bead on my cell phone location."

She didn't like the way he was studying her as though she were a specimen under a microscope. He said, "Are you sure the name of the airfield didn't accidentally slip out?"

Her temper began to rise. "You're wrong about Angela. She was heartbroken when Eddy was murdered. She never would have ordered his death. Or mine. She wouldn't want me dead."

"But she set you up, Eden. You're forgetting what happened when Angela loaned you her brand-new Corvette."

"I didn't forget," she snapped.

He looked at her with suspicion in his eyes. Disbelieving. "Calm down," he said.

"I will not. You're treating me like an idiot. Like you don't trust me."

"Trust works both ways, Eden. Why haven't you told me about all these chatty little girl talks?"

"There was only once that I called when you weren't around. Yesterday. And I told you about it as soon as I saw you." Flustered, she planted her fists on her hips and glared at him. "I shouldn't have said anything. I should have known you wouldn't understand."

"You're right. I don't get it." He strode past her toward the door. "Get yourself and Josh packed. We're leaving this afternoon."

"Maybe I don't want to go with you," she said.

He turned and stared at her. "This is a safety issue. Even if it's not Angela, somebody in your family wants you out of the way so they can take over."

"I don't care."

"Are you going to put Josh in danger? Just to make a point to me?"

The door to her bedroom swung open. Josh stood there, trembling with rage. Through tight lips, he said, "My mom doesn't want to go with you."

Eden gaped in horror. This was the worst possible confrontation she could imagine. "Josh, please go to your room."

"I won't." He stamped his foot.

"Listen to me," Payne said. "I'm not asking you to like me, Josh. But you need to trust me."

"You can't tell me what to do," Josh said.

"I want to help you and your mother. I'm going to protect you, to take care of you. Both of you."

"You don't want to take care of me," Josh shouted. "Why should I believe you?"

"Because I'm your father."

Eden felt like she'd been slapped in the face. Shock waves pounded against her consciousness. Why had Payne told him? Why like this?

Josh froze like a fragile statue made of ice. If she breathed on him, he might melt. If she touched him, he might shatter.

"Liar," he yelled. "My father is dead. Tell him, Mom."

"Oh, Josh," she whispered, "I didn't know he was still alive. I meant to—"

"I hate you both!"

Josh turned on his heel and flew from the room.

Chapter Fifteen

Horrified, Eden stared after her son. She heard the outer door of the suite slam with a resounding thud as Payne stepped outside her bedroom. He instructed the bodyguards to go after the boy and bring him back.

Through a haze of anger, she watched Payne return to her bedroom. How could he have told Josh like that? Just blurting it out: I'm your father.

Damn it, why had Payne lost control? His words had wrought a ton of emotional damage. How would they ever sift through the rubble?

"I'm sorry," he said. "I didn't mean to—"

"I know."

She turned away from him, unsure whether to scream in rage or burst into tears. This was, at least partially, her fault. She should have told Josh the moment he met Payne. They should have taken time at the cabin in Colorado to go through a sensitive discussion, sharing the joy and the turmoil of finally being reunited as a family.

But she'd known the discussion wouldn't be happy. The relationship between Eden and her son was intense. For all Josh's life, she was the only family he had. No aunts, uncles or cousins. No great-grandparents. He had only his mother. It would be difficult to make room in their relationship for anyone else—even Josh's father.

Payne touched her shoulder. "Can you forgive me?"

With her back to him, she held up her hands to cover her face. Her quiet voice came directly from her heart. "I don't know exactly what I expected. Maybe a beautiful moment when the three of us would hold hands and walk into a sunset."

She had no basis for such a lovely fantasy. She'd never really known what a normal family was like. Her mother had died too soon. She'd never known unconditional love without fear. A shiver trembled through her, but she continued, "I've lost everyone I truly loved. My mother and father. Eddy. And you, Payne. I lost you. Josh was all I ever had. I might have spoiled him, indulged him, smothered him. But, oh, how I have loved my son."

"You've found me," Payne said. "I'm here with you, and you're not alone anymore."

"It's hard to believe. To trust." She lowered her hands and leaned back against his chest. His arms encircled her. She whispered, "I'm so afraid."

"Don't worry," he said. "We'll talk to Josh. He's a smart kid. He'll understand."

There was a shout from the outer room of the suite. One of the bodyguards came into the bedroom. "We lost him," the man said. "The kid took off and we can't find him."

Eden's fear closed around her—a dark shadow that would blot out every ray of light. If anything happened to Josh, she would surely die.

Payne turned her to face him. He stared hard into her eyes. "Where would he go? Where should we look?"

"I don't know." Her tears streaked down her cheeks in cold rivulets. "He's just a little boy. He doesn't know his way around Las Vegas."

Speaking to the bodyguards, Payne issued a quick series of orders, setting up a search party. He turned back to her. "You stay here. I'll have Melissa come and keep you company."

"But I want to help."

"Somebody has to stay. In case Josh comes back here." He led her toward the bed. "I'll find him. It's going to be all right."

She balked, wiping the dampness from her cheeks, pulling herself together for Josh's sake. "I'm coming with you. Josh is more likely to show himself if he sees me."

Payne studied her carefully, assessing her mental state. Then, he nodded briskly. "I want you close to me. Within arm's reach. Do you understand?"

"I'll be careful."

"Stay with me." Payne wanted to imprint those words on her brain. He needed to be sure she would take every precaution. Like it or not, Eden was a target. The Verones wanted to get their hands on her. And there were a lot of them in town. Gus and Sophia. Robert Ciari. Angela and maybe even her husband who wasn't supposed to leave the Chicago area without notifying his parole officer. Outside the door to this hotel, the Verones were waiting like voracious predators with talons unsheathed and fangs bared. The most dangerous predators. Payne could only pray that they hadn't already grabbed Josh.

Holding Eden's hand, he went to the elevators. Payne was sweating beneath his lightweight blazer and short-sleeved shirt. Fury simmered in his gut; he was mad at himself. He'd lost control with Josh. Never should have spoken. Looking down at Eden, he said, "I really am sorry."

"You never meant to hurt me. Or Josh."

God, no. Hurting them was the farthest thing from his mind. He wanted to dedicate his life to protecting them. "We'll find him."

The elevator doors opened onto the main casino. With rows of slot machines and flashing lights and the crowds of gamblers, it seemed impossible to locate an eleven-year-old boy who didn't want to be found. This was a huge hotel. He could be in a bathroom or in the coffee shop or hiding under a gaming table.

"The hotel with the bird," she said. "Earlier, Josh said he wanted to go to the hotel with the bird that's next door."

"Why?"

"Something about bears." When she looked up at him, he saw renewed hope in her eyes. "We have to go there."

Payne sensed a trap. He hadn't wanted Eden to leave this hotel where she was relatively protected. But he couldn't deny her logic. Josh had mentioned the hotel with the bird. And the boy was more likely to come to his mother than anyone else.

Payne led her through the rows of slot machines, through the neon lights toward the front exit. In a moment, they were out on the street in the relative calm of sunshine and palm trees.

Aware of heightened danger, Payne released her hand. He needed to be free to draw the gun from the shoulder holster. "Stay with me, Eden."

"Of course."

As they approached the hotel next door, Payne was on high alert. If they were to be ambushed, it would happen fast. He guessed they'd be hit as soon as they walked through the doors to the neighboring hotel, before their eyes accustomed to the casino lighting.

His hand was on the glass door when he heard the shout.

"Mom! Hey, Mom! I'm over here."

By the time Payne turned, Eden was already sprinting toward the sound of her son's voice.

"No," he shouted. "Wait."

But she was across the curb and into the street. He saw her dive into the rear of a pale sedan which sped away.

EDEN HELD HER SON, clung tightly to him with her eyes squeezed shut, blocking a million tears. "Thank God, you're safe."

"I'm okay, Mom."

She doubted his statement as she opened her eyes and saw the other person, sitting beside Josh in the rear of the vehicle. "Hello, Gus."

Her grandfather removed his sunglasses to confront her directly. "Your son is a handsome boy. Strong. Smart."

"I know." She stared into Josh's face and brushed the black hair back from his forehead. He seemed to be all in one piece, and she was too grateful to scold him. He had no idea what he'd done.

"I'm sorry, Mom."

"How did you find your great-grandfather?"

"Remember when I looked up the Verone family on the computer in Colorado?" he asked. "When I figured out I was really a Verone, I thought it was cool and I wanted to meet everybody in my family. So, I sent an e-mail to Gus."

He turned his head and smiled at his great-grandfather who beamed proudly back at him and said, "This is a very smart kid. Takes after my side of the family."

Oh Lord, I hope not! "Then what happened, Josh?"

"Before we left Colorado, I sent Gus an e-mail and told him we were going to Slippery Spring Airfield near Las Vegas, and he promised to meet me."

Josh was the informant. A few things came clear to her. Josh had demanded to stay in the co-pilot's seat because he was anxious to see his new family. And what about his desire to visit the hotel with the bird? "Let me guess," she said. "As soon as we got here, you used the computer in the hotel bedroom to chat with Gus. And he told you he was right next door."

"Yeah," Josh said. "When I ran out of our suite, I knew where to go. The hotel with the bird on the side. Room four-two-four."

She should have guessed. In the back of her mind, Eden cursed every computer class Josh had taken since kindergarten. He had too damn much access.

"Mom? Are you mad at me?"

"I'm glad you're safe." Grounding him for life would come later. She looked toward Gus. "We are safe, aren't we?"

"Sure, honey. We're on our way to a house in the desert where your grandma is baking cookies. She's going to have a cow when she sees this handsome boy." He nudged Josh's shoulder. "Is that what you kids say? Going to have a cow?"

"Sure, Gus."

"You can call me Grandpa," he said. "I know I'm really your great-grandpa, but that takes too long."

Eden leaned back against the seat. Sooner or later, she'd have to tell Josh that his grandpa was a bad person, not cool like gangsters in the movies. Gus Verone made his living by taking advantage of others, hurting them. She would have to explain this criminal heritage to her son...if they survived long enough for a meaningful talk.

AT THE PALATIAL HOUSE in the desert near Las Vegas, Eden faced her grandmother with wariness and cool suspicion. Sophia had betrayed her, had offered her into the hands of her enemies. Yet, Eden knew better than to expect an apology from this proud matriarch.

"Twelve years ago," Eden said, "you helped me."

"And I have never regretted that decision."

A twitch at the corner of her eye betrayed strong emotions that would never be spoken. Eden was not so constrained. She warmly embraced her grandmother. "I forgive you."

Josh bounded up beside them. "I'm hungry."

Grandmother Sophia turned to him and beamed. "Cookies for you, young man. Wash your hands first." Josh stayed with her in the kitchen while Gus pulled Eden into a large den and closed the door.

When he faced her, his genial grandpa attitude vanished.

He became the patriarch, the leader of the Verone family. "You've caused me a great deal of trouble."

"So, shoot me," she said. He probably intended to, anyway.

"I wish you no harm. And your son? A good boy. You raised him well." He settled majestically into a brown leather chair. Despite his age and his mane of white hair, Gus looked strong and virile. "If I didn't love you, Candace, I would—"

"Eden," she interrupted. "My name is Eden Miller. It's the name I chose."

"Edie," he said. "It sounds like Eddy. A memorial for your brother."

"I didn't plan to use a name that sounded like his, but maybe I picked it on a subconscious level. To remind me of Eddy. My murdered brother." She stopped herself before she went too far down this path of remembrance and recrimination. "Let's not waste time, Gus. What do you want from me?"

"I've made a decision. I'm old, and I'm going to retire. Sophia and I will leave Chicago."

This was good news. "To Florida?" she asked.

"California. I bought a small vineyard where we will live out our days in peace. I hope you and Josh will come to visit, to renew our family."

She was skeptical, waiting for the other shoe to drop. "Are you saying that Josh and I are free to go?"

"There is one thing," he said. "I have enemies within the family. Are you aware of this?"

"Yes," she said. "They ordered Eddy's murder."

"Not true." He held up his hand to silence her. "If I were to believe they killed my grandson, I would stand and fight. For the honor of my name."

And so, he would lie to himself and deny the truth. Her family was a psychological nightmare with all these archaic codes and unacknowledged deceits. "What about these people?" she asked.

"They've agreed that if I retire and move away, you and your son will not be bothered."

With his retirement, he'd bought her a treaty. She would have safe passage with the Verones. It was the best gift her grandfather could give her. Eden felt like kissing him.

Then, he said, "Payne Magnuson is another matter. Twelve years ago, he betrayed our family. He must pay. Vengeance must be served. They ask that you use your influence to deliver him to them."

"I can't do that. It's horrible."

"You have no choice," he said. "Give them Payne Magnuson. You and your son will never be threatened again."

Eden sank into a chair opposite her grandfather. The cost of a safe, secure life for her and Josh was Payne's death. To save her son, she must sacrifice his father.

THE LONG SHADOWS of dusk spread from the jagged rock formations and mesas across the desert. Less than ten miles from the outskirts of Las Vegas, the traffic thinned to a trickle. Payne sat in the passenger seat, uncomfortable not to be behind the wheel. Danny-O was driving.

"I negotiated a good deal for you," Danny-O said. "All that Angela wants from you is an apology. Then you're free to go. And you can take Eden and Josh with you."

It was the tenth time he'd told Payne this story or a slight variation on the same theme—as if repeating the lies would somehow make them come true. Danny-O was a man at the brink, desperately trying to salvage a bad situation. His dreams of wealth and influence had gone rotten and begun to stink.

For the last few miles, Payne had been trying to decide how he could turn Danny-O's desperation to his advantage. One thing was clear: Payne needed an edge. Something unexpected.

An hour ago, Payne received the phone call from Eden. When he recognized her voice, he was elated. "Are you all right?" he'd asked.

"Fine. I'm just fine." But there was a tremble beneath her words as if she was underwater, drowning.

"Where are you?" he asked.

"With Gus and Sophia. They want you to come to me," she said. "They say if you apologize, we can all leave."

Listening hard, he tried to find double meanings, clues. But there was nothing, no hint of what was really happening. Aware that he was signing his own death warrant, Payne said, "I'll do whatever is necessary."

She told him the street corner where he was to wait for a pickup. "And you must come alone. Unarmed and alone."

When he hesitated, she continued, "There's really nothing to worry about. Sophia has made some delicious cannolis. Do you remember the cannolis we had in Lawrence, Kansas? At Motel Comanche?"

"I remember." They'd made love for the first time that night. He wasn't likely to forget.

"At Motel Comanche?" she repeated.

"In Kansas." Payne was certain she was giving him a clue, but he wasn't sure what it meant.

"See you in about an hour," she said.

And the call ended.

Motel Comanche? He remembered that when they checked in she'd been talking about the history of the place. Comanche was the name of a horse, the only survivor at Little Big Horn. An ambush, Payne thought. She was warning him about an ambush.

Not that her warning made a whole lot of difference. He had to follow her instructions. In order to insure the safety of Eden and his son, Payne had to face the Verones and accept the consequences.

Before he left for the pickup, he quickly arranged a few

precautions with Skip and his men. Payne wore a homing device and a microphone in the heel of his shoe that would let them know where he was. After his location was pinpointed, the area would be surrounded.

An assault was planned, but Payne didn't have high hopes for his own survival. He couldn't arm himself. The Verones would never allow him to enter their lair with a weapon. He fully expected to be dead before the feds arrived to take the others into custody.

He waited at the street corner and was only slightly surprised to be picked up by Danny-O who drove carefully, following a map.

"Are we almost there?" Payne asked.

"I think so. It's just a couple of miles from this turn. Kind of isolated."

"Isolation is something you should get used to," Payne said. "Most feds who go to prison end up there."

"What are you talking about?" Danny-O laughed nervously. "I'm not going to prison."

"The FBI isn't going to forgive you," Payne said. "If you're not an agent, you're not much use to the Verones, either."

His face twitched. Danny-O tried to summon up a flare of anger, but he was whipped. He'd lost everything. "There's got to be another way out."

Payne made his offer. "The only way you'll get out of this in one piece is to turn state's evidence and go into the witness protection program. And the only way you'll get there is on a recommendation from me."

Danny-O's lip quivered. He looked like he was going to cry. "You'll do it, won't you? You'll recommend me?"

"That depends," Payne said. "I need to be alive to help you. If I get killed this afternoon, you're going to jail."

Shaking his head, Danny-O turned away from the windshield to stare at Payne. "They promised me they wouldn't hurt you."

"I think we both know better. From the very start, from the time we were at the restaurant in Brooklyn, killing me has been part of the plan."

Danny-O returned his attention to the road. "This isn't right. I was running an undercover operation. How could this turn out so bad for me?"

"It was worse for Samuels in Abilene," Payne reminded. "He's dead."

"We better not drive any farther. I should take you back to Vegas," Danny-O said. "You can get me into witness protection."

"Not yet." Payne still had to rescue Eden and Josh. "I have to do this meeting. And you have to back me up."

"You got it, Payne. You can count on me."

The promise of support from this redheaded snake wasn't much, but Payne would take it. He needed every edge.

At the secluded house—an irrigated acre of green grass that was miles from anywhere—Danny-O parked in front where there were several other cars. Payne recognized the pale sedan that had been used to whisk Eden away. He hoped she was here. At the same time, he wished for her and Josh to be far away—somewhere safe.

The door was opened by two wise guys in running suits. They gave Payne a thorough frisk before leading him through the house to a long room that looked out on an azure swimming pool and palm trees. Danny-O followed him. When the door closed, they were alone.

No witnesses, Payne thought. This might be planned as a clean hit. One gunman. A quick bullet to the head.

He went to the sliding glass doors and pushed one open, giving himself a route for escape. Outside, beyond the swimming pool, was a stucco fence. Beyond that, an outcropping of rock. Then, desert. Not much chance for escape.

"It's going to be okay," Danny-O babbled. "Just tell them you're sorry, Payne."

The door opened and Angela Benedict strode inside. Her bearing was regal. She wore a blood-red dress, short and snug, with enough gold jewelry to rival King Tut's tomb. "Good afternoon, Payne."

"Hello, Angela."

He was disappointed to see her. Though she'd been his primary suspect throughout the investigation, Payne hadn't wanted to believe she'd been swept into crime.

Hands in the pockets of her dress, she stared at him for a few moments. "I speak for the family," she said. "You betrayed us."

Apparently, this was the moment of truth. Angela wouldn't kill him. The dirty work would be left to her henchmen. But she would outline his transgressions against the Verones and tell him the punishment for his behavior.

She said, "Because of your testimony twelve years ago, my husband went to prison. I can never forgive you for that."

"Nicky was in jail because he broke the law." Payne wouldn't take the rap for Nick Benedict's crimes. "There are things I'm sorry about. I'm sorry for every innocent member of the Verone family—the wives and children. I'm sorry you had to suffer. I'm sorry for Eddy's death."

She inhaled sharply through clenched teeth. "So am I."

"Wait a minute," Danny-O interrupted. "I thought you were the one giving the orders, Angela. You put out the hit on Eddy."

"Shut up," she snapped.

"But I thought—"

"Murderer!" Her dark eyes blazed like embers. She despised Danny-O, and Payne knew in that instant that Angela had never ordered Eddy's death. She wasn't in charge of the family. She was as much a victim as Eden.

Payne said, "You didn't want him killed."

"Never."

He stepped close to her. Speaking in an almost inaudible whisper he said. "Somebody else gave the order. After Eddy was dead, you found out who. You were paid for your silence with a shiny new Corvette."

"Correct." She met his gaze. "But the car isn't enough."

"You loved Eddy," Payne said.

"As much as Eden loves you." In a formal gesture, she held both his arms. Coldly, she brushed her lips past both of his cheeks. It was the kiss of death.

Before she separated from him, she passed him a palm-sized gun. "Don't miss."

As Angela retreated to a far corner of the room, the door opened again. Four men entered. Payne registered their presence but reserved his attention for Eden. Her cheeks were flushed. Her eyes were red. She'd been crying.

Breaking away, she flew across the room into his arms. "Oh, Payne, why did you come? Didn't you understand what I was trying to tell you? Comanche. Little Big Horn."

"Where's Josh?" he asked.

"He went back to the hotel on the strip with Gus and Sophia."

Finally, a positive note. Payne assumed that the three of them would be in FBI custody by now. They'd be safe. "I wish you'd gone with them."

There was no way out of here without violence. Even now, Skip and the feds would be tracking the homing device in Payne's shoe. They'd be planning an ambush of their own.

A harsh voice snarled, "Get away from him, Candace."

"Eden," she said. "When are you people going to learn that my name is Eden Miller?"

"I'll call you whatever the hell I want."

Nick Benedict stood in the center of the room while the other men spread out around him. It was a standard move. Even if Payne had a machine gun instead of a tiny pistol that probably only held one or two bullets, he couldn't shoot all of them. He waited until they were positioned. By a stroke of luck, no one blocked the glass door leading out to the swimming pool.

Payne carefully led Eden to a chair beside that door. "Sit here," he said, glancing toward the open doorway. He hoped she would understand that she had an escape route.

Turning away from her, Payne strode toward Nick. "You're the new boss."

"About time," Nick said. "Gus is old and soft. It's time for him to retire. Time for new blood."

"Eddy's blood."

"He was in my way," Nick said. "Like you."

Nick Benedict had more reason to hate Payne than almost anyone else. He'd spent six years in prison based on Payne's testimony. He'd lost six years of his freedom, and he'd also lost the love of his wife, Angela, to Eddy Verone.

"Go ahead," Nick said. "I'm ready for your big apology."

Danny-O moved closer to Payne. "Do it," he urged. "Give him what he wants."

Payne looked Nick straight in the eye. There was a cold understanding between them. Payne said, "Whether or not I apologize, you're going to kill me."

"I have a vendetta," Nick said. "I deserve my revenge. My slow revenge. You owe me, Payne. For six years in prison."

Payne steeled himself. He refused to grovel before this thug, wouldn't beg for his life.

"Well, Payne? Have you got anything to say?"

"As the new boss of the Verones, the honor of the family is in your hands. I have one request. Eden and her son go free."

"I already promised," Nick said. "She made the deal. She gave you up, Payne. She doesn't care about you."

"That's not true!" Eden surged to her feet. "Payne, I love you."

One of Nicky's men stepped over to her and shoved her back down in the chair. Her eyes blazed. She'd reached the end of her self-control.

Payne knew what was coming next. He remembered when she almost killed Danny-O in Chicago. The same desperate determination tensed her muscles. Her rage would not be denied. Eden wasn't a woman who allowed herself to be insulted or pushed around. She snatched the gun from the thug's holster and whirled toward Nicky.

Payne reacted just as quickly. The small gun Angela had given him was in his hand. He fired at one of the other men.

Suddenly, everyone was armed. The sound of gunfire erupted. Danny-O dodged in front of Payne. He took a bullet and crumpled to the floor.

Payne grabbed Eden's hand and yanked her through the glass door. They leapt into the swimming pool as an FBI helicopter swooped down from the skies.

Armed agents in full riot gear closed in on the perimeter of the secluded house. A loudspeaker blasted warnings to throw down all weapons and come out of the house. There was a burst of machine-gun fire.

In the deep end of the pool, Payne held Eden's arm and pulled her to the side. "Are you all right?"

"I'm sorry. I'm so sorry."

"Did you plan this?" he asked.

"A little. I made sure Josh was out of here. And I knew the feds had forgiven you so there would be backup." Water streamed down her cheeks. "I didn't mean to grab that gun. Kind of dangerous."

"But everything turned out okay." He gazed into her beautiful eyes, aware that the chaos around them had taken an organized form. The Verones were surrendering. "By the way, I love you, too."

"I couldn't let you die on me. Not again."

"We're going to live for a very long time. Together. You and me and our son."

When she flung her arms around him, they bobbed under the surface of the cool azure water. Washed clean, they had a chance for a new life.

Epilogue

Five months after the shoot-out in Las Vegas, it was September, the beginning of a new school year.

Early in the morning, Eden rushed around in the brand-new kitchen of the house she and Payne had bought together in Denver. With two stories and a finished basement, their new home was almost too big. Their two guest rooms had been full ever since they moved in. Gus and Sophia had stopped by on their way from Chicago to their new vineyard in California. Several of the Borellis had come during the summer. Angela—in the process of divorcing Nicky Benedict who was back in prison—had brought both of her sons, one of whom was interested in a career in law enforcement. Even Skip and Melissa had visited from Las Vegas. Eden wouldn't have been too surprised if Danny-O, who had survived a bullet at close range, tried to take time out from the witness protection program to spend some time with them in Denver.

Right now, she had only two guests and was busily whipping up biscuits to go along with a breakfast of huevos rancheros and fresh fruit. Today, both of her men would be in school. Their large house was still in the same district as her former home, so Josh would be at the same school with his friends. And Payne was starting his new job at

University of Denver, teaching various classes on law enforcement.

Payne joined her in the kitchen, slipping his arms around her waist and kissing the back of her neck. "Good morning, darling."

She turned around to kiss him back. When she checked out his outfit for his first day at the new job, she grinned. He was wearing a tweed jacket with leather patches at the elbow. "My, don't you look professorial."

"It's like any undercover assignment." He poured himself a mug of coffee. "You've got to dress for the part."

"But you're not undercover."

"Don't tell the students," he said.

The timer on the oven sounded, and she removed a tray of fluffy, fresh biscuits. Whirling back to the countertop, she finished slicing cantaloupe. Formerly, she complained about not having any family. Now Eden longed for a day when she could sit back, relax and enjoy a moment of loneliness.

Back at the sink, she replaced the diamond engagement ring on her finger. She and Payne planned to get married as soon as they felt the time was right. The relationship between Payne and Josh was still a little prickly, and she wanted the transition to be perfect. Some day, her son would accept his father.

Payne caught hold of her left hand. With his thumb, he brushed the surface of her ring. "When can I change that diamond to a wedding band?"

"Soon," she said.

"Not soon enough," came another voice. Sister Max appeared in the kitchen, still moving "in mysterious ways." She was attending a seminar at the Denver Botanical Gardens and staying with them for the week. "It's high time you two were married."

"Yes, Sister."

When Eden began to prepare a plate of food for her,

Sister Max stopped her. "Not a full breakfast for me. I have plans before my seminar today. I'll just have a biscuit."

"Plans?" Eden questioned.

Cody sauntered into the room. "Plans with me. I'm going to teach this good woman how to fly an airplane."

"Closer to heaven," Sister Max said.

"You're not going to believe this," Cody started in, "but I once saw a real angel with a wing span of five yards on either side."

"You are the most dreadful liar," Sister Max said with a twinkle in her eye.

"What kind of nun doesn't believe in angels?" he questioned.

"Well, of course, I do. But you didn't see one."

Arguing good-naturedly, they went out the back door.

Josh rushed into the kitchen. "No time to eat. I'm meeting my buds to walk to school."

"Forgeddabouddit," Eden said. "Breakfast is the most important meal of the day."

With a groan, he sank into a chair at the table in the kitchen. "I don't want to be late."

Eden placed a plate in front of him. "It'll only take a few minutes for you to inhale this."

And she was correct. Within five minutes, he'd shoveled down a decent portion while Payne sat beside him, reading the newspaper.

"I've been thinking about mountain property," Payne said. "Building a cabin."

"Closer to snowboarding," Josh said. "I'm for it."

"I'd need for you to help," Payne said.

"Can I bring a friend?"

"The more the better. As long as they can hold a hammer."

Josh swallowed his last bite of breakfast and bounded to his feet. He kissed Eden's cheek and ran for the door. As usual, he completely ignored goodbyes to Payne.

Then Josh turned. He smiled at her, then at his father. "Good luck on your new job, Dad."

Then he was gone.

Amazed, Eden stared at the door. "He called you Dad."

"He did," Payne said.

"And he was polite. Thoughtful, even."

"The kid is coming around." Payne rose from the table and came toward her. "Now, can we set a date for the wedding?"

"I can't wait to be Mrs. Payne Magnuson."

Happily, she kissed him and snuggled in his arms. She loved her family and her friends. More than anything, she loved Payne. Being with him was the only home she ever really needed.

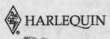

INTRIGUE

COMING NEXT MONTH

#697 HER HIDDEN TRUTH by Debra Webb

The Specialists

When CIA agent Katrina Moore's memory implant malfunctioned while she was under deep cover, her only hope for rescue lay with Vince Ferrelli. Only, Kat and Vince shared a tumultuous past, which threatened to sabotage their mission. Could Vince save Kat—and restore her memories—before it was too late?

#698 HEIR TO SECRET MEMORIES by Mallory Kane

Top Secret Babies

After he was brutally attacked and left for dead, Jay Wellcome lost all of his memories. His only recollection: the image of a nameless beauty. And though Jay never anticipated they'd come face-to-face, when Paige Reynolds claimed she needed him—honor demanded he offer his protection. Paige's daughter had been kidnapped and nothing would stop him from tracking a killer—especially when he learned her child was also his....

#699 THE ROOKIE by Julie Miller

The Taylor Clan

For the youngest member of the Taylor clan, Josh Taylor, an undercover assignment to smoke out drug dealers on a university campus could promote him to detective. Only, Josh never anticipated his overwhelming feelings for his pregnant professor Rachel Livesay. And when the single mother-to-be's life was threatened by a stalker named "Daddy," Josh's protective instincts took over. But would Rachel accept his protection...and his love?

#700 CONFESSIONS OF THE HEART by Amanda Stevens

Fully recovered from her heart transplant surgery, Anna Sebastian was determined to start a new life. But someone was determined to thwart her plans.... With her life in jeopardy, tough-as-nails cop Ben Porter was the only man she could trust. And now in a race against time, could Ben and Anna uncover the source of the danger before she lost her second chance?

Visit us at www.eHarlequin.com

HARLEQUIN®
INTRIGUE®

**Elevates breathtaking romantic suspense
to a whole new level!**

When all else fails, the most highly trained, covert
agents are called in to "recover" the mission.
This elite group is known as

THE SPECIALISTS

Nothing is too dangerous for them...
except falling in love.

DEBRA WEBB

does it again with an explosive new trilogy for Harlequin
Intrigue. You'll recognize some of the names from her
popular COLBY AGENCY series, but hang on to your
hats this time out. Because THE SPECIALISTS are more
dangerous, more daring...and more deadly than any agents
you've ever seen!

UNDERCOVER WIFE
January

HER HIDDEN TRUTH
February

GUARDIAN OF THE NIGHT
March

Look for them wherever Harlequin books are sold!

HARLEQUIN®
Makes any time special ®

For more on Harlequin Intrigue® books, visit www.tryintrigue.com   HISPEC

HARLEQUIN®
INTRIGUE®

Cupid has his bow loaded with double-barreled romantic suspense that will make your heart pound. So look for these **special Valentine selections** from Harlequin Intrigue to make your holiday breathless!

McQUEEN'S HEAT
BY HARPER ALLEN

SENTENCED TO WED
BY ADRIANNE LEE

CONFESSIONS OF THE HEART
BY AMANDA STEVENS

Available throughout January and February 2003 wherever Harlequin books are sold.

HARLEQUIN®
INTRIGUE®

Opens the case files on:

TOP SECRET
BABIES

Unwrap the mystery!

January 2003
THE SECRET SHE KEEPS
BY CASSIE MILES

February 2003
HEIR TO
SECRET MEMORIES
BY MALLORY KANE

March 2003
CLAIMING HIS FAMILY
BY ANN VOSS PETERSON

Follow the clues to your favorite retail outlet!

HARLEQUIN®

Makes any time special®